HAND-TO-AIR COMBAT!

He took one of the crossbow bolts and loaded it in the pistol. He poured a little fluid from his cigarette lighter onto the shaft. Then he lit it and fired in nearly the same movement.

The crossbow quarrel penetrated the cargo vert's light skin and passed a fuel line. The vert flared for a moment and then exploded with such violence that the paving shook and Sylvia could feel the heat bake his face and the back of his hands.

Steel swore slightly. "Do it again," he shouted over the roar of the fire. . . .

CYBERNETIC JUNGLE

S.N. LEWITT

ACE BOOKS, NEW YORK

FOR EVERYONE IN THE CROWD: Amelia G and Red Steve, Scott and Gothic and Julia, Ken and Tanya and Tis, Sarah and Bells and Dee, Johnny Slaughter and Deborah, Gypsy, Grinner, and everyone else who is guilty, you know who you are . . .

CYBERNETIC JUNGLE

THE old woman moaned softly. "Ogun, Oxala, Yemanja, protect the marked ones, give them justice, give them victory." Her red head scarf was the color of blood, her face dark and beaten like the earth floor of the *axe*. She held a rooster by a neck as scrawny as her own, a rooster with black feathers and a brilliant red comb. For one second Paulo Sylvia thought that the woman and the rooster looked the same, red on top, black all over, old and mean and too tough to die. Then the woman's hard gnarled hands twisted around the rooster's throat and it was suddenly, violently dead.

She used a knife on the altar, a kitchen knife sold out of a bin in the budget housewares store like a million others, and opened the veins in the bird's neck. The blood was as bright as its comb, as the woman's head scarf. She took the carcass and shook it at them, splattering them with sticky red blood like the aspergillum of the priest on holy days.

Paulo Sylvia was revolted. If he had known beforehand that he would be required to do this, he would have insisted on Francisco Pope coming along. There was no way he should have to endure the indignity of this alone.

But this was the Serps' territory, not his. Suddenly he longed for the neat, sterile *superquadras* of town, the stressed concrete and glass arteries and the endless exposed sky. He was not some ignorant scum from the inland who believed that the Yoruba gods walked and that there was any power here, except the power of theater.

But Sylvia kept his horror in check. There were other considerations. He had agreed to this run because it would make the Serps obligated, and it would link his own new cadre, Bakunin, to the traditional tribes in the *favelas* and satellite cities outside the grassland belt around the city. Pope might see it as part of their scheme, to get in on the highwire deals and burn them out. Sylvia was only interested in the power. To increase their profile among the tribes, Bakunin had to strike acknowledged runs. This was a first. And if the idiots who ran the Serps wanted a blessing from the Yoruba gods, then he wasn't going to blow the whole deal over superstition.

He wished he could. No matter how many times he told himself how useful this run was, he couldn't shake the feeling that something about it was off. Maybe, he told himself firmly, it was only this requirement of attending the *axe* rite. It was not the Serps who bothered him so much as the rooster blood and the chanting and the drums.

But the Serpentes had suggested the action and there was no way Paulo Sylvia could refuse. A delivery case with Cadea Company stamps all over it could be the highwire the Serps insisted it was, or it could be nothing. One thing Paulo knew for certain, it was going to be trouble.

The ancient priestess had finished with the blood, had laid the body of the rooster in a large bowl and emptied a bottle of *aguardente* over it. But there was no way to tell the Serpentes that something was very wrong, without sounding like a coward. And if he sounded like he was afraid, then everything was ruined.

He was certain that the older favela tribes were just testing them. Bakunin, Sylvia's tribe, was barely two months old in the new favela of the southern *blocos* inside the greensward. The older, more traditional gangs were from the outlying satellite cities beyond the ring of grassy *cerrado*. Those tribes, like the Serpentes, were products of the corrugated tin towns. Many of them were illiterate, most were simply desperate. But they were not as desperate as Paulo Sylvia and Francisco Pope.

Sylvia knew it, and he knew that the others knew it too. Obviously he was desperate or else he never would have consented to the *candomble* ritual. It was laughable and crude. He might have very little left to hope for now, but once he had had an excellent education. He had sat in quiet and careful classrooms and been exposed to great ideas, had read for himself everything he could find from Machiavelli to Fasco Batista das Meinhas.

They were passing around a cup now, filled with the sharp cane liquor and blood. Each of the Serpentes took a swallow and passed it to the next. Then the cup was passed to him. It was old and chipped—even crazy and poor Francisco's mother would not have kept such a thing. He looked at the soft rose liquid, smiled wryly and gulped it down. Sorrel, one of the leaders of the Serps, was watching. And Sylvia neither respected nor trusted Sorrel.

Paulo knew that the Serps wanted to see just how far Bakunin would go, and just how far they were willing to trust Sylvia and Pope. The leaders of the traditional tribes had not liked Sylvia's nickname, Jackal, the only name they knew him by. A jackal, they argued, turned on its friends. There was no crime worse in the favela, in the world.

Which he agreed with, firmly and quietly, so everyone could see he was sincere. The meeting was not in his district. It was in the Serpentes' headquarters far to the north of the city proper, in a flimsy shack made of mud and rough boards with a corrugated green plastic roof. Only they were wrong about the animal, Sylvia pointed out carefully. The jackal is dangerous and smart, but it never turns on its friends.

The meet two days before the action with the Serpentes had been important. No one from the outlying towns would even talk to Bakunin for the two months they had sprayed their name on all the concrete they could find in the hallways in the southern superquadras. They were not family, they were nobody. But a lieutenant of the Serps had a mother who was *comadre*, with Pope's father, of a child who as yet had no tribe connections whatever, being only two. The cogodparent relationship created enough of a family connection that Pope was able to ask a favor, and the "relative" was too uncomfortable to deny him.

The leaders and lieutenants who had been at the meet grumbled a little, shrugged, adopted a wary attitude. That was when a lieutenant from the Serpentes suggested the action. The Serpentes had planned it alone, but they would share, this once, in exchange for the opportunity to work together and pay the family favor.

Such an offer had given Pope and Sylvia no choice. And, given that the cargo was highwire, it was a brilliant opportunity. Sylvia had seen the humor of the situation when he and Pope worked out the specifics at Pope's bare desk. There wasn't anything they found lower than highwire and a highwire death. It stank of submission.

They flipped *dinheiro* on who was going out and who was playing war chief. Pope won the toss, heads, and he had been the one at the leaders' last planning parley. Both of them figured Sylvia had really won. He might have to put up with someone else yelling orders at him, but he was going to be in on the kill. That was before they knew about the rooster.

The ritual was over though, finally, and the group shuffled back into the sunlight from under the miserable dry winter heat of the small *axe*. It was only a few meters down the dirt main street of the town to the Serps' headquarters. And if he and Pope had been dismayed by the tin and cardboard walls, the corrugated green plastic roof and the open chinks between the two, there was still the fact that this was one of the more substantial structures in the shantytown. Even the poorest people, dying highwire addicts in the southern sector of the city, could break into abandoned apartments and live in the hallways. And if they didn't have the nerve for that, there was the shaded, protected area under the residences themselves, where they were supported on pillars above the ground. Some of the buildings housed illegal *barzinhos* or highwire offices, but those that were less well off could shelter the addicts and destitute and the street children. There had been times when Paulo had assumed that anything that was not the endless monotony of the southern structures was desirable. He had been to satellite cities where people lived in brightly painted stucco houses with flowers growing up the walls. He had always despised the suburbanites for their neat, pretty smugness. In this suburb that smelled of open sewage and no facilities, he was not so sure.

He suddenly wished that he had won the toss and Sorrel wasn't looking at him and smirking. He didn't want to be careful around the Serps; he wanted to assert his position and smack that grinning idiot across the face. Inside, the rage smoldered and threatened to flare. It was the rage that he lived by, that fed his soul. It was the only reason he had to live, and it was the only dream he had left, he who had once had so many dreams in the soft life of the middle class. In the life that he and Francisco Pope had shared, and had both lost.

Sylvia and Pope were equally the leaders and founders of Bakunin. Paulo Sylvia was the dreamer and the fighter, Francisco Pope the strategist and planner. Between the two of them they were better than half the companies in Brasilia together, let alone the tribes. They had grown up together, used each other's refrigerators and copied homework. And both of them had fallen together, tumbling down the class structure from the solid comforts of the managerial class to the festering concrete cages in the southern city. Victims.

The day after Paulo's seventeenth birthday, he and Francisco had left the remnants of the shabby party and two-day-old cake, the older relatives talking about the glories of the past before the Forestation Reforms. So different from two years before, when there had been nearly a hundred guests and two huge tables heaped with appetizers and candies and two maids helping out making the *batidas*. When Paulo still had his own parents to live with.

Francisco's family had tried to make Paulo's seventeenth birthday special. They had done for him as they would for Francisco himself, but there just was so little anyone could do anymore. So the boys had left the intimate day-after party and had gotten on their beat-up powerbikes and gone over to South 109.

South 109 was crowded. Young boys in longcoats, aping the cadres, stood around under the buildings, lookouts for the drug traders, or spotters for the legal dealers in leather and food and art. There were some people there who were obviously from the northern sector of the city, most likely the South Lake Mansion District, where all the wealthiest houses were. They wore bright colors and gold jewelry, although it was stupid to wear gold into the southern section. Even with tracers, the runners here in 109 were expert in security systems.

Still, it was the crowd, the bustle of this center of the tribal city, that they wanted. Here two young men could buy and sell and be lost. None of their relatives or neighbors would be here, most likely. They were not alone, but there was a privacy that did not exist in their own artificial neighborhood, lost among the soccer fans who gathered to watch the afternoon games in the World Cup bar.

Francisco had held up a hand and gone into the shadow of a thick pillar and talked to a man with scars on his face. He came back and handed Paulo a black Teflon knife. It was beautifully balanced, and the grip felt as if it had been made for Paulo's hand.

"Someday it's going to be different," Paulo had said softly, holding the knife carefully. Francisco had just looked ahead, and his face had tightened.

"It isn't fair," Francisco said with some confusion. "We aren't like them." He gestured at two young boys with shoeshine boxes, sitting in the sun, too tired to even run after customers.

"No," Paulo agreed. "We aren't. So we're not going to end up like them. I'd rather end up dead."

Francisco had stopped and stared at Paulo for a long time. "You probably will," Francisco said softly. "But I'd rather end up back at the Minas Tennis Club with a membership pass."

"How about elections?" Paulo had asked.

Francisco had only laughed bitterly. He remembered elections the way he remembered the Minas Tennis Club. That had been over two years earlier, before the Forestation Riots had reduced half the city and surrounding land to burned waste, and the government to a military dictatorship. A dictatorship beholden only to the rich *fazenda* families who already had more than their share.

In those two years Paulo had spent too much time among the favela toughs and *capoeira* artists. He was sick of the slurs on his background and how he had fallen; on his pale skin that burned too easily in the summer, fighting *roda* outdoors.

So Paulo had to remind himself that it was the fazendas with their insular wealth and complete contempt for even the hardworking bureaucrats of Brasília, and not the favela tribes, that he hated. He had to remember the tribes were his allies and that he had to prove it to them before they would join Bakunin's scheme. And he had to prove more than that he was smarter and stronger and crazier than they were. He had to prove that he was equally sincere.

But here, at the edge of the wild lands, he was only too aware of how close they were to the primitive. There was something about the Serps that made him wonder if they could possibly understand about the city, about unity of all the favelas and the tribes, all the things he and Pope had spent all those nights dreaming about deep in their dreams with the music up loud.

That calmed him somewhat as he checked the black Teflon knife on his wrist. The crossbow pistol, which was his favorite weapon, lay light in his belt. Eight painted wood quarrels were stuck in a leather band around his boot as if they were simply decoration.

"You don't have any energy throws?" Sorrel asked. Somehow, Paulo didn't believe it was merely chance that Sorrel was the Serp lieutenant responsible for Jackal's section, the group honored to carry the main weight of the action.

He shook his head. "They'll read on cityscan," he replied. "And this"—he patted the miniature crossbow—"is as powerful as any projectile ever made, as long as the space is limited."

Sorrel shook his head and spat. Sorrel didn't approve, Jackal thought, but then Sorrel didn't seem to approve of anyone else, either. It wasn't worth the argument, and so he kept quiet. But he still wondered where the Serpentes would get throws. They were the favorites of company security pigs, terribly expensive and not generally available without company sanctions.

They probably just stole a shipment, like everything else, Sylvia thought. And then kept the goods rather than selling them on the street. But having met Sorrel and a few other of the Serps, he was just a little confused. They didn't seem the type to keep weapons they could sell for a serious profit and then spend the proceeds on aguardente and gambling and cheap painted girls.

Sorrel walked around some more, talking softly to people Jackal didn't know. And then Sorrel gave them the order to move out for the rendezvous down across the lake from the Minas Tennis Club, in one of the residential sections of the city. Seven of them in the section, and only Jackal and Steel were Bakunin. The other five were Serps.

They took the bus the fifteen kilometers downtown. There wasn't any other way of getting to the city, not when they didn't have a vert. And only the rich had verts. Or the well-to-do.

He had been quite upset about not using the powerbikes that were common in the city. Even he and Francisco had them, strung together from castoffs and reconditioned parts. Still, the bikes ran.

Sorrel had made a face when Paulo had suggested it. "Oh, and how do we get all three groups on six powerbikes? Or do you rich city boys have extras stashed away back home? You think a crew coming in on bikes and wearing weapons will get past the roadblocks? Let me tell you, city boy, they check out anyone coming in from the satellite cities before we get too close to town. Or is it too hard for you to try and blend in as one of the ordinary people on the bus? Is that beneath your pride?"

Sorrel's sneering tone tempted Paulo to violence. It took more discipline than he had ever shown in his life not to slam the Serp lieutenant in the face, but he managed. There were things more important than his immediate gratification, though at the moment he was hard pressed to name them. And so he went along and got on the crowded bus and argued with the ticket-taker over the change.

There was something that struck Sylvia as very silly about going down for a run on the broken-down blue bus with heavy women in too-tight maid's uniforms and young girls in too much makeup and old bent men carrying baskets of bread and eggs and coconuts and bottles of hot palm oil to sell. That they had to stand and hold the handrails, when they were armed and dangerous.

"Miguel, I saw your mother yesterday," one of the older women stuffed into a pink flowered dress said to Sorrel. "She told me that you were looking for work in the city now. *Aaaie*, she must be so proud of you, with Theresa pregnant. When is the baby due?"

Sylvia told himself he imagined it, but Sorrel blushed. "In September," the Serp lieutenant mumbled.

"September," the woman said. "Springtime, very nice. Have you chosen godparents yet, or will you wait and get caught out and have to make someone unhappy about not being chosen? This is a very important matter. So tell me, who did you have in mind?"

Sorrel rolled his eyes and gulped nervously. Sylvia enjoyed the show. The bus lurched to a stop, nearly toppling him onto a man with a cane and a white hat. Sorrel looked only too relieved as they climbed across the crowd to the front and down to the street.

Even in daylight, walking through the empty streets of Brasilia was depressing. There were no corner pubs, no local spots, no community services, not even any trees to block out the blazing sun in the residential housing blocks they passed. They walked under part of the monorail structure, a useless thing that had never gone into operation, built by some former Congress to get votes from the shantytowns. The people in town were dismayed by it. After all, the one good thing anyone could say about Brasilia was that there were never any traffic jams. Ever.

They weren't going all the way into the protected environs of the government district or the South Lake Mansion District; they were going to be on the wrong side of the lake for that, but they would still have to pass several cityscans on the way in. A measure to keep police presence at a minimum and, incidentally, to keep the cost of municipal protection low. The scans were hidden in the street lights, the entrance blocks, the crossings at major avenues. Jackal was pretty sure when they hit a scan, and exactly what the scan revealed. Thus the crossbow and the Teflon-coated knife. Nothing with a charger to set off the alarms, nothing with enough steel mass to trigger the detectors.

They weren't stopped, so Sorrel must have taken the warning on energy levels seriously. That, or he took orders from his leader, like the revealed word of God.

As they approached, the city didn't become any more inviting. No one loved residential Brasilia any more than rats enjoy experimenters' cages. Still, the Serps looked around like tourists on the rubberneck float. They didn't get into town too often, weren't real familiar with paved streets and flashing lights.

Then Jackal had to hold himself in tight. It was too easy to sneer at the Serpentes. He had to remember that some of them were *capoeira* artists; a few might have even studied with his own teachers.

Contempt was more dangerous than stupidity; overconfidence could kill him faster than betrayal. *Capoeira* had taught him that, and *capoeira* was the heritage of the favelas. If the Serps had never heard of Machiavelli, they still knew how to weave low, to dodge, to simply not be there when the blow was struck. He had to remember that, and remember too that the Serps would be watching him. Not just for his actions, but for his attitude. And if he didn't want to blow the whole thing, he'd better play along. It shouldn't be so hard to have a little respect. Even if they were beneath him.

Two

THERE were few people on the streets. Inhospitable, the streets of Brasilia were frequently empty. Sylvia wondered why the cityscan didn't set off at the presence of the group, who were converging from different streets, closing in around a single corner. The other groups were still far enough away that he couldn't see them, pick out their leathers in the white glare of the harsh sun and the endless sky. Just as well.

The scan was set for some specific number, so that there was no possibility of demonstrations and public outrage and ministers pulled out of their offices and torn apart by the crowds. The new military government had learned from Chile, from Argentina and Peru. From the fazenda security forces from whom they took their orders. They took no chances.

Which was why the gangs had split into attack groups of fewer than ten, and not all of them would meet. The three rooftop teams should stay out of sight. They had been planted in case the cargo vert came down on the roof instead of the street. The rear guard under Iago, one of the more intelligent Serpentes, should never catch up.

The whole thing was Pope's plan; the Serpentes didn't know enough about making a city run to split for the scanners. And they wouldn't have thought of a roof landing, either. That wasn't common, but it was sometimes done. Of course, Brasilia being what it was, there was more likelihood of being seen on a roof than in the street. Pope had counted on this when he planned for a major street offensive.

Paulo Sylvia sauntered through the street. Some members of his attack group were on the other side, several were a few meters behind. They didn't want to look as if they were together, at least not to the scans. The scans weren't smart enough to make anything out of the fact that all the seemingly unassociated people on the street were young and dressed in the painted white longcoats preferred by the favela gangs. A false economy when it came to security, Sylvia thought. And then he turned his attention back to the task at hand.

Already a few of their teammates had dropped back into the shadows of doorways. There was little cover in the unforgiving geometric lines of the local architecture. The one girl on their team had draped herself around Sorrel like a *carioca* on a date, hiding both their faces but giving him a decent lookout along with an excuse.

For minutes nothing moved. Sylvia began to wonder if the Serpentes had accurate information, if they had any access at all, or if the whole thing was a setup. The idea of a setup seemed very possible and grew more likely every second that the sky remained clear.

Then he heard the wind-beating blades of the cargo vert before the cool shadow fell as it drifted down. Oversized and ungainly, it came down roughly on its skis. Sylvia got the definite impression that the driver preferred pontoon landings on Lake Paranoá.

There were two armed guards who jumped down first. Steel was behind one of them with a silk ribbon. The girl had turned from Sorrel and let go with a blowgun. A dart caught the other guard under the ear. The girl was good. Maybe he should recruit her.

There was no sound at all over the slowing rotor blades of the vert. Sylvia joined Steel, tossing the guards for code keys, speakers and weapons. Steel crunched the speakers under the heel of his boot. He smiled.

Sylvia took the code keys, and both he and Steel stuffed the small finger chips in their pockets. Then they bracketed the sides of the back door, waiting for another guard to jump out, or the driver.

Sylvia counted to sixty slowly, taking a deep breath with each number. No more guards. He took the code key and inserted the magtape into the lock. There was a grinding sound as the mech cycled through, did a recheck and test and cycled again.

This gave Sorrel enough time to gather the rest at the driver's door. They didn't try anything as subtle as a silent assault. Sorrel flashed his homemade brightgun at the driver, who opened up without a fight.

The damned thing couldn't have fried an egg, Sylvia thought with disgust. The driver was a coward and an idiot. All he'd had to do was start the rotors again and try to lift. That would have been enough to shake them off. But he wasn't smart enough to think of it, or he didn't care enough to try. Sylvia hoped it was the second. He didn't have the luxury of time to find out. He and Steel sealed the locks behind them. There was one guard waiting outside, who surrendered politely. Obviously the company didn't pay them enough to risk anything for their employer.

Sylvia left Steel in charge of the cargo and went up front. Sorrel and one of the Serps were sitting at the vert's controls. Sylvia tapped the soldier Serp on the shoulder and pointed toward the back. The sound of the blades made talk impossible.

Sorrel shook his head in fury, gestured to Sylvia to return to the cabin. Sylvia refused. He hadn't trusted Sorrel from the start, and he didn't care whether the delicate negotiations on the action had agreed on the vert drivers being Serpentes or mechs right out of the factory. Paulo Sylvia was going to watch them all the way.

In front of them, on the street, the few team members left were securing the building. The girl and two Serps were the only ones he could see down there between the vert and the door. Two hauling mechs came out, along with one deathmech that opened fire as soon as sunlight hit.

Sylvia had never seen a deathmech on go. He could hardly discern the shape of the firing platform under all the smoke and flare. The Serps went down. The girl blew a dart out. Sylvia admired her for that one, before the mech got her across the chest.

Even with the doors locked and the rotors on high, the stench permeated the control sector of the vert. Why the hell weren't they moving yet? Get out of there while the deathmech methodically raked the area. Did it do that all the time, just on general principles to clear the landing zone? Or did someone know they were out there? That seemed far more likely.

Suddenly Sylvia glanced at Sorrel. The Serp was smiling, watching the carnage. And then Sorrel flicked on the green to lift.

Sylvia slammed his hand against the board. His other hand held his wrist knife. He cut Sorrel's throat execution-style and pushed the body out of the vert. Maybe there would be trouble with the Serps over that, but he knew a setup when he saw one, and he knew a stooge.

He'd driven a vert only a couple of times and didn't have his license but he knew enough to throw the lift. The heavy cargo hauler strained upward and listed to one side. Sylvia was worried. With a partner driving, he could tell Steel to shift the cargo, distribute it more evenly. And, to be honest, he didn't want to handle the vert alone.

At three meters he did a quick check on the ground, running a visual of the bodies that had been left. There were the charred remains of the two soldiers who'd gone in to the deathmech, and Sorrel looking like a rag someone had tossed away. The girl, though—the girl was moving.

Sylvia swore under his breath. It could be rigor. He didn't know much about the mechanics, but he had seen chickens beheaded and walk around in circles until they fell. He had heard the same was true of humans. And he didn't want to go back. Landing was hard enough on a proper pad without the threat of deathmechs coming through the doors.

She moved again. She was hurt bad and he had to go back. Jackals don't leave their friends. Killing someone who had betrayed them wasn't nearly as important as saving one of their own.

He took the vert down, trying to keep it slow, but lurching hard and grinding against the pavement. The jolt of his landing went straight through his spine.

He got out, hoping it would only be a moment. He went over to the girl and she was still alive, but barely. Sylvia thought for a second, maybe two. He wanted to take her with them, slip her into the second driver's seat. But her breathing was ragged and she was losing blood fast. He didn't know if it was better to save her.

There was pounding from the back of the vert. Swearing lightly, Sylvia left the girl and opened the back door for Steel.

"What the hell is going on?" Steel demanded furiously.

"Girl's down," Sylvia replied.

"That's not all," Steel said briskly, pointing at the vert's shredded legs.

Sylvia ignored him. He took the girl in his arms and carried her to the vert. She was light and he could feel the bones in her against his arms. The blood running down her chest against his jacket made him angry.

"She isn't going to make it," Steel said after a quick glance. Then he pointed up.

Fiscal responsibility notwithstanding, there were two baby-blue police verts in the sky, hovering over their position. It was over. But Sylvia wasn't thinking straight. Something in him seemed distracted, diffused. As if nothing at all was real, and soon, very soon, he would wake up in his old bed in South 713, with Francisco's mother fixing breakfast and his father packing lunch.

He took one of the crossbow bolts and loaded it in the pistol. He poured a little fluid from his cigarette lighter onto the shaft. Then he lit it and fired in nearly the same movement.

The crossbow quarrel penetrated the cargo vert's light skin and passed a fuel line. The vert flared for a moment and then exploded with such violence that the paving shook and Sylvia could feel the heat bake his face and the back of his hands.

Steel swore slightly. His knife wasn't good at that range. "Do it again," he shouted over the roar of the fire.

Sylvia was already loading the crossbow as Steel spoke. He gave Steel the lighter, but only a few drops of fluid remained. No instant explosion this time.

He knew enough about the theory to know that he had to take out some vital piece, but he didn't know enough about verts to know where to aim. The crossbow was a very delicate weapon, very accurate. He could try for the window, the driver.

Instead, generations of instinct took over. From the primal emergence of man on the ice, he knew that the vulnerable point of a killer was its belly. And so, without thinking why, he aimed and shot out the belly of the police vert.

He froze. There wasn't time to get the second police vehicle. He didn't even know if he'd done decent damage to the first. And then the vert lurched and plunged and tilted like something in a game arcade.

The second vert tried to steer away from it as it spiraled down, the pilot making violent attempts to regain control.

Steel pulled him along at a run. Down the perfectly straight street where there was no cover as the police verts descended, one of them smoking. The deathmech came out, but its readings were on the burning verts and not the two young men running away. Running faster and faster, burning around his chest from not enough air, Sylvia fled.

Steel grabbed his arm and threw him into the dark mouth of a doorway. Nem Brito was standing there, smiling. Nem Brito was one of theirs, not a damned Serp no one could trust. The roof patrol was ever ready.

The three of them took an elevator to the top floor and then the service stairs to the roof. No one liked the rooftops of Brasilia any better than they liked the canyons. Flattened against the top of the residence, they watched the police below them, only two scurrying around.

"Maybe five minutes to reinforcements," Steel said.

Nem Brito smiled. "Then maybe we shouldn't stop for coffee," he said as he jumped easily over a low barrier to the skybridge that led to the monorail line. Sylvia was impressed. He knew he and Pope had recruited well; he knew he would have thought of a building grab that had a monorail link, but he wasn't in the habit of trusting anyone else to think of it. This came as a pleasant surprise.

The monorail was not operational, and by popular opinion, it never would be. Isolated on a peninsula, without a rail link or a vert, it was easy to secure. Already Sylvia could see the blue and yellow police verts filling the sky. Even ordinary traffic would have a hard time. Below, barricades were set for groundcars, and individuals on foot were being searched.

The three gang members pulled themselves through the locked gates to the monorail station and began to walk the line in the opposite direction. Not back out to the cargo vert they had left behind, but across the expanse of the lake and toward downtown.

No one was searching in this area. No one expected them to be able to get downtown without passing the barricades. Everyone forgot that the rail was built and ready to use, that it was politics and the fact that Brasilia had been perfectly planned for ground traffic, if not humans, that made the system a white elephant.

The rail was wide enough for two of them to walk, but it still seemed too narrow and too high to Jackal. He didn't like the glare of the sun off the water blinding him, distorting images and distances. He kept his eyes half-closed, looking only at the surface of the high bridge. There was nothing to hide them at all, and if any player from the tennis club

chanced to look over, the three would be perfectly clear
against the sky.

And so they walked carefully, five meters above the lake.
If a police vert saw them and buzzed them, they would be
dead. Their one protection was that no one looked. That no
one ever considered the rail course, that everyone was used
to the idea that part of the northern residential section was a
peninsula and there were plenty of bridges that would all be
under scrutiny now.

They climbed down in the pristine, unused University station and walked to the library. No one would look for them
there, and they could blend in with the students and bums
who sought out its cool shade.

"The Serps aren't going to like this," Steel whispered as
they settled behind piles of books at a table in the reading
room. An examination was just starting, a proctor handing
out papers to everyone there. Paulo Sylvia took one with a
smile. It might be interesting. Besides, this would give them
plenty of time to catch their breaths and let the trail grow old
before they caught the loop bus south and changed for the
line back to the residence on the edge of the city. "You
torched the cargo," Steel said. The proctor glanced in their
direction.

Sylvia smiled thinly. "That was the idea. Pope and me, we
agreed in the beginning. Highwire. We don't do highwire.
And our allies don't do it anymore either. The corps want the
stuff, sell the stuff, we're going to torch it. And there's no
way any of the Serps can touch me. We were justified."

Nem Brito smiled serenely and Steel just rolled his eyes.

Three

D INNER in the Vielho-Markowicz fazenda was an edifying affair. Appropriate to its place as the one time of day that the entire management level of the compound spent together, formal dress and manners were required. From the youngest manager-trainees in short pants or ankle socks to the CEO, everyone participated.

Zaide Soledad was not the youngest, but at seventeen she was only two classes more advanced. She wore a print dinner dress with a lace collar and matching peach pumps. She sat at the far end of the table and listened carefully while she used the correct silverware without thinking. All her thought was centered on the speaker.

"The attack on the Cadea shipment today is the first time any of the gangs have ever come in so close to the center of the city," Julio Simon was saying. "They were not prepared, obviously. The deathmech was effective, and it was innovative given the fact that they had no warning. I believe that the police said they thought the gang members had throwers. Naturally, we will have to reevaluate our own security measures in light of this."

"But surely, Julio, they lost. And they won't be so anxious to try again. Four dead and the vert blown? I would say we don't need to worry about them trying anything very soon. And I surely don't think it means that your department will be in line for a major increase this year." That was Sonia Leah, one of the "aunts" and very high up in the Financial Division. She wore a large aquamarine pendant, the gemstone of economists, although some people whispered that she had never attained a degree. Sonia Leah smiled carefully down the table to the youngsters there, to let them know that she had scored and they should study the technique.

Zaide Soledad studied Julio Simon. His face was smooth and relaxed, he ate his shrimp with appreciation. There was no tension she could see and she envied his control. Being lectured in front of "Uncle Victor," the CEO, by someone like Sonia Leah was not the way to advance a career. Especially when she was right. But Julio Simon had been campaigning for increased funding for a long time, and the attack on the Cadea shipment just fed right into his program.

Zaide felt a certain sympathy for Julio Simon. She and he were both "S" series. There was a certain bonding between the various series of DNA adaptations to fit into the fazenda/corporation scheme. Julio Simon had played mentor to Zaide Soledad, teaching her tricks about security and finance and even trade negotiations among the familial/financial groupings that were never covered in regular training sessions. They weren't even available in the databank that trainees could access.

That would change when she went through the final surgery and learned to ride the wave, when she became a true Changeling. Though it was hard to imagine how access to the quantum consciousness of the city could possibly be as much of a privilege as Julio had hinted to her, along with the other "cousins" in the corporate/family structure.

In any event, it was the supreme rite of passage. Then she would become a player, an enemy in the treacherous back alleys of the Vielho-Markowicz fazenda. And already there was destined to be tension. Julio had been adopted under the name Markowicz and thus owed his primary loyalty to that faction, while Zaide was Vielho. The merger was only a generation old, and there was still a good bit of rivalry.

"Are you sure about the idents on the bodies?" Miguel Leal asked, picking up from Sonia Leah. "It is very convenient when the Board will be voting on next year's fiscal policy next week. You didn't happen to have a hand in it?"

Zaide tried not to make a face at Maria Susana sitting across from her. Miguel Leal was not subtle and was not going to advance very far. He was over thirty and was still only an assistant Director. Zaide was embarrassed for him. His accusation was stupid, even if Julio Simon had set up the raid to make a case for a larger budget.

Julio smiled sadly and placed his knife and fork together precisely, indicating that he was finished. He had eaten maybe half his meal and Zaide was surprised that he had managed to ingest anything at all. She had a lot to learn.

"If our profits were to increase, there might be a margin for additional funds," Julio Simon said reasonably. "Cadea has been expanding into our traditional market in the north very slowly, but the drop in revenue has been steady. If Cadea decided to compete elsewhere, we stand to increase profits by nearly seventy per cent. I have the projections if anyone is interested."

"And that wouldn't have any effect on the rumors of free elections?" Zaide Soledad asked carefully. She didn't often speak at dinners, but she was surprised that this evening no one else had brought up the current politics which had been the topic of mealtime conversations ever since she had been brought to the big house from the village.

Sonia Leah looked at her as if she were studying a specimen in a jar. "That's very astute, Zaide," said the financial Director, giving her grudging approval. "This could be a very reasonable argument for postponing those elections, though we never did discuss a date for them. I, for one, think we are much better off dealing directly with the military. The entire election process is a waste of energy and funds."

Julio Simon looked down the table, caught her eye and winked. For herself, Zaide couldn't see what he would have against elections. But making points with Sonia Leah was reason enough to do anything.

The main attack over, rum cake was served. Zaide only

had a few bites. She wanted to do well in the evening's soccer game. "Uncle" Victor took the evening athletics very seriously. Competitive spirit and teamwork and all that. Soccer was not Zaide's best sport. She excelled in swimming and tennis, neither of which were team sports and therefore didn't count so much with the aunts and uncles.

So, much as she loved Bebe's rum cake, she pushed it aside after a taste. She needed to be light and fit to run as hard as any of the cousins in the trainee program. Even the younger full managers like Julio were still counted as cousins and played. At least teams were easy. As always it was Vielho against Markowicz.

"Want to go out?" Susana asked as the two of them walked back to the house together. The game had gone well enough. Zaide had fallen and skinned a knee on a save, and that should have gotten her some points with the higher-ups.

Now all she wanted to do was to sink into a hot whirlpool, put on Susana's collection of North American rock and roll and steal a little time to feel young before she slept and got up and put the *fazendeira* mask on again. She hated that mask, hated the rules and petty denials that came with it. But she feared the alternative.

Like everyone else in the management trainee program, she'd been adopted out of the breeding pool after extensive DNA analysis. The rest of the pool were shipped into the city, into the great residential superquadras to the north. And if the aunts and uncles decided that she had not lived up to her potential in service to the Vielho-Markowicz, she would be sent back with the next batch of rejects.

The family was very careful before they paid for the final surgery to ride the wave, to make her a true Changeling. They had already invested a good chunk in her—the series alterations that permitted her system to use the microwave chip once it was embedded, the highwire feed and Changeling programs, the training, the excellent food and the expensive clothes, and the room she shared with her cousin

Susana, which had two four-poster beds covered in plum chintz and lace dresser scarves.

And if she washed out, they had no choice but to take back what they'd given her, burn her mind into the oblivion that would have been her natural state had she not been chosen from all the others. There were drugs for that. Julio had told her about them. Julio knew a lot about drugs, about the various things the fazenda sold to ease the pain of the favelas and erase the minds of those who had crossed the company.

There were other things Julio knew, too, darker things. He hinted and teased about them but never quite told her. And, of the male cousins, he was the only one who was not interested in taking her to bed. His pleasures were somewhat more rarefied, he had said. And he was always given charge of the fazenda prisoners.

Zaide thought of all that. But Susana was waiting for an answer, and Susana was two years older and would be blamed if they were caught. Besides which, she had always enjoyed her adventures with Susana. They were friends in a house where there were very few allies.

"What did you have in mind?" she asked cautiously. She was tired and didn't want to stay out long in any case.

"Just to go over to the Alado fazenda and see if we could talk Veronica into coming with us. You are still coming to town for the Saint Anthony's Day celebration with me, right?" Susana said.

"Yes, I'm still coming to the Saint Anthony's Day celebration. You must want a husband really badly," Zaide joked. Neither of them wanted a husband, and certainly not any time soon. "But maybe we don't have to go to the Alados' tonight. Maybe we should work on our costumes. We only have two more days, and I've got a heavy schedule."

Susana wrinkled her brow, considering it. "Yes, you're right," she finally agreed. "If we're going to have decent costumes we'd better work on them. Did you have anything in mind?"

"I thought you'd help me," Zaide said, throwing her hands up. "I've never been to any of the Saints' days before."

They had reached the main house, and split up, Zaide to get washed after the game and Susana off to the attic storeroom where there were treasures left from past ages. Zaide loved the attic, the ancient puppets and chipped plaster saints and costumes from when the whole fazenda would celebrate Carnival. But Susana was mistress of that space, able to unearth things that Zaide would swear existed only in her imagination.

Zaide was still in the tub when Susana came into the room they shared, the room Zaide hated with its plum-colored chintz on the bed, the chairs, the windows. It was frilly and depressing, and there was not one thing Zaide could do to improve it. Even worse, Susana liked it and had pinned up extra lace on the already ornate canopy. Secretly, Zaide believed that all the bedrooms in the house were deliberately hideous, to make people want to leave and spend time together in the family lounges or the porch. Teamwork yet again.

She got out of the bath and wrapped a towel around her long, almost black hair. There wasn't time to dry it before Susana dragged her out and began throwing the contents of a decaying suitcase over the furniture. Zaide threw an oversized man's shirt on over her underwear and put on dance music to get in the mood. The beat of the drums filled up her world, and she got off the bed and started to dance barefoot on the carpet. She had to watch her feet to make sure she didn't trip over any of the bright, unidentifiable items Susana strewed all over the floor and on top of Zaide's bed. Then Susana began to dance with her.

"No, no, no," Susana corrected her. "In, out, quick, tight. Keep it tight. Keep your steps small."

It was Susana who had taught her to dance. It was the sort of thing Susana learned merely to horrify their elders, although where she had picked up the samba and the *quadrilha*, Zaide couldn't guess. Maybe just from watching the tapes. Susana was good at that sort of thing.

Zaide followed directions, weaving around Susana in a brisk, provocative circle. They danced until the song ended and they both collapsed on Susana's bed.

"I thought the game wore me out," Zaide said, out of breath.

"The drums are like that," Susana told her. "Some day I'm going to take you to the *axe* where they do the *candomble* rites. Not just the little paper boats and perfume to the Lady of the Waters—that's almost a civic holiday. I mean, the whole fazenda family, even Uncle Victor, goes out on that one. I mean the real *candomble*, where they kill black chickens and sprinkle the blood on your forehead and the old African gods come down."

Zaide laughed at her. "Where do you come up with that shit?"

Susana put her hands on her hips and snorted. "If you ever talked to Bebe down in the kitchen, you'd learn a few things, too. You know she was once Carnival Queen? Not here, in Rio. That's what I want." She looked at Zaide and her turquoise eyes snapped with desire. "I want to be assigned to the field office in Rio. I want to get out of this fazenda a million kilometers from anything, away from this deadly boring city—you can't even get anywhere without a vert. I want to be out of the Planalto, I want to be in civilization, in Rio or São Paulo, where there are nightclubs and glitter and people dress up and the city doesn't close down at ten. God, I hate Brasilia."

Zaide began picking through the garments Susana had brought. She had heard this line before. It had even tempted her a year ago. Then she realized that she had hardly ever been to Brasilia, had hardly ever left the fazenda since her entrance into the village school at the age of six.

Besides, Susana was full of dreams and ideas, and not very practical really. She was slated for Product Development, where her originality would be a benefit and her wanderlust would be satisfied. And she would never be in the running for CEO.

No one from Product Development ever became CEO. Finance and Marketing were the two high-powered divisions in the company and accounted for most of the Board-level management. In one of her more political moments, Zaide had requested a career assignment in Marketing. She respected Sonia Leah but didn't trust her at all, and "Aunt" Sonia was way too smart. Also, she had no desire to move from her current position. While the Marketing people, well, there was a nice concentration of Vielho there and a couple of potential allies.

"Did you catch what Julio Simon was saying and not saying just before dessert?" Zaide asked cautiously. She wasn't sure she had really understood the threat, or if she was overreacting as usual. Susana rolled her eyes. Susana was more interested in ideas and products than corporate politics. "What? Did he mean that he was going to hold Uncle Victor hostage or something?" She giggled.

"No." Zaide sighed. She wished Susana cared more about the delicate games of position and power. She had been certain that Julio had meant that the attack on the Cadea family benefited them directly. And if that were so, knowing how subtle Julio was, he could have very easily had something to do with the attack in the first place. It was Julio's style. It hurt Zaide that she couldn't discuss this with Susana, that her best friend didn't care to speculate on Julio Simon's and Sonia Leah's hidden meanings and concealed tactics.

But Susana was great for crazy ideas, like going into town for Saint Anthony's Day. There was no reason they shouldn't, Zaide reasoned. And it was supposed to be a great public party with bonfires and fireworks, almost like Carnival. Of course, she had never been to Carnival, either. No one from the Vielho-Markowicz fazenda ever paid the least attention to the superstitions of the outside world, of the people who believed in old African gods or a near-Asian one who never died on a cross. At least, they didn't act like they paid attention.

There were some proprieties that were observed, for the sake of good public relations. Everyone in the family was baptized Catholic and was married in the Church. Everyone had a certain amount of training so they could appear in public as perfectly normal citizens. The fact that it meant nothing, well, that was for the Vielho-Markowicz alone.

The three Saints' days in June were mere superstition, and Carnival was a waste, some of the aunts and uncles said. Others, including Sonia Leah, pointed out the benefits of tourism and increased spending. Trust Sonia Leah to find the bottom line in everything.

The Vielho-Markowicz went through the minimum required motions of traditional religion. What they worshipped was the bottom line. The first thing the trainees learned was that the profit margin was God and that Hell was the anteroom to red ink.

So Zaide and Susana knew about Carnival, had some idea of the history of the celebration and its customs, and a very good idea of its profit and loss statement. It was very profitable indeed.

But they still had never gone to any of the popular celebrations downtown. No one from the plantation went. It was déclassé.

Susana suggested they ought to try it once. While they were young they should have a few adventures, before they became part of the Vielho-Markowicz machinery forever. So they planned, and Susana had already signed for a vert, proffering an invitation from the Alado-Merea-Dee fazenda for a trainees' seminar to cover for their absence.

Then Susana had insisted on costumes, the whole thing, before they actually went into the streets of Brasilia on their own. She had brought a wide assortment of scarves and old dresses that had been stored up in the attic. There were even a few period-like pieces, historical things that Zaide thought might have come off the giant puppets she had once found when she was rummaging up in storage.

The historical dress actually suited Susana. With her ash-blond hair and fine skin, the pale rose damask was striking. Zaide had never thought about Susana as beautiful before. She'd never given much thought to their looks at all, as long as they were neat and professional. That was the highest compliment anyone could pay, that they looked professional. It never occurred to Zaide that Susana could be pretty, that her figure was more voluptuous than heavy, and that dull greige suits didn't flatter her at all.

"That's it," Zaide said. "It's perfect."

Susana nodded. "I thought so when I saw it. Upstairs. I'll bet it was for some theatrical or something, a long time ago, when they had things like that."

"Before Sonia Leah worked the household budget into the books." Zaide giggled.

Sonia Leah didn't skimp on things she considered important, and so there were always three courses at dinner, and shoes always had to match dresses. But theater and music and dancing were lost on Sonia Leah, who thought that television and films were suspect, unless someone was laid up with a sports injury.

"Do you want a historical too?" Susana asked generously.

But Zaide had been thinking about it. "No . . ." she said slowly. She picked through the pieces that lay on the bed and let them all fall to the floor. The bright colors didn't attract her and the rich fabrics seemed too stiff and smiling. Disappointed, she took the whole heap, turned it over and threw it back into the suitcase. And, turning it, she exposed a material that caught her imagination.

It was black and translucent and shot through with threads of glittering silver and violet. Its colors changed and shifted in the light.

Zaide picked it up and draped it across her arms, over her chest. It was generous, and flowed over her, making her long-boned thinness almost ethereal. "This," she said.

"What as?" Susana asked, for once the practical one. "A Gypsy?"

Zaide shook her head. "I'll put it together and think of something. Maybe one of the wind spirits."

"How about Death?" Susana suggested. "You can get one of those great feathered masks down on the Esplanade—they sell them all over. And you wear a black tonga under it and your hair all wild. I wish I had hair like yours. Oh, well. It'll be great."

Zaide thought about it. She liked the way it sounded. Not with a tonga underneath; that wouldn't give quite the elegant line she needed, and besides there wasn't any beach around and she didn't have an all-black one anyway.

"You'll have to call yourself something," Susana told her. "I can't decide if I should be Queen Juana. But you'll have to use some kind of name. No one uses their real name."

The towel slipped off Zaide's head. Her near-black hair tumbled over the fabric, making her skin look bloodless white. Her eyes were like sapphires in that face, hard and unknowable.

But mostly she was black, hair, clothes, mood. Black. She thought about it for a minute. "Noire," she said at the mirror. "I'll call myself Noire."

Four

S USANA drove. They waited until after the evening athletics, swimming tonight, and took time drying off and doing their makeup. The costumes were stuffed in portable cases with shoulder straps that went well with their proper professional beige. Susana slipped her request disc into the valet, and a vert was delivered from the garage. She got in and Zaide followed.

Susana drove west first, for as long as the local trackers would be on them. Then she angled north to the city. Zaide, over the city night, wondered if this was such a good idea. And then, as they came in straight over the north-south highway, she began to see signs of celebration and she was riveted.

The central Esplanade of the city had become fairyland. Colored lights were draped across the buildings and strung on poles to create a whole new world. This Brasilia was soft and comforting and full of people on the streets. The central area was divided into five arenas by painted wooden archways covered with lights and flowers, sparklers and streamers. Then long garlands of color defined two avenues running up and down the sides, and smaller streets branching off between the monuments, statues and government buildings of the esplanade.

Zaide begged Susana to land. They had to go down to the Northern Commercial District and use the company lot. The bio-ID on the building gave them immediate access and a decent place to dress.

"We'll have to take a taxi, but we've got a place to change," Susana said as they sprayed their hair in the over-sized mirror of the executive ladies' lounge.

"I told you before, you're a genius," Zaide agreed mechanically. She patted her hair once more, pleased with the way the sparkles on her costume caught the color of the optic fiber ribbons at her shoulder. Then she hung up her dress in the locker and helped herself to the French hand cream in a porcelain container. The company did not stint on comfort for their executive class. Not even under Sonia Leah, although Zaide thought it was a good thing that the pink marble flooring and vanity had been installed before she had gotten hold of the budget. For sure, Sonia Leah would have insisted on something more modest, like tile.

But she wanted out of the rich, perfumed lounge. She wanted to be on the streets with the people, the music, the beat of the drums and the smell of flowers and warm, home-brewed *pinga* and broiling meat. She wanted to be in the press of the crowd.

Finally Susana was ready. "We meet back here at five, no matter what," she instructed.

Zaide raised an eyebrow.

"In case we get separated," Susana explained, then blushed. "In case I meet a guy. Or you meet one. Anything can happen. Anything can happen and it doesn't count. I mean, what did you come for anyway? You didn't really plan to just play dress-up and listen to some sambas, did you?"

Zaide rolled her eyes. It sounded like Susana had memorized a tourist ad. There were times when Susana believed it all too easily. Zaide knew perfectly well that five in the morning meant that they would be drooping over breakfast and people would ask why. She planned to return by one or two and stretch out on the plump chaise in the lounge and sleep. At least a little. If Susana wanted to attract attention by being tired and ill-prepared, that was her choice.

"Okay, if we get separated," Zaide agreed.

Susana practically dragged her down the stairs and into
the streets. It took them quite a while to get a cab. Here it
was as deserted as if it were Sunday. Zaide and Susana were
the only living beings there. It spooked Zaide, and she
walked a little faster, eyes glued firmly on the distance, on
the fireworks exploding over the Esplanade.

As they got nearer she could hear the music, the seductive,
invasive beat of the samba. They asked the cab to let them
out on the edge of the Esplanade. Zaide was relieved. She
didn't want to be seen coming out of a cab, didn't want to be
associated with the fazenda. This night was magic, not part
of her real life or the real world.

She started to walk toward the lights while Susana paid.
The drums got in her walk and exaggerated the swing of her
hips. She wanted to dance. The drums were the pulse in her
throat, in her wrist, between her legs.

And then they were at the festival of Saint Anthony, surrounded by lights and crowds and music. It smelled like incense and burning wood and roasting meat; it smelled like
sweat and desire. Zaide tasted it on her tongue, and flicked
the pink tip over her black-painted lips.

There was too much to take in at once. At first she was
content to be overwhelmed by color and costume alone. In
the multicolored light the most offensive bright pink and
searing aqua became merely cheerful and festive. Costumes
were not fantastical like they were for Carnival—great
feathered headdresses and dripping beads over the tongas
that were favored in Rio, mythic animals, samba clubs done
up as the sun and the moon with papier-mâché and glitter.

The costumes here were simpler, more rustic. There were
a large number of people in brightly patched clothes resplen-
dent with ribbons, and others in traditional country dress.
Susana and Zaide were a bit on the fancy side.

Many people wore only masks. There were mirror masks
and feather masks and leather masks. Zaide was sure they
had bought the masks cheap at earlier festivals, from the
boys wandering with dozens hanging from their arms. After

some deliberation, Zaide selected a black satin half-mask with strings of glass beads hanging from the edges low enough to drop over her throat.

There was a man dressed as a pirate with three parrots on his shoulders and his head, and a transvestite in a peach silk negligee with an ocelot on a leash. There was an entire dance team wearing jaguar hoods and little else but glitter paint, which made Zaide turn away. There were certain things about the past that shouldn't be played with or prettified, she thought. There were the requisite skeletons and ghouls, some of whom must have spent a lot of money on a special-effects makeup job.

Then there were the more mundane costumes, the clowns and hobos, the transvestites in tongas, the things that were featured in every tourist brochure. Bit by bit Zaide separated them and appreciated the very best, ignored the commonplace. She felt a little embarrassed that her own costume was so funereal. But at least it didn't look exactly like everyone else's—the unending hot-pink and green and orange patches on baggy drawstring pants, the ubiquitous oversized painted fans and paper-flower necklaces.

First they went to the center archway, covered with real flowers and ribbons, and coins glittering over the statue of Saint Anthony. The tradition was that unmarried girls went to Mass and then gave the saint thirteen centavos. Zaide felt a little uncomfortable about that and looked away as Susana added her few bright coins to those at the statue's feet.

"Come on, it's part of the celebration," Susana hissed. "It doesn't mean anything."

But Zaide still refused. It did mean something. Most of all, it meant that she felt attracted. There was something about the cheap lights and the noise and the press of people that made her feel nostalgic. She couldn't figure out why. She'd been born and raised for, and in, the compound. She might have been brought down to such a festival once with a group of children in the village school when she was very young, but that wasn't enough to explain the strong attraction.

She turned away from the statue and began walking, anything to fill her mind with other, more comfortable images. There were plenty of them. They passed a game arcade, young boys yelling their pitches at the strangers in the night. There were food vendors, too, whole alleyways full of them selling sweets and ice cream and roasted meats and soft drinks. Folding chairs had been set up on the street near each stall so that people could sit to eat and then move on.

Susana tugged her past the food sellers and back to the main area where there was music and dancing and several large fires going. Zaide watched indulgently as her cousin flirted wordlessly with one masked stranger and then another until someone finally led her out to dance.

Zaide turned away. She wanted to see the places she hadn't been. There were people on the edge of the shadows engrossed in their own games. Zaide drifted over, certain that Susana was much happier in the dancing than wandering the festival.

Mostly what she saw wasn't very interesting. Portable tables set up with con games and fortunetellers and lottery cards, mostly. But she wanted to be sure she had seen everything, experienced the whole range of the fair. After all, she had never done this before and she needed to touch, see, taste, every part of it. Then she would be content to go back to the dancing that was not so different from the dancing at any young people's party in any of the golf and tennis clubs that bordered the lake.

She heard the drumming again, closer and stronger than before. The rhythms were complex, weaving against each other to make complex music with only the pounding of the great ceremonial drums. It drew her into itself, into the pulse of the festival, of the city, of the land. But the land of the rhythms was older than Brazil. The patterns of the music were pure African, the Yoruba heritage that was as much a part of the Brazilian identity as the Portuguese language or the native cuisine. It made Zaide feel proud and feminine in the early winter night.

Then the crowd parted to reveal a platform, and a group of men mounted the stage. The music intensified. The performing group were all dressed in loose drawstring pants and vests, each in a different color to go with their different skins. All Brazil was in the group, and all were masked.

Pleased to find a performance of some type, Zaide staked out a patch of ground and watched the men form a circle. The drumming slowed slightly as the men swayed together and the traditional music of the three instrumental African bows whined high and sharp and full of African syncopation. And then two of the men came to the center, weaving and swaying and tumbling in a combination of gymnastics and dance. Their bodies glistened under the festival lights, arms floating forward and away, feet kicking in slow motion. It was formal and hypnotic at the same time.

Zaide was fascinated. She had heard of *capoeira* but had never seen it. In combat that was dance and drama, one of the men forced the other to the edge of the circle. The two merged with the group, and two more came forward and the ritual conflict began again.

As she studied the circle, Zaide met eyes behind a mask on the stage. She held the gaze, flirting the way she would at any party at the golf club. But the expression she could see under the thin fabric mask was more dangerous than those of any of the cousins, even when the cousins were ready to cut her dead. He had far too much pride.

Then, deliberately, he nodded in her direction and turned his attention back to the *capoeira* circle. It was his turn, and he came forward only two deliberate steps. His opponent had black skin, and he was moonlight white, but both were hard-muscled from labor as well as the discipline of the fighting circle. Even at this distance, Zaide noticed a few scars. The black man wore spotless white, and the pale one who had caught her eye was in black. Both outfits were trimmed with red braid that was like blood, the only color between them. Under the harsh stage lights the contrast between the two men was artistically composed and primitive. But then, *capoeira* was above all an art form.

She had never known people who looked like this. Men of her class were fat or thin or ordinary, but their bodies were not hard and their movements were not fluid. They began the slow, circular movements of the game that was both dance and martial art. The drumming built to a frenzy; the music from the master's bow controlled the precise kind of *jogo* to be played. Zaide merged with the crowd, the combat, the primal test of strength and will.

Savage and controlled, the dancers weaved and dodged, kicked, swept and rolled across the floor in what was part choreography and part true confrontation of force. Black and white, yin and yang, each always completing the circle the other started. Like dinner conversation at the Vielho fazenda, like negotiations with governments and industries, Zaide suddenly saw. They were all the same. Words or bodies, testing, thrusting, pushing the other out of the arena.

And then they each touched one of the waiting men in the circle and it was over. They both returned to places in the circle. And then the same man caught her eye again, and this time he smiled. Just a little, to let her know that the show had been for her. Ever so much better a compliment than the usual speech or flower taken from the table arrangement.

Zaide considered walking away. It would be easy—blend into the crowd and the night and disappear forever. She was surprised to find she didn't want to. She wanted to see if he would come over after the game or if he would slink into the dark. Since coming to live at the big house, she had rarely talked to anyone who was not of her own class or background, except for a maid or a garage tender.

The next two sets of competitors were not quite as good as the earlier ones. The contests were over too quickly and none of them used the languid drops and theatrical gymnastics of the dance that had been performed for her benefit. The bones of the *capoeira* were exactly the way she had perceived them, the constant balance of the *tao* alternating in the eternal circular whole.

Then, abruptly, the music stopped and the dancers jumped off the stage. Zaide was still watching the platform, wondering if they would acknowledge the crowd that had gathered or collect any of the coins tossed on the bare stage. She didn't notice him at her shoulder until he lifted a blue paper cup to her face.

"Would the lady care for a drink? Some man gave me a bottle of aguardente," he said casually. "I hate to drink alone."

Zaide grinned and took the cup. They walked over to the shadows and sat down before drinking. Zaide admired that, just a little. And, like at the dinner table, she chose her words.

"Your dance struck me very strongly," she said. "Like I was seeing it for the first time. Like it was an allegory of the universe or something."

He laughed softly and nodded, drank the harsh liquor. Then he called over a boy who was selling the traditional soft candies everyone ate during the holidays, bought a small bag and dropped four coins in the urchin's hand. He handed her a napkin and then held the bag while she dipped in and fished out one of the soft, sweet balls.

"The *capoeira* came from the slaves," he said, more as if talking to himself than trying to teach her. "The Yoruba weren't allowed to teach their martial skills to their children, so they hid it from the masters in the form of a dance. And when the slaves rebelled, they were able to hold off a superior force of Dutch and Portuguese with *capoeira* alone, against modern weapons."

The words sounded hollow to her, as if he were speaking in some room far away, as if the connection were no good. She was so very conscious of her breathing, her posture sitting on the grass, her glitter-black skirts spread around her.

She knew it was time to say something, to keep the conversation going, but this was not one of the golf-club boys she chatted with all the time. This person was more firmly real, and more dangerous. She knew she should just leave. She didn't want to.

Susana wanted the semblance of rebellion; Zaide wanted the real thing. The primitive, raw energy she had seen in the dance coalesced around him. In the soft cloth half-mask his eyes burned with a rage that spoke to her and somehow touched a fury of her own.

"Would you take off your mask?" he asked, teasing.

"Only if you do," Zaide returned, and pulled the satin and bead thing off with a flourish.

He took longer, and when he finally unknotted the long scarf that hid the top half of his head and face she saw that he was very young, very pale and tense. As if he was about to snap. Somehow the prospect pleased her.

"What are you called?" he asked, very polite.

She thought for a moment. Susana had said that no one used their real names all the time down in the festival. The night and the dark glitter around her made her wish for the same aura of danger and control that she sensed from her companion. "Noire," she said, remembering the name she and Susana had agreed on in the safety of the favela.

"Dona Noire," he repeated, and studied her with a respect she had done nothing to deserve.

Five

THE last time he had seen this girl she had been bleeding to death on the street. Expert with a blowgun, too, good enough to consider recruiting. She had seemed more intelligent than many of the favela girls he had known.

And the name she gave him wasn't the usual street-girl name. She was finer than that, maybe another one like Pope and himself, displaced from all the dreams.

But he had seen her die. He had felt the absence of a pulse himself, and Steel had seen it too. He studied her a little more closely. No, it wasn't someone who looked like her, not unless she was a twin. He hadn't looked at her too carefully before, not until he saw how good she was with a blowgun, how cool and fearless.

It was the same girl. He was good with faces, with names, with people. It was a paradox. It was impossible.

It was only a bad dream. The rational part of his mind, the part that had always screamed at the *candomble*, was screaming now. He should walk away. Later he would believe that it was just the light and the atmosphere and the quantity of aguardente he had drunk. If he left now, everything would make sense in the morning. He had merely had too much to drink.

And the part of his mind that kept bringing him back to the African rites—the part that couldn't leave sense alone like a scab on the back of his hand, which he had picked to scar—that part of his mind refused to listen. This was something important, it screamed at him. The *capoeira* was part of the whole circle and so was this person, dead and not dead.

His classical education for once joined forces against sense. Eurydice following Orpheus back from the underworld and dead Alcestis whom Hercules brought back, these had been taught to him in the same clean and quiet rooms that had seen his first attempts at algebra and Newtonian mechanics.

Paulo Sylvia did not believe that the dead could walk any more than he believed that he could fly. But he also knew that the world was not a clean and sterile and logical place. Life as he knew it was psychotic and perverse. This girl's appearance was one more proof of the twisted humor of the universe, which the *candomble* priests named the god-trickster Exu Tiriri.

"Let's play the arcade," the girl was saying.

Paulo followed, knowing that he was not able to leave. The mystery of it wasn't the only reason; although he was curious, he was certain there was an explanation hidden somewhere. More, he followed because he recognized in himself what he believed to be fate.

"I know this sounds very stupid, like an old line, but didn't we play a run earlier this week? You had a blowgun. You were very good. I was impressed."

"I think you're mistaken," she said firmly.

But he knew she was wrong. The universe was a cruel and perverse place and this was one more proof thereof. He knew better than to try and second-guess Fate. "Well, let's play the arcade," he said as if he hadn't mentioned the run at all.

The arcade was brightly lit and noisy. The games were old, many physical throwing and aiming things, a few tame interactives for the kiddies. The real interactives were too expensive for a mobile touring arcade down on a cheap one-day festival.

The prizes weren't all that appealing, either. Still, he played shooting ducks and won a large stuffed snake, which he draped around the girl's neck. She smiled as though impressed, as if her own skill with the blowgun wasn't twice his.

She had a pocket full of dinheiro, small coins that paid for the balloon toss and dunk-the-caller. He won smaller prizes at those, too, and finally she was so heavily laden with soft pastel animals that they both had to laugh. He had less money than she, only a few centavos that weren't meant for spending that night, but he needed to offer her another aguardente.

He saw her glance over at the dancers at the other side of the esplanade. "Do you want to dance?" he asked.

She laughed and touched the rainbow snake, the white and lavender giraffe, the little pink lion. "Where would I put them?" she asked lightly. "No, it's just that my cousin is over there. We came together."

He understood. He had been right; she was from a decent family, not come down to party alone among strangers. But the good families had their own parties at the golf and tennis clubs around the lake, parties where their daughters didn't meet people of the wrong class. This was absurd. Girls from good families didn't run with the Serps or get that dangerous with a blowgun, either. The contradictions piled up.

He led her to the dance floor set up over the grass, and cast a look over the crowd. Pope already had two girls in tow and Steel was lounging in a shadow with a bottle in a paper bag. Sylvia took the prizes and went over to Steel, dumped the soft toys all over Steel's legs. "Watch these for us, would you?" he asked, smiling. He didn't wait to see Steel's reaction as he led Noire away.

They danced, samba after samba, as if it were Carnival in Rio and not simply Saint Anthony's Day in Brasilia.

Only when the band took a break and he asked for her number, did Zaide become confused. She almost wrote it down without thinking, until she realized that the code would reveal that she lived at a fazenda. Above all she didn't want him to know she was one of "them," not even if it meant never seeing him again. So she just looked down and turned slightly red.

Paulo laughed softly. "Don't worry, I don't have a link either. What about Thursday night? Do you know South 109?" He was certain she did; all Brasilia did. And if she was what he thought, then there was no question.

Zaide smiled to cover her confusion. She had never heard of South 109 before. But she had nearly a week to figure it out. And he wanted her. She could taste it in the dry winter air. And then the band came back and they danced again.

"She was dead," Steel was saying firmly. "I felt her pulse. You're wrong, that's all."

Sylvia ignored him and dropped feeder into homemade solution. He'd filched the biochips from the freeze library where he'd worked for a few weeks last year, until they'd been bought out and closed down by the Alados. Now the third generation were growing in jam jars in the closet.

The first-floor apartment had once been meant for a caretaker. Now that the building had dropped from the white-collar middle class to favela on even the top floors, the first floor was fit only for a drunk or highwire addict. So it was fitting that Bakunin had moved out the addicts who slept and died there and had turned the place into their own.

There was still a lot of work to be done. The blood and vomit had been wiped off the concrete walls, and they had been papered over with flyers and concert schedules for underground bands. Pope had discovered a table and a rolled-up carpet on the street the day Mrs. Flora had moved to her daughter's house in São Paulo, and had hauled them down. The carpet had been dirty green and looked horrible with the red and pink, white, yellow and green flyers that covered the walls, but they had glued it down because there was nothing to sit on, and carpet was better than bare cement. The table sat to one side and was covered with more flyers, which served as scrap paper, a broken link sitting half-submerged in a pile of assorted second-generation discard chips, and a set of ancient dental tools.

Sylvia adjusted the lights over the row of jars and closed the closet doors, then made a few careful notations on the back of a favela under-building club schedule.

"You think that's going to do any good?" Steel spat the words out furiously. "You play with that shit like it's a lab or something. Well, this is just one more hole and one more gang, and you aren't going to access the Wave. Not ever. And if you do get in, there isn't anything you can do with it anyway."

Sylvia never raised his voice. "I didn't say I was trying to get in. You're angry because of the girl. You saw her. It's the same girl."

Francisco Pope had been listening to this for far too long. Steel never let anything go, and although he was useful, he was annoying. It wasn't important. Other things were more pressing, and he didn't want to discuss them in front of Steel. Steel was a good soldier, but Pope didn't want his opinions. On anything. And he was already tired of this debate about the girl. He'd heard it two days running, and if Steel didn't shut up soon, he was going to find his head on the other side of the concrete wall.

"I'm sick of this place, I'm sick of you sitting around like you're so superior," Steel said. "Today I'm going to place a bet on the Palmeiras for this week's game."

"The Palmeiras haven't won a game in seven years," Francisco said evenly.

Steel only shrugged and left. Neither Pope nor Paulo said goodbye.

"The Serps came back this afternoon with more data on highwire," Pope said. "They say there's another Cadea shipment due Thursday. They wanted to know if we're on."

"What did you tell them?" Paulo asked, not looking up from the scribbles he had made. The DNA matches he had recorded from the library weren't working out exactly right, and he wasn't sure why.

"I told them I'd talk," Pope said. "I was a little surprised that there wasn't any trouble that we torched the stuff. I was sure they'd charge us the street value."

"So why do they want back in with us?" Sylvia asked. "I thought they'd drop the contact, even though they could be really useful in the suburbs. When we're ready."

Ready. They'd talked about it a million times, ever since their families had taken the plunge downward from the carefully maintained northern superquadras and into the south. Paulo Sylvia didn't like to think about the time before that when he had actually aspired to something beyond destruction.

But most of the time he didn't believe it. There was no place for dreams in his life, and he was too full of them. He dreamed about learning how to grow altered cells the way Gilberto Reyes did in the frozen library. They'd talked about scholarships, about someday becoming partners in developing something more subtle and less debilitating than the current apparatus. So the wave would become a natural part of the individual, the link a seamless meld.

And Francisco Pope, his friend who was closer than a brother, Pope would run the business office and work with the companies. They would remain independent, deal with all the conglomerates and the government. Maybe one day they would move their headquarters to São Paulo, which was the technical center of the country.

When the dreams were gone there was only rage. Cadea, Vielho-Markowicz, Alado-Merea-Dee, any of the others, it made no difference to him. He just needed to make them hurt the way he hurt. So he had given up on Pope's ideas about the gangs and the favelas. He went along only because he wanted to believe.

"I don't know why they want back in with us, and it worries me," Pope admitted. "And it's Cadea again. You think they have any special source there? Some relative who works there or something?"

Sylvia shook his head. "Maybe. But security is pretty

tight, I think, for getting into those companies in the first place. And anyone who really knows anything is part of the family."

Pope snorted. "They aren't any kind of family."

"Whatever," Sylvia agreed. There was no use talking to Pope about families. "I still don't feel comfortable about this whole thing. Maybe they're trying to set us up. And why would they give us that much information up front?"

Pope was silent for many minutes, thinking. He knew Sylvia was probably right. But the Serps held Bakunin's reputation in their hands. And word on the street was that Bakunin couldn't keep up, wasn't willing to put it on the line. They couldn't afford that, not if they wanted to use the Serps, and the Crows, and perhaps count the legendary Jaguars as allies some day.

There wasn't a choice. Pope explained it and Sylvia knew it was true. Fate again, coming full circle. They had to prove themselves; Pope repeated himself twice on that. They had to win the other's respect.

"Why don't we preempt them?" Paulo asked. "They gave you enough information for us to use independently. So we set up and go in before they can get on that damned bus, and by the time they arrive we've got the initiative."

Francisco looked at him and frowned. "Tell me more," he urged.

"It is easier for us than for them," Paulo said quietly. "We only need to crash the vert, burn the shipment. They want to take it whole. We get there beforehand and we make them take a second loss on the street. Highwire is big income, but it isn't respected. We could earn some notches with the other gangs and take the Serps down a few."

"That might be seen as a betrayal," Francisco warned, his tone heavy with disapproval.

Paulo shrugged. "They gave us the information. We have the option of playing by their rules again, or of taking on the leadership ourselves. And there's another thing. I don't like them. I don't trust them. And this offer is too good for it not to be a trap."

"Then we put it out on the street that they meant to betray us." Pope said aloud what Sylvia had merely implied, tasting the words as he rolled them on his tongue. "I don't know. There could be problems. On the street . . ."

"There haven't been anything but problems since the Forestation Riots and General Risado decided that the entire country was his personal playground, and the whole universe collapsed," Paulo reminded him bitterly. "Who cares about one more?"

Dinner at the Vielho-Markowicz fazenda was rather dull on Wednesday night. Sonia Leah was distracted and Miguel Leal and Ana Lourdes dominated the conversation. Julio Simon said nothing until the strong sweet *cafezinho* was served after the dessert.

"I have a rather special event planned for tomorrow afternoon," he began judiciously. "Uncle Victor, Sonia Leah, I hope you will both be able to attend. If so, you will see the efficacy of our new policies with both the favelas and the Cadea competition in our market."

Zaide Soledad nearly dropped her cup. For Julio Simon to invite the CEO so casually was quite out of order. Junior executives, even those like Julio who were considered prime candidates for the seventh floor one day, simply did not invite Uncle Victor to anything without going through the usual scheduling routine. Even Sonia Leah wouldn't be so impudent.

But Uncle Victor merely nodded. "Yes?" he said in that deceptively gentle voice.

The cafezinho sat ignored on the table, growing cold.

"I have the Cadea shipping schedule for top-grade highwire into the peninsula, which is not our most lucrative market but accounts for a seventeen percent profit share. It would be a shame to lose it," Julio said. "Tomorrow afternoon they are planning another delivery. I have made arrangements for that delivery to be intercepted."

Sonia Leah yawned gracefully, half covering her mouth with her napkin.

"Not by regular security forces," Julio continued, ignoring Sonia Leah's disinterest. "The interception will be untraceable. And I know where the cargo will be taken afterwards. It should be easy enough to confiscate. And the highjackers will be disposed of. With credit going to us, and Cadea in our debt."

"Very ambitious," Uncle Victor said. "If it succeeds, you will have to show us all the tapes. If not . . ."

Uncle Victor shrugged and laid his damask napkin next to his plate. Dinner was over. Julio glanced at Zaide as they left the dining room.

"What did you think?" he asked in a whisper as they walked through the sun room out to the porch.

"I think you should have waited until you could show off a success," Zaide hissed. She thought he was getting too confident, rash. The thrill of the risk should be enough. Offering to fall flat in front of the CEO and assembled senior staff was merely stupid. For the first time, Zaide found herself wondering if Julio Simon might not be just a touch overrated.

THE after hours sub-building barzinho in the super-quadra was at its best just past midnight. The music was loud and the card players could barely make out their hands for the cigarette smoke trapped under the ceiling, the bottom of the six-story residence. Beer and aguardente were plentiful, and if it was hard to see well, then it softened the cynical lines on the girls' faces and obscured the raw plumbing and power lines overhead.

"You think Laurindo's going to make it?" Sylvia asked Pope. They were sitting away from the light, around what had once been a fifty-gallon drum, nursing beers that had lost most of their foamy heads an hour ago. There was an empty seat beside them.

"If he doesn't come tonight, then he'll be around before noon," Pope replied evenly.

"We could go to 109 and pick up immediately," Sylvia groused.

"And we'd pay more and we don't know about the quality," Pope reminded him quietly. "We've been dealing with Laurindo for a long time now; he's never cut us yet."

"You mean you trust him?" Paulo asked, smiling.

Pope smiled in return. "No. But I'm fairly certain he likes our business." Then he sighed and eyed the bar.

"Serps are a bunch of no-respect babies," Steel was saying loudly as he clung to the makeshift bar. "Bunch of skirts, and not too smart, either. You know, they go and give us everything and then the gutless wonders don't have the nerve to join in the raid. Makes you wonder about those outside towns, you know?"

Pope flinched.

"It might be better if we just got rid of him now," Paulo suggested softly.

Pope dropped his head to his hand. "If he weren't so damned useful, if he wasn't a Changeling and wasn't so damned fast, I'd do it myself. For the satisfaction. But he's too useful."

"The Ministry paid for it, and even they didn't keep him," Sylvia reminded Pope. "They couldn't stand him, either."

"Their budget went," Pope said. "Yet another example of project planning."

Paulo turned and looked at the haze dissipating out into the night. He had wanted to enter that program, and at the age of twelve had qualified in the physical and placed in high-officer capacity in intelligence. He'd gone through the prelims, the secondaries already in place and pumping his chems. But he'd been eliminated in psych. His parents had been both disappointed and relieved. The modifications to work in orbital could mean being unable to return to Earth, to live the way families ought to live.

Orbital was not to their liking at all. But with the secondaries, they had talked to Dr. Valdemar at the University, who had been one of Paulo's father's thesis advisors. Already roughwired for Changeling programs, Paulo might qualify for something a little closer to human. As long as the phrines were carefully monitored, he wasn't the monster the mindmen thought him to be.

Paulo had always been strange. Three years in the Observatory had not yielded a confirmed diagnosis. Seven genevirus intrusions had altered his personality only moderately. The rage had become bearable, controlled just under the surface. Seven allele changes was more than anyone should tolerate. But with the implant he was dangerous, some mindman said, a danger to society, to himself.

Once there had been a place for people like Paulo Sylvia.

The *candangos* who had built Brasilia in the last century had been a rough breed, playing out uncivilized genes against a wilderness. The creative outlets were all gone. How the genes had disappeared through the sieve of personality and reappeared realigned in Paulo was something of a mystery.

Candango genes, not very good with authority. Independent, from a time when the interior had been one of the great challenges. When the cerrado had been impassable, when the great forest had stood up and challenged men instead of being coddled by them.

Paulo Sylvia accepted that he was something worse than a monster. He was a person out of time. And because of that he had always been something of a loner. Even in the Observatory the others were not like him. The violent ones were not creative, the intelligent ones were torqued away from reality. His friendship with Francisco was the one real friendship he had.

In the end, that was the only diagnosis of his disease. He liked to be alone. And no one liked to be alone. No one ever wanted to go off by himself the way Paulo did all the time, into the twisted, scary universe in his own head.

Which maybe was good spacer material, and Paulo had always intended to try that. It was the one place where he was sure he could work, where his interests in bioengineering and mechanics and explosives would be useful. Like the early days in the Planalto for the pioneers. But everything had collapsed and he had been rejected for the orbital anyway.

"I can't believe they took him," Paulo said through clenched teeth, looking at Steel.

Steel was now talking to Old Hector, the blind bookie who drank down in the barzinho everything he did not have to pay out. "What do you say about those Palmeiras, huh?" Steel asked loudly. "Everybody tells me I'm out of my mind, and they pay off twenty to one. Palmeiras out of São Paulo, green and white, they're my boys. Bet their coach gets to pick the World Cup team."

Old Hector spat on the packed ground. "A lucky win, that's all. Bom Jesus, he's going to be disqualified for all those Changes, if not this season, then for the World Cup, I tell you."

Steel snorted. "What use is the hand, I ask you? And it isn't like he had it done on purpose—he had an accident as a boy."

"And the eye?" Old Hector asked. "And the knee implants?"

"That was because of arthritis," Steel protested vigorously. "It's old technology; they've been doing that for years. It isn't like he's been wired for speed."

"Not like you, you mean," Old Hector said meaningfully, and spat again. "Take your money, boy, and buy an old man a fresh drink."

Steel gestured to the bartender, who took a new bottle and poured *pinga* into Old Hector's empty jar.

"He keeps us in dinheiro, though," Pope said. "His bets pay off. You can't deny that."

Paulo didn't reply. Instead he watched an old woman in a red headrag come into the light and sit delicately on a broken stepladder that served as a barstool. She looked as if she had survived from the days of the great cacao plantations, before the candangos came and built a city in the grasslands. She was withered and frail but with the straight back and elegant manners of the old days. She was served *pinga* in a glass jar, which she sipped very slowly. Around her, people showed respect. The men excused themselves when they swore. The young whores working the room spoke to her softly and bowed their heads like convent school girls asking a blessing from one of the sisters.

Paulo knew he was being rude, but he couldn't stop. He was certain that she was the priestess from the *axe*. There was something about the way her fingers curled around the glass, the way she moved her head and made the fringe of the head scarf flutter, that brought back visceral memories of the *candomble* ritual he wanted very much to forget.

"Where are you, the moon or something?" Pope demanded.

Sylvia blinked hard. He hadn't told Pope about the ritual. Of all the things they had shared together, that one thing he had missed. Paulo didn't understand why he felt so ashamed that he needed to hide the ritual as if it had never happened.

"Have you ever seen that woman before?" Paulo tried to keep his voice even. "She looks older than Brasilia."

"No," Francisco answered. "Why?"

Paulo felt distinctly uncomfortable. He shrugged. "I hope Laurindo is coming tonight," he said, changing the subject. "I hope he'll have phrines."

Francisco smiled. "He'll have. Laurindo likes to live nice, you know."

Steel lurched at the old woman, fast, even if unsteady. He was drunk. Sylvia wondered where he came by the instinct that kept him in funds for beer and aguardente every night, but Steel's pockets always seemed to have the extra centavos. Steel always drank, while Francisco and Sylvia had money only for a single beer each which they had to savor all evening. When they had money at all.

The old woman looked Steel dead in the eye, firm and steady and righteous as his mother. "You," she said, and spat.

There was no mistaking the voice. High and musical and full of power, there was no doubt. Paulo could feel the anger rise, and he wanted to kill her. He wanted to eliminate all of the strange and offensive ritual, his own part in it and his own acquiescence.

"You are cursed," the woman said to Steel, not terribly loudly but with such authority that everyone in the makeshift bar paid strict attention. "A bad curse is riding you and you will bring evil and death to one of your friends, and a heavy heart to another."

Sylvia went pale. Pope smiled grimly. "That lets us out," he said. It hardly reassured Sylvia.

Steel sneered. "You old bag," he said hoarsely, "I don't

believe your bullshit, okay? So go sell your fortunes somewhere else."

Several hard, frowning men formed a semicircle around
Steel. He looked at all of them, at their bruised fists and hag-
gard faces. These were not people who had anything to lose.
One, a tall black man Paulo recognized from a *capoeira* circle, wheeled around slowly, and with perfect elegance,
kicked Steel in the head. The young man crumpled, as much
with drink as with the blow. The group around him dis-
persed.

"Damn," Pope said under his breath. "How the hell are we
going to get him out? It'll screw us completely with the people here."

"Laurindo isn't here yet either," Sylvia pointed out. "And
I don't want to run this without phrines."

Francisco shrugged. "Laurindo isn't here. It's better if we
weren't either." His gaze returned to Steel, lying prone on
the scuffed concrete floor. The old woman was still drinking
as if she were at the head of the table at the finest fazenda.

"Leave him, then," Paulo said.

"We can't," Francisco objected flatly. "He's still
Bakunin."

"He's trouble, even if he is Changeling," Paulo stated.
"You know he's a liability, admit it."

Their eyes met. Paulo knew Pope didn't let his personal
feelings, be they prejudices or liking, get in the way of making use of usable people. But this time was too much, Steel
had gone too far. Not just safety in the barzinho, but the reputation of Bakunin on the street had been jeopardized with
Steel.

"He isn't street," Francisco finally agreed.

They left through the cigarette haze, skirting the bar and
the tables, and even the girls, as they kept close to the pillars
that opened on to the night. Paulo pushed the red steel door
and they slipped into the main building onto the first-floor
corridor. The door gently folded back in place.

Their office was only two doors down, behind a door with

the oversized words NO UNAUTHORIZED PERSONS PERMITTED. That sign was the reason Sylvia loved their place so much. The humor of it had not worn off. He also appreciated the fact that it had once been a broom closet and janitor's lounge. Now that there was no money to pay for cleaning supplies, let alone someone to use them, there was no reason for the two large, well-situated rooms to be ignored. Francisco and Paulo had a far better use for the space than the few addicts who had made their way up the front stairs and into the broom closet to die.

Since there was no band in the barzinho tonight, it was silent here. Everything was clean, pristine, the way Francisco liked it. No papers anywhere, all the pens neat in the jar that still sported its imported mustard label.

"I don't like it," Francisco said softly. "We don't have the phrines, the Serps are going to be real unhappy, and this thing with Steel. She was an old woman, what was she going to do? Say a couple of things, so what? She's an old, old woman."

"You think Laurindo will come by, maybe?" Paulo asked, trying to keep the need out of his voice. Trying to play casual, as if it didn't matter any more to him than to Pope. As if the secondary weren't there, filling him with inhibitors and stims at the same time. Making him more "normal." Making him crazy and angry and confused. Making it hard for him to influence the visions that filled the twilight, the chems that made his hand shake and not obey his mind. "If he goes in and doesn't see us, he knows we're right here. He should come. So we'll have the phrines. Laurindo's a businessman; he doesn't pass up a sale."

"What the hell are we planning to use for money?" Francisco asked bitterly. "Steel said he would pay, remember? He is useful."

Paulo paced, flicking the long black Teflon knife in ornate patterns, tossing it thoughtlessly from one hand to the other. Halfway across the room he dropped, caught himself on his hands, and executed one of the slow, round kicks that was the center of *capoeira*. He came up with a corkscrew twist that was both elegant and would take him out of an opponent's reach. Then he twirled the knife again.

"You know, maybe we should call the whole thing off," he said after he had completed a second circuit of the room.

"Because of Steel?" Pope asked. "Or the phrines?"

Paulo shook his head. "I have a bad feeling about it, is all. That old woman. She gave me chills, you know. She was like some messenger from Hell."

"You don't believe in Hell," Francisco reminded him softly.

Paulo crumpled against the wall. The chems started talking, although they used his mouth. "It's just everything is going against us now. The phrines and Steel and that woman showing up here. And the Serps. Why would they tell us anything at all that wasn't for their own benefit? They came up looking very bad after the last burn. Maybe they're setting us up."

A sound came from the metal door, more a soft scratch than a knock. The knife twirled faster in Paulo's hand. Francisco went to the door. "Come on, we'd almost given up on you," Pope said and stepped aside for Laurindo to enter.

For all his fine white linen shirt and pants, Laurindo looked pinched and pained. It was his whole aspect, not merely his Changeling eyes. Paulo Sylvia secretly believed that the drug seller should have been a priest. While Laurindo seemed to have all the luxuries the southern sector of the city offered, he never quite gave the appearance of enjoying anything at all.

There were rumors about Laurindo. That he had been the most brilliant student of genetics in the history of the University of São Paulo, until he took one too many of his own creations. That he plundered the dead for the organs he used to make the phrines he sold, that he even processed the tissues of highwire addicts and other city refuse, to continue some experimental work that no one quite understood. That he bought *pivetes*, the urchins who roamed the streets and cerrado, and tortured them alive to produce the phrines no one could synthesize. That he was the son of one of the wealthiest families in all Brazil, that he had killed a gardener's child in some early game, and his family had hushed it up.

Paulo didn't believe any of the rumors. Laurindo always dealt with Pope in person. Laurindo was a snake-Changeling, and not even the most eccentric São Paulo family would ever permit that. No, Paulo was quite certain that Laurindo was merely one more manufacturer of cut-rate phrines, most of them probably refined from cadavers instead of being decently organ-produced in a lab.

Laurindo nodded at Paulo and took a small envelope out of his pocket. "Only the best for you, Seu Francisco," he said quietly. Pope examined the merchandise, tiny white pills with a horseshoe stamped on one side. A horseshoe so small that it would take a microscope to see the detail. Pope looked at the figure as if he wished he had access to equipment to check the authenticity of his purchase.

After he had taken long enough to show Laurindo that he did, indeed, appreciate the best, he replaced the pills in the envelope and handed it back. "Steel has our money," Francisco said softly. "He's drunk. We won't have it for a few hours at the least."

Laurindo's narrow eyes raked Pope over, and then inspected Paulo, still crouched against the wall. He seemed to hesitate, undecided. Then he blinked and Paulo caught the reptilian membrane under the eyelid as it closed. He had never quite figured out why Laurindo seemed so cold. The snake eyes with the extra lid that never blinked now became the whole of Laurindo's face for Paulo Sylvia. He wondered if Laurindo was a Changeling cut from some other program that had been discontinued for lack of funds. Or if maybe he was something else, if the alterations had been his own idea. If anyone had the connections to become Changeling, it would be Laurindo. Or so the word on the street had it.

"I will trust you for the dinheiro," Laurindo said, placing

the envelope precisely on the corner of Pope's desk. "If you will do one thing. Promise me that this highwire will not reach the street. It is bad for business, you understand."

"We don't work for anybody," Paulo growled from the wall.

Laurindo turned his head and regarded Sylvia without blinking. Then he shrugged. "We have interests that coincide," the snake-mod said. "I want to see Antonio Suertes suffer."

"Will you tell us why?" Paulo asked.

Laurindo smiled. It looked like a new mask, something that would shed and reveal his real, scaled skin. But it didn't crack. "Let's just say he is trying to impose his poetry as well as his pharmaceuticals on the world. He should stick to pushing poison."

Paulo shrugged. Francisco immediately turned and walked between the two of them. "Thank you, Seu Laurindo," he said with all the hearty enthusiasm he normally reserved for enticing Serps to deal. "I think we can agree if our final goals are similar, although we do have different motivations. It all comes out the same. And highwire off the street does drive your prices up for everything else, doesn't it?"

For a moment Paulo was certain that Laurindo would hiss. Snake-mods were fairly unpredictable under stress. But Laurindo must have had a loop memory that prompted him to smile. He looked almost human when he did that. The hiss, when it came, was one of victory and agreement, not warning of a strike.

"I believe that our interests coincide," he repeated. Then he let himself out, seeming to slide over the carpet as he did so. There was something faintly reptilian that lingered, although Laurindo was gone.

"See?" Francisco crouched next to Paulo and poked him playfully in the ribs. "We got the phrines. Steel isn't here. Those are pretty good omens, I think."

Paulo waited a long time before he nodded. "Let's go upstairs, then," he said. "If you think we can make it past your mother."

Francisco laughed. "If she asks I'll tell her. It's better than listening to the sermon again."

Paulo did not join in with the laughter. Francisco's mother had become one of the believers who attended a white church every Sunday and read her Bible aloud after dinner every night. When she was there at all. More often, her mind wandered farther than a highwire addict's. Usually he found it as laughable as his friend did, but for a moment Francisco's mother merged with the ancient black-skinned priestess in his mind.

And then the association broke, and he nodded. They left the office and began the long, long climb to the Pope family cells.

Seven

AT noon Paulo and Francisco wakened to the scent of fresh coffee and frying manioc. A little sunlight filtered through the dingy window in the bedroom they had shared for the past year. Francisco went to the window and peered out. It was a perfect, bright winter day, the endless sky a dazzling cloudless blue, the shadows on the street crisp and clear. None of that clarity invaded the room with its two mattresses thrown on the floor, piles of used clothing and neatly stacked books that Francisco kept in strict order. Not bothering with the light, both Pope and Sylvia pulled on the clothes they had been wearing the day before. Paulo ducked into the bathroom to throw some water on his face, leaving the kitchen and his mother to Francisco.

But Dona Elena, pouring out the coffee and slicing the manioc onto plates, was in her absent mood. Which was easier than her saintly one, but it still hurt Francisco to see her staring at nothing, humming tunelessly. She set the plates and cups on the counter for them to take. The plates and cups were from a better time, from a home with a housekeeper, where Dona Elena never had to stand over the stove and fry manioc. The china was delicate, so translucent that Francisco could see through it like an eggshell.

His mother patted his shoulder while he washed at the kitchen sink. "You are so big now, Francisco," she said sweetly. "You will be going to university soon. I remember when I went to the *colégio*, how the nuns were so very strict. Of course, I wanted to go to a proper university, but my parents thought that the morals were too loose. They preferred the *colégio* instead, and since I wanted to teach at the time anyway, it was a fine choice. It was the nuns, you know, who influenced me to go on into journalism. And I was afraid of the *vestibular*. But the teachers all say you should have no trouble with the test at all, even if there are only six hundred places. Even if there were only sixty places. And you are going to study engineering and everyone will call you Dr. Francisco like your father. . . ."

Francisco grabbed his plate and took it back into the bedroom to eat. He tried to chew the manioc, but his mouth was dry and his stomach complained. He drank the coffee instead.

Paulo came in with his own plate and coffee cup. He was able to eat. For him, there were worse things than Dona Elena crumbling in front of him. Francisco tried to remember that, but with Dona Elena's vacant chatter running through his head, he honestly wondered if it had been worse for Paulo.

Of course it had, he told himself firmly. Paulo's parents had died in the riots, his father disappeared and his mother sliced with a bayonet from an antique prize. Paulo had been there, had tried to defend his mother and his sisters. He had been brushed aside like a mosquito, held in restraints while the rioters broke in and committed murder and revolution.

Paulo looked at Francisco's uneaten manioc. "You will need the energy," he said. Pope nodded and choked down a few bites. Paulo knew he wasn't going to get any farther.

Pope swallowed two of the white pills with the last of his coffee, held out two more to Paulo. Sylvia swallowed them both and then held out his hand. Pope gave him two more, which he tucked into the small pocket in his belt.

He waited for the first touch to open the secondary glands, wondering just what combination Laurindo had created this time. Somewhere out there, Paulo was sure, Laurindo was laughing. Laurindo knew and was trying out different mixtures on him to see just how the embedded secondary reacted. It was always a gamble, taking any phrines at all except the legal ones. And he couldn't touch the legal ones, couldn't even walk into the clinic.

Paulo felt the first stirring of energy and it felt good. He strapped the knife to his arm and took the crossbow pistol and fastened it against his leg. Wordlessly Pope handed over two microwave receiver chips. Paulo emptied out his quarrels. The two he chose were hollow bolts. He unscrewed the hardened plastic shafts and fitted the chips into the empty cylinders, then packed them well with toilet paper. The impact shouldn't hurt them. Over it all he threw on the narrow gaucho-style ankle-length natural canvas coat, which had been painted all over with ancient Indian writings. Some, like those of the Serps, were painted with the *veve* of different Yoruba gods, their power talismans. But the coats were common enough among the University crowd and the young intellectuals who hung around 109 and played at being alienated gods. Francisco, too, put on his coat, brilliant with rainbows, after securing his directionals.

Pope then took the plates and cups back to the kitchen, put them in the sink. His mother was staring at the empty wall and hardly acknowledged him when he came in. If she were on highwire she would be more alive, he thought, and that was even worse. Paulo joined Francisco at the door and they walked the six flights of stairs down to the street.

After the red lights in the stairwell, the sunlight was blinding. Steel was loitering near the lobby entrance. He fell into step with them wordlessly. They were not headed for the office on the first floor. There was no need. They were not the Serps. The fewer on a run, the lower the risk. In fact, if Steel had not been waiting for them, they would not have been interested in his joining them. But since there was no way to avoid him, he had to come along. Paulo hoped that Pope was right and that Steel would be useful.

Three people, even in painted coats, didn't draw any attention on the street. They walked securely through their own territory, the center of the superquadra, to their powerbikes secured in code-lock bike boxes out by the main road. From there they rode slowly up through the unrelieved straight artery of the city. Most of the other traffic was cycle or motoped. A few individual groundcars went by. Almost no verts in this sector, although a few bright spots could be seen up ahead beyond the bus station.

Nothing made Paulo so unreasonable as waiting for action. And Steel didn't need any time to reflect on how much he wanted to flame and destroy everything around him. The less mess the better. Enough to show that something had gone down, but not enough to make the action look sloppy. None of the tribes wanted to work with sloppy operators.

The city changed as they came up to the Esplanade. Even from this far end, the view of the Towers of Congress was magnificent. The sun was too high to be bracketed between them, that most famous of all views in Brasilia, but it was impressive all the same. There were the stark sculptures and the linear thrust of the Cathedral, which made sharp shadows on the ground. And above were the lush water gardens, designed for a more civilized time. Gardens that were restricted now, where the gates were locked and a uniformed guard with an oversized charge gun stood watch. Still, it was beautiful.

That beauty fed Paulo. He belonged to the city, and he acknowledged that. The phrines were taking effect. In the stark landscape he felt brilliantly vital, shining like the sun, powerful like the Towers of Congress.

When they were built, no one ever thought there would be another military dictatorship here. No one imagined that international pressures combined with the internal problems of keeping the population productive and the rain forest safe could, together, destroy democracy in Brazil. Now the Towers of Congress were vacant, an unrelenting relic of his country's dignity, and his own.

They walked down the center of the Esplanade toward those imposing structures, so different from the night of the Saint Anthony's Day festival. He wondered about the girl, whether she would be at 109 that night waiting for him on one of the benches, eating an ice cream, or if she would be one of those who laughed and then got scared and didn't show. Maybe he shouldn't bother, he thought, but there was the blowgun and the idea he could recruit her, and the idea that he wanted her more because he had seen her dead. Fate, Francisco had called it.

Suddenly he knew that if he was alive, he would be at their meeting tonight and so would she. And he knew that he would be alive and free because the meeting itself was fate, and nothing could interfere with that. The run was optional. Something about the girl was not. She was important. He wondered briefly if she was Death.

The entire idea was so absurd, he laughed aloud. But the feeling of invulnerability had settled on him and he didn't sense the least, rational twinge of apprehension. Whatever Laurindo had given them this time was very very good, he thought. Better than he had ever had. His mind was as clear as the sunlight reflecting off glass, and his body was completely fluid and at his command.

They cut into the northern half of the city. Here the buildings had once been the mirror image of the south. But this area had been retained as the stronghold of the middle class. There was no graffiti written on the pristine walls here. The endless glass of the uniform six-story buildings reflected perfectly blank walls, not a pane of it broken. There were no young people loitering at corners, leaning against lobby doors, slouched under street lights. There were no young men in the long narrow coats that made them look lean and tall and dangerous.

Instead, there were ladies in the street who wore slender-strapped high-heeled sandals, girls in starched colégio uniforms, young men their own age in carefully pressed slacks in the latest Parisian style, with Italian loafers and gold jewelry. Some of them wore the worried concentration of the new managerial class, worried because there was so little left under their jurisdiction and so much to manage.

Suddenly Pope stopped. "Here," he said, his eyes raking an undistinguished building in the business sector.

"In downtown?" Paulo asked. Even through the phrinemask of omnipotence he knew this was reckless. The first run had been in a residential district, a private shipment to the Cadea distributors in the sector. This was different. This area was full of people, of cityscans, of corporate offices and fazenda holdings. And everyone here noticed them as outsiders, and menacing.

Paulo smiled very slowly. He turned his back to the building and pretended to study the headlines in the faxscan in front of the vendor's station. There were many interesting things at the stand, Paulo noted. He flipped through the reader displays with a sure sense that something would occur to him.

And then he saw the name. He knew that name very well, the regional distributor for Cadea. He had heard it only the night before. Then he requested the reference, and smiled. It was a local poetry publication. He was immensely pleased. He asked Steel to buy it. For the operation.

Steel grumbled, demanded to know if he really needed the whole thing. The single page-print would do in almost any case Steel could imagine.

Paulo wanted very much to strangle him. Instead, keeping his frustration and fury in check, he told Steel that indeed he did need the entire publication. Steel gave him a disbelieving look while dropping the centavos into the machine slot and stepping aside for Paulo to take the hardcopy.

Then, harder still, he had to ask Steel for yet more dinheiro. For tips.

"Tips?" Steel asked as if he'd never heard the word before. Which Paulo knew was ridiculous.

"I may have to tip a few people to help me," Paulo said carefully. He didn't have a plan yet, only the inkling of one. But on the phrine high that was enough. And it occurred to him that a few centavos would somehow be useful.

Steel parted with the dinheiro grudgingly. "I won't be able

to get any more for at least three days. Palmeiras don't play Vasco de Gama until Saturday."

Paulo rolled his eyes. In his current state he didn't edit his dislike of Steel's income. "Well, then why not bet on Flumine versus Corintans tomorrow? Don't you have a hunch on them?"

"No, I don't," Steel said nastily, turning his back and pretending to study the readerscan operating instructions.

Paulo separated from him and Pope, crossed the street and entered the building. The lobby was full of tropical plants and leather furniture. There was a guard at a large desk. This was all exceptionally luxurious. Sylvia had been in public buildings before and most were far more utilitarian. The guard was staring, so Paulo went straight up to him.

"Excuse me, sir, I am looking for a Dr. Antonio Suertes, the poet." He pulled the rolled-up magazine out of his pocket and opened it to the page. "I should very much like to make an appointment with him, if that would not be inconvenient. If he would do me the honor of autographing this copy of his work, it would mean a great deal to me."

"Dr. Antonio is a very busy man," the guard said.

Paulo smiled and pushed two fifty-centavo bills over the polished brass console. "I am so much impressed by what he has done, and I will not be in the city very long. I'm a student in São Paulo and I'm visiting my aunt this week, so this could be my only chance to tell him how much I admire his work."

The guard smiled and took the tip, then buzzed the line. There was a brief conversation Paulo could not hear. He remained earnest-looking, watching the people move through the lobby in the mirrored wall behind the guard. He adjusted his coat, dusted off the sleeves, then pulled out the band that held his hair back and raked his fingers through the shoulder-length tangle until he thought he looked effete enough. Which wasn't much. He probably should have done it before approaching the guard, but the man behind the desk was paying little attention to him.

"Dr. Antonio's secretary says that he will make a few moments for you," the guard announced in a bored voice.

Paulo grinned brilliantly. "Thank you, thank you," he repeated over and over, enthusiastically pumping the guard's hand.

"Sixth floor, Suite nineteen. It's on the door," the guard said, waving him to the rear bank of express elevators. Paulo nearly skipped away as the guard smiled indulgently. He had done a good thing, getting the kid in to see Dr. Antonio, the guard thought. Good for the kid, who probably was just another student in the poetry seminar with big dreams. And good for himself as well. Even down here at the security desk at Cadea, every person knew there was nothing Dr. Antonio liked more than to be reminded of his success as a poet. A young student with a copy of the latest magazine and asking for an autograph—that should put Dr. Antonio in a good mood. And he would be more receptive to the request put before him for the guard's youngest daughter to enter the Cadea Changeling program. Without mentioning the fact that the gratuity was small indeed for the level of service.

Paulo hummed as he rode in the elevator. Sixth floor. The very top. He got off and went down to Suite 19. There a very pretty woman sat at a large desk and looked severe.

"I am here to see Dr. Antonio," Paulo said softly, with the look that had gotten Luzia Amerida and Rosangela Baulindo and Estrella Quinta into bed with him when they were all respectable girls. The secretary's look softened slightly. She sighed and gestured. "He will see you. But only for a few moments. Do not ask him to read your poetry, and please do not get into a long critical discussion with him. He has a lot of work to do and is not really able to spare this much . . ."

"Come, Olivinha, a few minutes of poetry makes the work so much easier."

The man who spoke from the inner office had the soft, polished accent of São Paulo. Suddenly Paulo panicked. He hoped the guard had said nothing about him visiting from the university there. He didn't want to get caught out in a simple lie.

Dr. Antonio had come to the door. He was tall, and as elegant as his voice, in a silk suit and very thin, light shoes. Paulo was acutely aware of his own boots on the thick rose carpet. He hoped no one noticed. He looked down and blushed just slightly, remembering when he had worn such expensive, useless shoes.

Dr. Antonio took the blush differently. "Please, don't be shy. Come, sit down. Would you care for a cafezinho?"

"Thank you," Paulo refused politely. He had not been prepared for this level of enthusiasm from the Cadea executive, and he had not quite thought out all the particulars of the role.

"Please, Olivinha tries to protect me more from fellow poets than from corporate spies. Have some coffee and tell me what you are working on."

The older man smiled indulgently and looked far more like a professor than a businessman. He himself poured the sweet strong coffee into a tiny cup at the credenza and handed it to Paulo. It was the best coffee he had ever tasted.

Slowly Paulo pulled out the magazine, dogeared at the page. "I really only came to ask you to autograph this," he said, proffering the page. Under his coat the crossbow pistol bit into his thigh.

Dr. Antonio smiled indulgently. "No, certainly you have an opinion on that essay Velez wrote in last month's *Review*. I was quite pleased to see it. He stands for Brazilian literature against the Colombian and Peruvian influence, even if his own work is somewhat dated. . . . But what do you think about that? Or are you one of those youngsters in the University Circle who is actually a deconstructionist?"

"I must admit it, I am a deconstructionist," Paulo said playfully. He glanced out the window wall behind Dr. Antonio. He was perfectly situated to see the street, the landing zone, the vert approach. Suddenly his plan reversed itself. It was all he could do not to laugh. How Francisco would appreciate the finesse of the move! "But do you agree that Velez's points are important even in your critical area?" Dr. Antonio asked, his eyes intense.

"I think that how our language has evolved from European Portuguese, and the way our society is radically different from that of Colombia or Peru or Argentina, has already naturally brought about the result Velez argues for without any artificial changes in form," Paulo stated, despite the fact that he had never even heard of Velez. "There is no way to mistake the Brazilian spirit for the Argentinean or the Portuguese. And poetry is about spirit, not about national boundary lines. Maybe Velez has an inferiority complex—I don't know him personally."

As he spoke, he watched the window for movement. There was nothing outside but white cement and blue, blue sky that spread out forever. Not even the flicker of a bird across the glass horizon disturbed the view.

The Cadea executive nodded thoughtfully. "I had not considered that. I had been so concerned with his literary points that I had completely overlooked the underlying sociology. Which is why we need you young Turks running around, arguing, writing even mediocre experimental poetry."

Something caught Paulo's peripheral vision. A Cadea security vert, green moving against the blue. He paid attention. There, behind it, he saw the cargo vehicle. Small. This wasn't a big shipment. And if there was enough time . . .

"You yourself write experimental poetry," Paulo replied abruptly. "But if you would excuse me, sir, do you have a toilet here?"

The older man chuckled and waved his hand at a heavy teak door set discreetly into the side wall. Better and better. Paulo went in to the private executive restroom. The full wall window had been discontinued here, but there was a smaller window high up. Which didn't concern Paulo much. Being tall had its advantages. He felt around for a catch. In some of the offices the windows didn't open at all. But there was a catch, and the window opened out. He flushed the toilet, pulled out the crossbow pistol and loaded a quarrel.

Then he turned on the water at full force while he aimed out the open window. The crossbow was powerful and accurate. And silent. Sorrel's guns wouldn't be any use here, Paulo thought with immense satisfaction. He waited, and then waited some more. Time blurred in the adrenaline rush; time and no time merged. His arm was perfectly still as he sighted down the arrow to the distant cargo vert. Concentration perfectly focused, he fired.

And then immediately he wiped his hands, stuck the crossbow back down into his coat and emerged. He returned to his seat across the desk from Dr. Antonio. Outside the window wall he could see the cargo vert was having some difficulty. He hadn't blown anything major, but then he didn't have to. That was Francisco's job. He only had to get the receiver onto the vert. And from the clumsy way it was flying, he thought he had done it. He very rarely missed, even at that range.

"So you find my work experimental? But I write in the most accepted Portuguese forms," Dr. Antonio said as he poured another cup of cafezinho.

"But what you write about, when coupled with a traditional form, is a comment on that form," Paulo said authoritatively. He had always been able to fabricate easily and always sounded good doing it. Especially when he had no idea what he was talking about.

Dr. Antonio glowed. His aristocratic face turned almost rosy under the perfect steel-colored hair.

And then, just as the cargo vert passed the window, it exploded into flames, colors that defied the peaceful afternoon. The explosion was enough that Paulo joined Dr. Antonio in jumping away from the window as burning shrapnel hit the hardened glass.

It was magnificent. It was beautiful, a fireball against the sky, flutes of black smoke arcing down to earth.

Eight

SOUTH 109 was like nothing Zaide Soledad had ever imagined. It was not like the Sector of Diversions, the Gilberto Salomao down by the bus station, with its fine shops and expensive European pastry shops and video arcades all jumbled together. This place was just one more *supermanzana*, one more of the planned neighborhoods, in the residential area, but the whole central section had been turned into a more colorful square than she had ever imagined in Rio. There were fashionable déclassé restaurants and at least one club, and various small shops and vendors with tables selling leather goods and jewelry, all made on ancient Indian patterns. There were brightly colored scarves and candles with the names of saints on them in glasses as big as her forearm. Incense covered the favela stench.

It took her a second circuit around the shopping and eating establishments to pick out the real poor at the fringes of the crowd. There were plenty of *pivetes* hanging around, their eyes like buzzards looking for something to pick over. There were three men in white linen, each sitting on a folding chair, looking very distinguished and holding court with a few other men. Zaide did not know who they were, only that they seemed to be important here in this world that was half legal and half Hell.

She had come alone this time. Even Susana didn't know where she was. Never before had Susana been excluded from any part of her life, and certainly Zaide had never considered excluding her from something this momentous. But this time she just couldn't confide.

At dinner Julio Simon had regaled the family with his coup. A shipment of Cadea highwire had been burned just outside town headquarters. He had given a tribe just enough information to take them out, and they had done so. He had been glowing, trying to sell them on his victory.

Sonia Leah had said nothing at all. Neither had Uncle Victor. Zaide read that as ominous. Julio Simon's plan had failed, the Cadea cargo had been destroyed, not confiscated. Then Zaide realized why the elders said nothing. They were waiting. They were going to let Julio Simon go on and either extricate himself from this mess or hang.

And Susana had wanted to spend the evening in the Cousins' Room of the fazenda. There were games planned for the evening by the younger ones, chess and cards and Investment Brokerage. Everyone had been invited; attendance was expected.

Zaide had some difficulty coming up with an excuse. Finally she said that she just wanted to practice in the vert for a little while and would show up for games night a little late. People shrugged, Susana had been more than a little wide-eyed, but Julio Simon began to hold forth again and Susana was caught between them. Zaide slipped up to her room and changed her dinner dress and tan pumps for jeans and embroidered gaucho boots and a bulky black sweater. She took off her jewelry and laid it on the dressing table. She could not wear real gold to the middle of town, and who knew where the boy would take her?

She picked up the vert at the garage, ready for her as ordered. She had flown herself a few times, but never alone, and never at night. She found herself immediately disoriented and afraid. She stood at the garage door and looked at the shiny green one-seater.

She could still turn back. She could pretend that the festival had never happened, that she was not expected in town tonight by some riffraff boy of no family. She could turn around and go back into the big house, back to the Cousins' Room and sit at the card table and ask to be dealt into a game of bridge. And if anyone asked how her practice had gone, she could shrug and say that she had decided to cut it short. She missed her cousins, she wanted to play.

The safe and familiar was very tempting. Zaide Soledad was vitally aware of this moment, that if she got into that vert and went to Brasilia, it would be the last of her innocence. She wasn't entirely sure what that meant.

Maybe he wouldn't come. She would go to South 109 and he wouldn't come and she would have stuck a toe into the unknown and found it benign and come back again. And she would never have to go out and explore that place in herself again.

She knew he would be there. She got into the vert. Her lift wasn't bad, given how tentatively she touched the controls. And controlling the vehicle took enough concentration that she didn't have to think about anything until she found herself landing at the Vielho-Markowicz headquarters downtown. Setting down on the urban garage was not easy, and momentarily she cursed herself for having decided to do something so stupid. Maybe she should forget the pass, lift, and go home where the autovalet would land her and claim the vert when she got out.

She swallowed hard, tried again, and this time settled roughly near the painted target. Shaken a little, she got out and stood, without moving for a moment, anxious only to be back on firm footing. Then she went to the private elevator, which accepted her ID and took her immediately to the executive lounge level. She rested for a few minutes and combed her hair before going down to the street and catching a cab over to the southern sector.

There were buses, but she had never used a bus in her life and didn't know the right one to take or how much it cost. Besides, she had no idea at all of where she was going.

He was not there when she arrived, so she walked slowly and inspected the tables of earrings and necklaces. The gold was only gilt paint and the beads were ceramic and bone, nothing nice or elegant or even interesting. Still, she looked at every stand as if she were seriously considering a purchase. That at least provided some camouflage. Inside she wondered if she should run. She had gotten here, and there was no sign of the boy and maybe it was all a mistake. No, she was *certain* it was a mistake.

She bought a coffee and a bag of soft candies at the indoor sweet shop, and found a place at a little table set up outside for customers. She sipped her sweet, dark cafezinho slowly, and decided to wait until all the candy was gone. When her snack was finished she would leave. She took out one of the caramel balls and began chewing. It was fresh and melted away as well as any Bebe had ever made for a holiday. She took another and watched the people around the square, aware of the quizzical looks from the locals. A woman alone, she was fortunate that so far none of the men had done more than show their appreciation.

And then Zaide knew he was there. How exactly, she couldn't say. The air warmed slightly and stirred, she felt him watching. A thrill stabbed her between the legs. If they were in the Wave she'd know this. They weren't and she didn't question. Only when she turned her head very slowly, she saw him over her left shoulder, smiling.

"I was wrong," he said very quietly when he took a seat opposite her. "I was certain that you'd get an ice cream."

She laughed and held out the candy bag. He took one while she finished her coffee. Then, when they left the table and looked through the stands she had not yet seen, he took her arm and showed her off. Not like the cousins at all, she thought, feeling frightened and conspicuous and pleased at the same time.

"Today is the best I've had in the past year," he told her as he steered her to a bus stop. "We showed up the Serps, looked good on the street, burned the highwire and you came."

"Burned the highwire?" Zaide asked tentatively.

"Burned it," he replied, glowing.

The bus pulled up and they got on the back, Paulo paying the conductor and arguing about the change. Zaide watched, fascinated. She also noticed the way the older people on the bus eyed her friend, pulling slightly away from him and averting their eyes. They studied her frankly and gave her disapproving glances when they realized she was with the young man in the long painted coat.

Swallowed up in the dark, she still could not miss how the neighborhoods changed. The superquadras were all identical to the northern in design. The only difference was the state of poverty around them. Some of the street lights here were out, and from the windows of the bus Zaide could see people in the street, sitting, walking, roaming. People sitting on the steps and on folding chairs, drinking out of jars and cans, yelling at each other, using creative obscenition she had never heard. And then it was time to get off the bus, the man holding her shoulders as he steered her toward the exit in the front. His hands were very large and very strong, she realized. And then she understood that he really could be very dangerous.

They got off the bus in a place where the concrete walls were brightly colored with layers of spray paint. Some were gang names and some were lovers, and some were merely drawings to enliven the unyielding, inhuman ideal of Brasilia. He kept an arm around her shoulders, protecting her in this place that was at once threatening and fascinating. But she was thrilled, not afraid. People on the street reacted even more strongly to her friend, very deliberately keeping out of his way.

Some of the younger men on the street nodded to them. One raised a large can in their direction. Paulo acknowledged the salute and went on.

"Your cadre?" Zaide asked.

Paulo nodded and steered her under one of the buildings, no different from any of the others, its doors painted over with gang slogans and its security wires dangling. In the deep shadow under the large residential block, she could hardly make out the figures in the center between the massive pillars that served to mark nonexistent walls. He held her closely and steered around the massive piling. She stopped with her back against the concrete.

"You know, I don't even know your name," she said, shaking her head.

He laughed. "You want someone to hold a candle for us?" His pleasure at being caught unawares only added to the other pleasures.

Zaide was more shocked at his using the old-fashioned phrase for a chaperon than by anything else that had happened. That was something she would have expected from a person with an education far more classical than her own. One of the intelligentsia of São Paulo, perhaps, or someone from the Arts Institute in Rio.

She stepped back, grinned, and held out her hand. "I am Zaide Soledad," she said formally.

"And I am Paulo Teodore," Paulo said, taking her hand as if she were a business associate. And then they both laughed and continued into the gloom to the place where the illicit and cheap was served, and laughter and stories were the only defenses against the winter.

The barzinho was packed, but the table where Francisco and Steel and Nem Brito sat was the center of activity. Two girls were pouring biting cheap *pinga* into large jars, and Francisco was talking so loudly that he could be heard from the far pillar.

"And so when Paulo disappeared, I didn't know what to think. He had to get in there somehow to get a decent shot at the vert. He used a magazine to dupe the guard—Can you believe Paulo as a poetry student?"

"Wait a minute," Paulo protested from the door, and then brought Zaide to claim the last remaining seat in the circle. He settled Zaide on his lap, took a jar of the white rum and offered it to Zaide as he spoke. "The Cadea exec was more than happy to talk to a poetry student. And you should see how I laid it on. Something about rebel deconstruction. And the way I asked for his autograph. You should have seen that vert blow right in front of his picture window. It was so beautiful, all the flames just about bathing the glass. And let me tell you, that poem of his that I got autographed, it's really bad. Horrible."

"Do you still have it?" Zaide asked. "Read it."

There was some general laughter as Paulo rummaged through his deep pockets and located the magazine. It was still open to the poem. Paulo read aloud to the appreciative hoots of the assembly.

"They shouldn't publish shit like that," one of the older men, already half drunk, commented. "The only reason they do is to suck up to the Cadea Corp, you better believe."

"Anyway," Francisco interrupted loudly, "you haven't heard the end of the story. So Paulo shot the vert from the bathroom window, but what he shot it with was a microwave receiver. And I had this wonderful little pulse device. I wasn't sure if Paulo had gotten the thing— I saw it quiver for a moment, but then it seemed fine. Maybe he had missed, maybe he hadn't been able to take the shot."

There were a few boos from the girls and older men. Francisco held up a hand for silence. This was his show, his moment of victory, and he was going to revel in every quantum particle of it.

"I was on the street at the news vendor's with Steel. I saw the vert come into position. I pointed the pulse at it and pressed the button, not knowing if anything at all was going to happen. And the whole thing burst into flame. Like a million butterflies in the grassland, flitting above the buildings in the business district, it hovered for a moment and then delicately the debris floated down, burning. Cinders drifted on the wind and we could smell the highwire smoke, just a little, before the breeze carried it away."

There was a moment of silence as everyone present appreciated the results of the action.

"And then," Francisco picked up again, his voice filled

with urgency, "then the Serps arrived. Maybe twenty of them, dressed like rubes from the 'burbs. Coats dirty, no shoes, no firepower. And they thought they were going to take charge of the action. Imagine the surprise on their faces when they saw the building cordoned off and pieces of charred plastic lying on the ground. They knew what had happened. And they saw us at the stand. Xavier, their lieutenant in charge of operations, came over to speak to me. He was very angry. And he looked at me, and he looked at the burned vert, and he looked at me, and he didn't have any words at all."

Francisco mimed it out, facing one way and then another, the expression on his face terribly exaggerated, to the amusement of the spectators. "You could just see that he wanted to accuse me," Francisco went on. "But he couldn't. You could see him trying to think behind his forehead, an exercise that is not common, I assume. He had put it together— that much was not difficult. Especially when I smiled at him and held up the pulse. But he finally figured out that he couldn't say anything without condemning himself. The surprise as he understood exactly his position, that was worth everything."

Someone pounded the table as general laughter ensued. The girls brought more drinks, beer and aguardente in assorted cracked containers. Paulo took up the near-empty jar and toasted his friend. Then he told his own story, Dr. Antonio's pride and poetry, and how he shot the vert from the bathroom window with no one the wiser. How he had a perfect alibi in the Cadea executive.

"But what I wonder is where the Serps are getting their information and why," Paulo said when all the healths had been drunk and Steel had stood them all to another round. "I wonder about their connections, and why they would have any connections at all. They're just one more tribe, not even much of a cadre, to have all the data they seem to be getting."

Zaide's recognition was enough to rock her from Paulo's lap. She saw it; she understood perfectly. This was the other end of Julio Simon's plot. This was the attack on Cadea he had planned with an ending he had not anticipated. And everyone knew except the Serps.

Even Julio didn't know how serious his failure was. Yet. To choose bad allies was a serious crime in the Vielho-Markowicz family. To fail in front of the population was another. The fact that Julio was trying to use the Serps to serve his own ends was not something either Sonia Leah or Uncle Victor would approve. Street tribes were notoriously difficult to control. Julio Simon needed a visible triumph so badly, he had chosen a very risky course of action. One that would profit the fazenda very little, and could put them at a serious disadvantage.

It would take very little for the Cadea to discover the source of the attacks on their shipments. It would become clear that they were being hit more than anyone else, and it would not take top management to trace the sabotage to Vielho-Markowicz.

Julio Simon was not as smart as he thought he was, Zaide realized. So far, his greatest ability was in taking risks and impressing the elders, but the substance underneath was not firm. He had taken a few risks and had won by chance. It had given him great visibility. It had not given him a long view, or a global perspective. And without those things, Zaide saw clearly, he was creating his own spectacular failure.

As it fell into place, she suddenly understood her premonition of the early evening. Only it wasn't Paulo who was making her a new creature. It was the knowledge of why Julio's plan had failed. He had been given to her, a gift, to use in the intricate politics of the family. She was the only one who could point a finger at his disreputable allies and prove his lack of judgment. She could either ride on Julio Simon or deliver him to Sonia Leah and her faction. Or to Uncle Victor.

A slow, secret smile on her face, Zaide leaned against Paulo's shoulder and let the members of Bakunin talk about their actions around her. She felt lightheaded and extremely pleased. She had never known how power tasted, and she was surprised to find that it was sparkling and light and very very strong.

Nine

THE offices of Bakunin were quiet. Everyone was still in the barzinho enjoying the victory, enjoying the Serps' fallen reputation, drinking on Steel's money and the bartender's admiration. When Paulo slipped out with Zaide, there were a few knowing glances, a few winks, and everyone else looked the other way. Except the girls who worked there. They liked Paulo; he was young and good-looking and very clean. Now they would only have Pope to argue over. Nem Brito had a girlfriend and was in love; people joked about that. And Steel, well, his money was good, but he wasn't dangerous like Paulo Sylvia or fiery and inspiring like the red-haired ice-eyed Francisco Pope. No, the girls were sorry to see Sylvia leave with Zaide, but they were not jealous. He would be back to them soon enough. They had seen it all before.

He did not take her far, only up the stairs and into the main building to the Bakunin office. It was quiet and close. And if it was ugly and poor, well, he had no desire for her to see any more of the inside of the building than necessary. He did not know where she was from specifically, but there were a lot of places in the southern favela of the city that were not fallen so hard as this building. Let her imagine that this was a place without red lights in the hall, where the elevators were still safe and where there were no rats or highwire addicts or cannibals squatting in the unoccupied apartments.

Zaide inspected the premises. The office surprised her. It was far more orderly than she had imagined. In fact, she had never considered that the gangs would even bother with a desk, let alone a working datapad and lock files. She wondered vaguely where they had picked up the merchandise, and then thought that it probably was stolen. Only datapads had identification markers, and gene lock files were made only by Vielho-Markowicz and had to be geared to the users. They were bought exclusively by the wealthy. Even the middle class could hardly afford the bioware to work one.

Her curiosity rampant, she tried one of the desk drawers. It opened to reveal nothing at all. It was somewhat disappointing. Like the favela, like Bakunin, the drawer was more dangerous and alien in her imagination than in fact. She had never quite imagined the swagging tribe-boys bragging in a crummy former broom closet, drinking something called *pinga*, which tasted like sugared turpentine.

Paulo's hands on her waist startled her. "Do you know how to use a blowgun?" he asked.

"Of course," she replied, somewhat offended. It was one of the first things she had learned, even before she had been accepted by the family, when she was still in fostering.

He nodded slowly, as if he had known the answer to his question and had merely confirmed something. She didn't know what or why.

But he didn't tell her any more. He locked the door and turned down the lights enough to change the ugly colors and scarred ceiling, the open plumbing and the exposed wiring, into something forbidden and exotic and desirable. And since he, too, was forbidden and exotic, sex with him was far more exciting than she had known with the cousins.

Afterwards he didn't get up and get dressed the way the cousins did. He stroked her back and muttered inanities about stars and death and all the things that were foreign to her. She looked at the scars on his body, which showed dark against his white skin. She traced the ones she recognized as knife slashes, the tiny stars that were most likely taser wounds pulled out, the very old one that she thought might be a burn.

Julio Simon had taught her about scars, had showed her the pictures to entice her into his own sensuality. She had been fascinated and horrified, and the horror fed the fascination. She had looked at his pictures and listened to his voice quiver with excitement when he described the various tortures that created this pattern or that one.

She ran her fingers through Paulo's hair. It was very long and thick and lay over his shoulders in dark waves. Untamed, unlike her cousins. She sank her hands into his hair and there, just behind his ear, she felt the hard metallic nub of the secondary glandular junction. Reflexively, her hand jerked away.

"What the hell are you, anyway?" she asked softly.

"I don't want to talk about it," he said, also softly.

Zaide had the feeling that she could push him and he would answer. She could force him in the moment. And then she would never see him again, never come back to Bakunin and never find out what he really was.

He got up and dressed briskly, businesslike, his back to her.

Zaide lounged against the green carpet. "I always wanted to be a Changeling," she murmured. "I saw the Lighters and the Sights and I wanted to go with them so bad. Anything to get away, maybe—I don't know. I thought it would be wonderful to be a Sight, to see the infrared and ultraviolet, to see the radio universe, to see the Wave forming and weaving. I wanted that."

He turned very slowly and faced her. There was something she couldn't quite read on his face, something between pain and desire, the way Julio looked when he talked about scars. "Why didn't you?" he asked.

"Because . . ." Zaide said, and then she hesitated. She had to tell him the truth. Their link was too delicate to withstand anything else. "My family had other plans," she said finally.

"I'm sorry," Paulo said, but Zaide was sure he was talking about himself as well as her.

Zaide shrugged. "The world fell apart anyway. It doesn't matter anymore, I guess."

But she let him pull her up, and she dressed carefully. She didn't want to return to the fazenda, to the cousins. She wanted the night to last forever, and whatever she did here didn't matter. It wasn't real.

Paulo unlocked the door. "Will you come back tomorrow?" he asked very quietly.

Speaking was too hard. She nodded.

"The same place," he suggested.

"Here," she said. "Write it down, where we are. I didn't watch on the bus."

Paulo looked at her almost suspiciously. Then he took one of the black pens from the mustard jar and a brilliant green flier for a *grunhir* concert from two weeks ago, wrote the number of the supermanzana and the building in the neighborhood. "But you shouldn't come to the barzinho alone," he said. "They're old-fashioned. It's better if we meet at 109 again."

Zaide took the paper and looked at the handwriting. She could read it clearly, 713 South. His handwriting was educated, there was no doubt. She bit her lip. Something was not making sense. "I'll go to 109, then," she said. "But it's time for me to go now. Or my family will worry."

"Can I walk you home?" he asked.

She managed to say no. He ignored her. "I can't let you walk around here alone," he insisted.

She lingered, let him kiss her for a very long time. And then she darted out, disappearing through the doors as if she didn't want to be followed. Paulo let her go. He knew the superquadra was dangerous and he shouldn't. But he didn't believe that she could be hurt. Not tonight. There was an unreality about their meeting, about her being, which made him too comfortable being that close to fate.

And how she had found the implant so quickly. Suddenly Paulo sat up so hard his head swam. The junction. How the hell had she known? Why had she looked? The question bothered him, floating in his *pinga*-soaked mind like the only thing of consequence.

He felt ill, defensive, ready to attack. The phrines, that must be it. He grabbed at the pocket in his belt and there was still one tiny white pill left. Then he hadn't taken enough, maybe, and this was just the crash. He hated the crash.

Or maybe it was the phrines themselves. He never did know what Laurindo created, and there had been enough stimulation in the day itself. He felt enzyme tides flood his body and withdraw, and in his most primitive mind he wondered whether it was like this to be a Changeling. He wondered if they were geared and phrined as well, or if the conversion seemed natural after a while.

Memory stalked and frightened him. He shivered against the carpet. It was winter, the dry time, that time when the dust devils would blow up on the cerrado and there wasn't a cloud to create the great shifting skyscapes that were the single great beauty of the city. They had just been coming out of a winter like this one, arid and chilly enough to want a coat every day, when the universe had fallen apart. When his dreams had fallen apart. Maybe he was crazy the way everybody said, because he wanted sometimes to be alone. Maybe he was a monster. Maybe he was some terrible thing that shouldn't live.

But whatever he was, he had survived the collapse, the Forestation and the termites and the destruction of all order.

It had begun simply enough. He had been in school that day, in history class to be exact. He had lived in the northern section then and gone to one of the best high schools in the city, he and Francisco Pope. Pope was a year ahead of him and had perfect grades. Sylvia never bothered with grades. Building things and breeding DNA chains and creating artificial viruses was more interesting than studying the War of Liberation.

So he had blown off school by lunch time, gathered Francisco and talked his friend into taking off for the grassland. Pope had little interest in the cerrado that surrounded the city. It was full only of termites and buzzards, he said.

But in the cerrado the butterflies were swarming. Paulo had gone before and seen them, the iridescent blue wings that the *pivetes* caught and sold to the junk dealers. The butterflies showed up under glass, embedded in ashtrays and shipped out to Rio and São Paulo, Belo Horizonte and Recife, for tourists to buy. Blue butterflies like the sky and the lake and the ravines when the summer rains came hard.

Even Francisco had been impressed with the sight—the street children, tossed aside by families who couldn't care for them, running through the grass catching the great blue butterflies as if they were the ordinary children of the middle class. The beauty of the open grassland and the tough plantation eucalyptus of the Forestation Program only made the great cloudscapes of October more pronounced against the uniform structures of the city.

They could see the monotonous six-story buildings of Brasilia in the distance, a blur on the horizon that could be mistaken for a dust devil or storm, only this was not the right time of year. Paulo Sylvia had looked at the city from the distance, somehow feeling unprotected this far out in the open land. There were dangers in the cerrado, he knew. There were poisonous snakes all over, corals and rattlers and fer-de-lants. Wild snakes were of greater concern to him than angry favela boys with weapons. The city streets were his territory; this feral preserve belonged to the snakes and the termites, the butterflies and the wolves.

He was watching the city—and his feet, to make sure there were no unwelcome visitors—when he first smelled the burning. He was confused. It did not smell like a barbecue, like anything he had smelled before.

Immediately he looked for Francisco, raised his eyes and saw to his right a wall of fire. The eucalyptus of the forest plantation had turned brilliant orange and yellow like the sunset on the clouds. Francisco was yelling at him, but the words were drowned by the blaze. He forgot the snakes and tried to run to where Pope stood, near the side of a paved road that ran into the plantation. It was impassable now.

A flock of verts came down, big pumpers, yellow and red like the fire itself. There were people with shovels, and truckloads of men with picks on their backs going to fight the fire. Great plumed geysers of both sand and water shot into the butterfly-blue sky. Paulo thought of the Plumed Serpent god and tasted ash.

The street children had abandoned the butterflies and had clustered around the firefighters. Paulo and Francisco held back. There was something about the power of destruction that filled Paulo with desire. And Francisco said flatly there was nothing to be done. Nothing at all.

Looking weary and bent, as if they had been on the fire lines, they were able to catch a ride back to the city with a truckload of men who were tired and hurt and making way for another human wave. They talked, and Paulo listened. According to the men, Francisco was right. The fire was out of control. The Forestation Program was over, the years of work and money to save the land were being eaten before their eyes.

They returned home that night and ate dinner and went to school the next day, and the fire was still burning. It burned for nine days, moved south by the winds away from the grassland and Brasilia into the heart of the rain forest.

The government declared martial law. The army was called out to fight the fire. Help came from Argentina and Mexico and Paraguay. And when the fire was over, the investigation began. The published report pronounced it an act of terrorism by one of the more insular and extreme cults in the Valley of Dawn. That gave the military government an excuse to go in and clean out the spiritualists and utopians who had lived near Brasilia since the city was first built.

But the rumors on the street had it that the fazendas had torched their own preserves. No one in Brasilia liked the fazendas. They were too rich and had too much control. They had preserved the rain forest, and in return enjoyed the monopoly on the rare drugs that they alone were permitted to harvest there. And they were well-loved outside the country, in the places where people worried about the air and about their supplies of pharmaceuticals. The fazenda families were a law and a world unto themselves. To some they symbolized the great newness and pioneer spirit of the interior. To most they symbolized how that great tradition had been exploited.

Over the years of their ascendancy, the fazenda families had made themselves the only Waveriders. It was the one Changeling ability that was not controlled by the government and was not open to admission via testing and desire. No, admission to the Wave, the very heart of the energy center of the world, was open only to those whose names were Cadea and Alado and Vielho and Markowicz.

They had created the drug highwire originally to burn out secondaries in Changelings. The secondaries with the chemical levels of the Change already in place were susceptible to the drug and it burned through them hideously. There were stories about the early days on the fazendas, where street urchins were seduced from the favelas and made into Changelings, and then burned hideously in the research process. The research showed that for an unadapted person highwire was useless, highly addictive and in the very long run fatal. Someone with secondaries became a vegetable.

There were even rumors that on the fazendas the families used highwire against each other, against themselves. That was the most horrific thing about them, and the most cold. No wonder they had been able to consolidate and increase their power when everyone else was falling.

As for the cultists, well, they had lived in the Valley of Dawn for almost a hundred years with no incident. They were strange, people said, but everyone knew they were harmless. Now they were mostly gone, enough of them dead so that the stink of unburied bodies permeated the city for days. Others had melted into the satellite cities and some into Brasilia itself. Some of them, so the rumors went, were now organizing for vengeance. But there were always rumors, and it was hard to know which ones were based in fact and which in wishful thinking.

Paulo hadn't been much concerned about the rumors. What mattered most then was that his father was one of the Ministry of Economics functionaries who had disappeared, and that the riots that began in the satellite cities of Sobradinho and Gama and Taguatinga spread as fast as the fire and much farther. They did as much damage, too.

After the first wave of looters hit the northern sector, the private police were called in from the fazendas. They restored order, cordoning off each of the middle-class supermanzanas and killing any indigent who dared attack. The looting ended very quickly.

Then the police rounded up every possible suspect for interrogation from those who were left in the Ministries. They went door by door through the endlessly monotonous buildings, eliminating those who had not survived the political spasm. Those who were displaced, angry and unemployed, drifted to the southern sector.

Paulo had drifted with Francisco and his family. The Sylvias were gone. And he had no family in the city; his parents had come from Recife with his father's promotion to the capital. He couldn't travel to Recife to his aunts and uncles, not now when his *identidade* had the surgical pointers and police notations.

Of course the boys could not remain in school, not in the fine high school with an excellent record of students placing on the *vestibular* and winning a place at the University. Paulo did not miss school particularly. He could learn what he needed from books; from Professor Dario, who had taught genetics, and Dr. Valdemar, who had once been the head of the Changeling program. Neither of their University chairs had survived the fazenda families' purge of the intelligentsia.

Professor Dario had known Paulo's father, and so Paulo agreed to help when the professor's wife, Dona Rachel, begged him to do something to make the professor a man again. For weeks after the purge he had done nothing but sit at the window and stare down into the street. Dona Rachel thought he was in shock. She had talked to Dr. Valdemar, who was a friend in a similar position but not so broken. Dr. Valdemar had suggested bringing the professor's current experiments into the lab he was in the process of setting up.

Dona Rachel explained to Paulo, who was delighted to have a chance to do anything useful. Francisco and Nem Brito helped him move the experiments into a large apartment Dr. Valdemar had obtained in 703. It all had to be done at night, very carefully, with the police around and all the samples taken one at a time. There were a few things Paulo and Francisco and Nem Brito hadn't been able to bring over, some of the larger pieces of equipment. But the professors had been very grateful for what had been done, and Dona Rachel had been extremely grateful. Since she was very young to be the wife of such a distinguished professor, no more than ten years older than Paulo, he enjoyed her gratitude enormously.

So Paulo had not missed school. What he missed were his dreams.

Ten

THE Vielho-Markowicz fazenda was to the southwest of the city, over the impassable cerrado and beyond, into the beginning of the mist forest. The house and grounds themselves had to be constantly cleared. The forest persisted, it invaded. It never gave up, and when there was the smallest breach in their watchfulness, it reappeared, triumphant.

But the small cleared area was not all of the fazenda. The Vielho-Markowicz land extended far beyond, encompassing the most spectacular falls at Itiquira. It extended up through the dense rain forest to the burn lines left from the fire. Three years past and there was already the beginning of life invading.

Zaide Soledad stood at the foot of the forest and smelled the mist. The humidity gathered on her skin and beaded in her hair. She was alone. The parrots were screeching and the forest was waking up for the day. Zaide Soledad hadn't slept.

She wanted to. Sleep would make the night disappear, and she could believe it was only a trick of memory. Instead, she couldn't get it out of her head. Not the people. And not the knowledge. She was anxious to see Julio Simon, to see him without his aura of power. Her knowledge of his misalliance had stripped that from him in her mind. Now she wanted to see it.

And she had to decide what to do. She could confront him directly and see if she could use what she knew as leverage for her own advancement. But that would depend on where he was heading in the family, and if he kept making mistakes of this magnitude, he wouldn't last. Or she could let Uncle Victor know, maybe through Sonia Leah, and so put the head of Finance in her debt. That could be useful. Zaide considered the possibility.

But without sleep, she knew she lacked judgment. And there was no time to sleep. She had already turned the vert in to the valet and walked back to the house, up to her room. Susana was deeply asleep, fighting off the early sun. Zaide was very quiet. She opened one of the little boxes on Susana's bureau, and then another. Susana had such a collection. One held coins and bills, ordinary dinheiro for going into town. Another had hairpins, and yet another a collection of single earrings whose mates had been lost. It wasn't until the fifth box, the one with the enameled Russian scene on the top, that she found the phrines. She didn't usually take phrines; it wasn't considered a good thing until after the final surgery. So far, only the secondary sequences were in place and the first of the DNA viruses had been induced.

Zaide didn't care. She looked at the pills in the box, tiny white ones and orange shiny ones and ones the color of Sonia Leah's aquamarine. She took one of each and lay down on the plum flowered bedspread and waited for the effect.

She was just coming out of the shower when Susana woke. "Where were you?" her cousin asked sleepily.

Zaide smiled slowly. "I met a boy at the festival," she said.

Susana's eyes went wide. "You didn't tell me," she accused.

Zaide was apologetic. "I didn't know if he meant anything," she said. "Why talk about something until it's fact?"

She heard herself say the sentence, but it wasn't about herself. It was about Julio Simon. And then she knew what she would do. It was dangerous, but she would never succeed without risk. The trick was to know which risk to take, and when. Julio Simon had gone over the boundaries.

She had to wait until lunch to make her first attack. It was tradition; it was the way things were done on the fazenda. The phrines she took got her through mergers and contracts and a workshop in international negotiation and a quiz in Japanese. It was boring beyond belief.

She dressed carefully for lunch, very professional and neat, with her long black hair pinned up in a grown-up French knot and nothing straggling in her face. A pink patterned kimono-style jacket softened her plain ivory dress and made her look just a little innocent. She didn't plan to let Julio Simon see what was coming.

She sat at the long table in the dining room. Dinner would be more formal, with the damask cloth and three wineglasses and everyone dressed for evening. Now everyone wore jackets and suits and discreet scarves; all the symbols of power were muted.

Zaide Soledad waited. She waited while she ate the soup and the steak. She waited while Cousin Ze Ladislau (Vielho) of R and D chattered about some project coupling the Wave receptors into a single biochip that could be engineered from a person's own DNA. Very interesting. Zaide didn't hear a word. She waited until after the dessert, until Bebe brought in the coffee tray and set it on the sideboard. She asked Susana to get her a cup, and Susana gave her a puzzled look but complied. Ordinarily, everyone got their own coffee at lunch. Even Uncle Victor and Sonia Leah went to the tray and poured for themselves.

She waited until everyone was sitting down again, sipping the hot, strong coffee and planning their tasks for the afternoon. That was when she smiled at Julio Simon. "Well, Cousin Julio, I have been anxious to hear about why your attack on the Cadea highwire shipment didn't go as planned. It would be beneficial for me to learn from you. I heard that the wrong street gang got data and burned the wire, but of course that was only a rumor at the Alado fazenda."

There was dead silence. She sipped her coffee. Julio Simon had gone the color of quartz when she spoke. Now she dared not look at him. She dared not look at Uncle Victor, either, or Sonia Leah.

"Yes," Sonia Leah purred, and even without looking, Zaide knew the aunt was pleased. "Do tell us what happened, Julio. We have all been waiting."

Only then did Zaide look at Julio Simon. He settled his cup into the saucer gently and laid the spoon carefully on the side. She wondered if he was buying time. Then he spoke. "While there were some deviations from my original plan, you cannot deny the operation was an overall success. The raid did take place on the Cadea highwire shipment yesterday, and both the full shipment and the vert were burned. Which is better for us actually, and no evidence remaining."

Zaide smiled. It was not pleasant. Uncle Victor looked at her with special interest, as if he had never quite seen her before and was trying to get a fix on who and which project she had been.

"You're using the Serpentes?" she asked softly, her voice carefully neutral.

Julio Simon stiffened in his seat. "I see no reason why my methods are any concern of yours. As long as they are successful."

"Of course," Zaide agreed. "As long as they are successful. But I believe the way I heard the story is that you leaked information to one group, the Serpentes from Cuidad Libre, but they were not involved in the action at all. I think I heard they sold the data at street value to someone else. Of course, this is only rumor. Perhaps they are more reliable. But if I'm misinformed, we should let the Alado know about it, or they might not be so interested in the joint venture on the upper river."

Susana dropped her spoon. The rattle against the china saucer echoed in the silent dining room. Sonia Leah studied Zaide Soledad and licked her lips. Uncle Victor remained perfectly neutral, watching the interplay as if it were a performance for his benefit.

Julio Simon did not move. His hands lay flat on the table,

relaxed, and he stared at them and took two deep breaths. "I don't believe that's relevant," he hissed. It was as close to anger as she had ever seen him come. "Since you have no knowledge of the overall plan. I was hoping to keep it secret. I was hoping that you would all join me in the Cathedral on the Feast of the Assumption of the Blessed Virgin, to see the final outcome of this plan in public. Cadea will be crushed and discredited, I can assure you. And you may assure your Alado contacts of that as well," he said, sneering and looking directly at her.

Zaide merely studied him with candid interest. She had once read something about Roderigo Borgia, Pope Alexander, that he could lose all the battles and win back more in his surrender negotiations than he had lost in the war. That ability intrigued Zaide, and she wondered if Julio Simon thought he was capable of such a play. She wondered if he really was capable. It was possible that Bakunin had been used by him for his own means. But she had been there, had heard Francisco and Paulo talk and she knew that it was not likely. More likely that her first analysis was correct and that now he was trying a save.

But she didn't need to do any more. After all, this was just her opening. She knew the basic thrust of her attack now, and had started things. That was all she needed.

"We will be pleased to see what you have in mind," Uncle Victor said. But he looked back at Zaide with the ghost of a smile on his face. And she knew that she had done well. Very well.

Maybe too well. She finished her afternoon apprenticeship working in the Accounts Division and went back to the house to change for dinner. She hadn't been able to concentrate on Accounts all afternoon. Now she wondered what Julio Simon had been doing in the intervening hours, what Uncle Victor thought, how Sonia Leah might become an ally. She was so full of these things that she didn't see anything as she walked across the porch, and promptly bumped into Uncle Victor himself.

She looked up, blushed, and started apologizing profusely. He held up a hand. "I came down to see you before dinner, so you have actually saved me some time. I have decided that it is time for your surgery. This new angle on Julio Simon's plan is very interesting to us. And how you obtained the information, how you manipulated it to your own advantage, speaks well of you. I think it would be to our advantage if you were to enter the Wave as soon as possible."

Zaide gasped. There was nothing else to say. This was the final promotion and the final acceptance. Once she had the complete range of implants, she was fully integrated into the company. The family could kill her. Worse, they could highwire her until her brain resembled manioc. But they could not expel her.

Which was why her attack on Julio Simon was so very dangerous. If he failed as spectacularly as he hoped to succeed, the family would have no choice but to eliminate him as flawed. Excellent genome, it would be quite confusing as to why he hadn't been able to control his position. But in any case, he would not be of much use and would be far too dangerous. The Wave made him more dangerous.

And in giving her entrance there, Uncle Victor was also giving her another place to pursue Julio. And where he could injure her. She would be very new to the Wave; Julio was an expert in its contortions.

Or he behaved as if he were. Zaide Soledad suddenly wondered about that. He had, after all, told her that he was the most skilled in the household in motivating groups of people. Last year, during her apprenticeship in Security, he had paid special attention to her.

"You are S-series," he had said after the third day of orientation, catching her alone in front of a model of the fazenda security system. "There aren't very many of us, and we can help each other."

She had waited for him to go on. It was true there weren't

many S-series in the family. They tended toward instability. Sonia Leah had considered eliminating the lot of them. But the factors that made them moody and difficult also made them charismatic. And so Uncle Victor had overruled her, and the S-series, the few who survived the secondary implants without undue emotional explosions, became part of the team. There weren't many of them. Julio Simon and Zaide Soledad were the two most promising. Sonia Leah had once remarked dryly that all the S-series would self-destruct before they reached majority or they would all make CEO. So far, Julio Simon was the only one to make it past his twenty-second birthday. Though there were bets on Zaide Soledad joining him.

They both knew it. Which was why Zaide was certain that he had approached her in the first place. He brought her into his lush office in the secondary installation where Security had its headquarters. He had poured her cafezinho and treated her very properly. Zaide had assumed that he had wanted sex.

"We can help each other," he had said a second time, after she had tasted her coffee. "In the Wave there are subtle ways to effect change. A small nudge in one place will multiply itself into new foci. But you're not there, so you don't know it yet. No matter. I just wanted to make the offer. For when the time comes."

"When the time comes," she had agreed, confused. He made no moves toward her, called up a schematic and went over the tripbeam plans.

She had had trouble concentrating. She knew about the Wave, of course. She had enough of a theoretical grasp to know that it was a chaotic system, where everything was pattern and nothing was the same. Ever. But that was only theoretical. She had not been in.

Now Uncle Victor was giving her the keys. And Julio Simon would be waiting at the other end. No one knew about the bargains made. No one knew that she had betrayed Julio's trust. He was the most dangerous enemy in the family, and she was afraid.

Uncle Victor didn't care about the outcome, she suddenly realized. He didn't care which of them was destroyed, which of them won, who died. All he saw was one more test, one more opportunity to judge their value overall. Whoever survived this would be in a very strong position. The winner would have magic for the rest of his life, no ambition too high. Not the Board, not even Uncle Victor himself. It was all pure Darwinism, even though the social applications had been refuted.

Uncle Victor believed in social Darwinism. He believed that those who survived were superior. Maybe he wasn't ever young. But Zaide was afraid she had been very stupid. Julio Simon was not an enemy she wanted to face alone.

So she bowed her head gracefully before the CEO with his white hair, standing before her like a benign and loving relative. "I am very young for this promotion," she demurred politely. "Perhaps it would be best if I finished my studies first."

"I think that we would all benefit from your presence as soon as possible," Uncle Victor contradicted her gently. "Your appointment has already been scheduled for next week. I hope that isn't too long to wait. And won't interrupt your schedule unduly."

His manner was so mild that they could have been discussing her choice of a dress, of her next internship before a first assignment. Either Julio Simon would destroy her or she would survive. It was a very simple solution to the problem. Elegant even. The part of her that saw the simple beauty in the plan had to admire it, even though the danger was too close to enjoy.

She smiled and thanked Uncle Victor for the promotion. Her face was properly arranged to express pleasure. That much training, at least, she had mastered.

By the time she had gotten upstairs, Susana was bouncing on her bed. "I heard, I heard about it, that's so great, Zaide!"

Her cousin was bursting with enthusiasm. "You'll see, it's amazing."

Zaide blinked at Susana. Either her cousin was an idiot, or living in some dream world that had nothing at all to do with reality. In the end the same thing. An idiot.

Guilt penetrated fear. Susana was her best friend. Susana had stuck by her since they were both little. Susana had shared her first secret dreams and ambitions, had encouraged her and petted her and never, never said anything unpleasant about her. Had always rolled her eyes when anyone called Zaide stupid or unsubtle or even plain.

"Maybe it's not such a good thing," she told her cousin, perching on the edge of the chintz-covered bed. That was one thing she could change once she had been altered, she thought absently. She could get rid of all the purple-flowered fabric on the beds, the curtains, the vanity skirts. Replace it with something cool and geometric and precise, not this suffocating growth from the ancient past.

Susana only laughed. "You don't like it because you won't be able to meet your new friend for a few days, that's all. You going out tonight? Want me to cover for you? 'Cause I don't think you're going to get much of a chance before the surgery, and it'll take a while to recover. Of course, if you want me to play go-between while you're confined . . ."

Zaide had forgotten that she was meeting Paulo tonight. She had been thinking so much about the Wave and Julio that her appointment with him had gone completely out of her head.

She would have to tell him something, why she wouldn't be around for a while. That worried her. But more, she was excited that she was going to see him again.

"Yes," she said slowly, enlisting Susana in her deception. If anyone was good at this, it would be her best friend. "I could use your help."

Susana giggled. "What are you planning to wear?" she asked Zaide, and the danger was brushed aside.

Eleven

WHEN Julio Simon surveyed his domain, he felt calm again. There was no threat here at all. His office was clear and bright, birds painted on the orange and blue walls, the enveloping white sofas soft and clean. Everything was in its place. No one had been here, no one could hurt him. And Zaide Soledad was merely an apprentice, and an S-series at that.

But he was not convinced. The stress was still there, the knowledge that maybe something could go wrong. Not because he had not taken every precaution and exercised every option. No. Because he had not made a mistake. But he was always afraid they would see the truth. And while there was nothing at all wrong with the truth, while he was certain he could win them over in time, he didn't have time now. The Vielho-Markowicz were scrupulous in their adherence to tradition. To some semblance of conventional behavior.

Which was not in S-series patterns at all. He wondered idly why the S-mix had been permitted to come through the sieve. They were unpredictable, expensive, and prone to early failure. How many Julios and Zaides were out in the southern favela now? He didn't want to contemplate the answer. But it brought it all home.

Julios and Zaides. Uncle Victor, Sonia Leah, they were no threat to him at all. They weren't S-series, they didn't have the wildness, the high-risk profile that made them special. More than special, made them the one mutation that could save the family.

Even Uncle Victor had to know that the fazendas were a thing of the past. Soon the Forestation would end, soon there wouldn't be any need for the individual hegemonies of the families protecting the oxygen of the world. There was even a plan to end the dictatorship and reinstate elections before the end of the year. And that was precisely the position he had investigated so carefully with the Alado. And the Cadea. Who had been horrified and shocked and immediately offended. All of which Julio Simon knew was merely an act to steal his idea, strike first and keep the profits. Without the Vielho Markowicz getting a cut at all.

Really it was very simple. After the reorganization, the fazendas had unlimited power in the forest. No one else could operate power verts here, and the security measures Julio Simon had developed in his three-year tenure had made it impossible to even fly over the region without suppressor programs running the idents. Outside the rain forests and the high central plateau of Brazil there was a stinking, ugly, polluted place where people still died of emphysema and influenza for absolutely no reason. Except the air. And the fazendas had a monopoly.

Brazil had thought it was a national monopoly, but nationalism was a dead thing. Julio Simon had never understood the stranglehold some outmoded eighteenth-century idea had on the present. His loyalty was only to himself and his fazenda. That was the way things should be, family above all, and competition to the death. Competition weeded out the unfit, the useless, the weary and old. Julio Simon knew that competition was one thing to be respected, and the only thing that he respected more was the bottom line. His own bottom line.

And so it seemed quite natural that this great resource, which had been so blindly entrusted to his family, should be turned to their greater benefit. The monopoly on medicinals, and the harvest of the forest itself, was minuscule compared to the possibilities. Didn't the charter give them the right to the entire harvest? And if that harvest included oxygen, wasn't that the main product of the endless, fragile green rain forest outside the house clearing? If their main work was to defend the region, then they were entitled to the benefits. Everyone agreed with that.

Julio Simon was frustrated. He couldn't understand why his family and his counterparts at Cadea didn't see quite so clearly exactly what their charters entitled them to accomplish. Under the fazenda system Brasilia had done well. Brazil had done well. Even the snobs from Rio and São Paulo, the proud aristocrats from Recife and the prouder criminals of Bahia agreed with that. And so they should all support him.

It was a grand vision. He knew that. Uncle Victor and his whole generation were too old to see the possibilities, to see the immense scope of just what they had inherited. The whole world was in their debt, and Julio Simon believed quite deeply that debts must be paid.

So he was somewhat unsettled by Zaide's behavior at lunch. He had assumed her help, needed her help. He needed someone else in the family to counter the old-fashioned thinking and voting blocks. Zaide was going to go to Management. She had been created to help in his plan; he had encouraged her and trained her for that role. And now she was betraying him, playing for her own stakes when she didn't realize that she had a place in his. A big place for a much bigger gain.

Perhaps she didn't realize that, he thought suddenly. He had never quite told her anything. He had never thought that he had to. The fewer people who knew, the safer it was. He knew all about safety. Security was his specialization, after all.

Yes, maybe he should tell her. But that didn't take the edge off his anger. She was S-series, she owed him, and she was supposed to follow his lead. Not come up against him, especially not in front of the family.

She had to be punished. To be shown the ignorance of her

ways. To learn that she was always to follow his lead, to support him. She was S-series, she had been made for his use.

But maybe he could use even this. The glimmer of an idea came through the haze of anger, a question that posed itself on the edge of his feelings. How did she know? Where was she getting her data?

And could he exploit that? Or stop it?

If she could be made to lead him to her contacts, he would have still one more coup on his record, and he would need it. Whether he used them or eliminated them could be determined at a later date. When he knew exactly what the stakes were. Lucky for him Zaide was so young, so innocent. He realized it with a shock that also brought pleasure. For the first time, in his opinion, he had an adversary as intelligent as himself. Only not quite so experienced, and he was not above using his edge. After all, he had earned it.

The pressure and anger collided and broke the calm of the office, the quiet of the soft samba music, the brightness of the parrot colors. He needed release. Zaide needed a lesson. She deserved it. And it would please him so very much, to see her hurt and begging his forgiveness.

He had never considered that he lusted after one of the cousins. But the image of Zaide, bleeding and broken and in pain, was more desirable than anything he had imagined. Not a prisoner. Zaide. His sister.

He put in the page immediately to have her report before dinner. An emergency, he said. He felt as if it were.

Her throat went dry when she saw the flasher on. She knew it was nothing good. Already there was the surgery, the Wave. Something else had to go wrong. But she wasn't prepared for the message from Julio Simon, ordering her to report to Security immediately. He had no authority to order her in that tone. He was still a cousin, not an uncle.

But there was nothing she could do but go. There was no good or valid reason to ignore it, and she was still junior. And now Uncle Victor was watching them fight with each other, isolated, uncaring if either survived. He wanted only the best. This was the winnowing, and she knew it. She'd been in the trough all her life.

Suddenly she wanted to be free. Then she thought of the favelas and wondered if anyone was ever free. Ever. And so she went over to the Security installation feeling bound and shackled like Paulo and Francisco and all the people drinking in the barzinho.

Julio was waiting for her. He ushered her through the first checkpoint, making certain that she had the "all clear" access which not even every member of the family was given. Then they went to his office. He settled both of them on the white canvas upholstered sofa, so stark compared to the brilliant walls. Or perhaps self-effacing so as not to take away from the tropical scenery.

He waved a hand, and the wall opposite them went blank, then reconfigured to show the Vielho-Markowicz security shield.

"I want to show you what you can have," he said, smiling gently. "I can understand that you wanted to show off for the elders today. I can even forgive it." He chuckled briefly in a studied manner. "I will have to, if we are going to be a team. Because you know that's what we're meant for, Zaide. In the next generation Vielho-Markowicz shouldn't only be one more rain forest fazenda. We should be a name that is written in small letters, something that is so much a part of people's lives that they can't forget that we own them."

Zaide blinked in confusion. "I thought you were angry at me," she said dully.

"I am," Julio Simon replied evenly. "But it occurs to me that it is my own fault for not having spoken to you earlier. For trying to let you have a childhood—I don't know. I had always assumed that we were natural allies in the family, that you would be my first lieutenant when the time comes. Because I'm not just going for Vielho-Markowicz. Much too small. How would you like to pull any strings you wanted in the world?"

Zaide said nothing. She wanted to see where he was going. And she knew that she didn't dare contradict him. Not here, not yet. She didn't have enough power to defeat him, and she couldn't afford a confrontation until she was certain that she could win. Everything.

She didn't notice Julio give the signal to dim the lights, didn't pay much attention as the screen brightened and the music stopped. There was nothing for a moment, then the screen filled with the image of a young woman. She was naked and tied to a chair. She had her eyes closed.

When she opened them, Zaide recognized her with a shock. This was Iraci das Chagas, the only woman ever to deal major quantities of highwire out in the satellite cities. Iraci das Chagas, who had contacts with every street tribe in the Planalto, who was a dealer and a murderer and rumored to be a *candomble* priestess as well. The stories were that she sacrificed her enemies to the old gods.

Those were rumors. Here Zaide saw only a woman perhaps a decade older than herself. She had the beautiful coloring of mixed ancestry, and the unfortunate tendency of those with rich cinnamon-chocolate skin to scar easily. Her body was covered with scars, raised and discolored, most of them quite old. Iraci looked warily at the camera. She had seen enough in her life to fill ten lives, and she didn't have any illusions that this was going to get better. Only that somehow she was going to get out of it.

"I told you everything," Iraci said to someone out of camera range, and Zaide judged that it was the truth. "You have the names, all of them."

A high-pitched giggle overrode Iraci's plea. "Yes, I know," the giggling voice said. It was a voice Zaide recognized. "We have the information, thank you. It will be most useful. No, this is not business. Just recreation." The giggle again. Zaide placed it too easily. Julio.

Her eyes slid sideways at him. He was breathing deeply, entranced by the image on the screen.

In the clip, a man wearing a soft Carnival mask approached Iraci and caressed her face gently. Then, with one hand he held her left eye wide open, as if to put in a contact lens. Only he used his index finger and did not stop at the cornea: the nail penetrated the eye until a jelly-like substance oozed down her face.

Zaide was sick. She wanted to leave, to throw up. Julio, sitting next to her, giggled in that same high-pitched way she had not heard before. He touched the back of her hand lightly. "Oh, that's just the beginning."

On the screen the woman shrieked but the sound was cut. The man in the Carnival mask had a miniature fiber-optic saw. He showed it to Iraci and turned it on. A spectrum sparkled between the quivering tips and the blade activated. The man held the tool down from her face. He cut off her nipples. He cut off her hands at the wrists. He turned the fiber-saw off and laid it aside, and picked up something that was even worse. In his hand he held a dental drill full to the camera, turning it, showing it off. The sound came on again suddenly, loud, the whirring scream of the drill. Iraci must have heard it. Mutilated as she was, she still sank deeper into the hard chair where she'd been bound.

The camera angle changed to a side view, so it was easy to see the man in the mask straddle Iraci. He laid the drill on her lap and forced her mouth open. She tried to bite him. He held her jaw wide, wider, the cracking sound loud as the massive joint gave.

He needed only one hand then to hold her head. The other one held the drill. The camera zoomed in for a close-up as he forced the drill through the palate, up through the roof of her mouth, shoving the narrow instrument in up to the handle.

He held her face up to the camera as the drill penetrated. The one remaining eye was wild with pain. And then he withdrew the drill and pushed it through her teeth and up. This time the drill was angled back in her mouth, and when the drill bit through the soft palate it pierced her brain. The one eye suddenly glazed in death.

Then the man in the Carnival mask dropped the drill,

unzipped his pants and masturbated on her mutilated remains.

Sitting on the sofa next to Zaide, Julio Simon giggled wildly.

Zaide Soledad did not appear for dinner that evening. Susana brought over broth and juice and toast, but Zaide couldn't tolerate even those. The images from the Security office were vivid in her imagination. She understood Julio Simon's threat. And with all her gibbering terror, she wanted to take his offer.

It wasn't worth that. Even becoming CEO was no compensation for what Julio Simon would do if she lost. Better to join him. It was a reasonable scheme. Someone would do it if not him, and if she was there she could perhaps mitigate some of the worst of it.

And yet she knew that was ridiculous. She would be terrified every minute they worked together. She wondered if she would ever be able to be in a dark room alone and not strain to listen for Julio Simon's giggle, not see Iraci's face and those streams of dark blood over scarred skin.

"So I suppose you aren't going anywhere," Susana said sympathetically. "I guess you really are sick. I thought it was just positioning after this afternoon."

Zaide blinked. She had forgotten about meeting Paulo. She hauled herself out of bed and into the shower. Hot water almost revived her, almost enough to drown the fear, to wash off the taint of being Julio Simon's series. Almost.

She dried her hair, put on makeup automatically, dressed again in the simple black sweater and jeans she had worn the day before. Only she looked far whiter and there were circles under her eyes. Susana only shook her head. "You shouldn't be going anywhere. You look like you've got the flu or something. Maybe we should call the doctor."

Susana's concern warmed her. Zaide wanted to tell her cousin what she had seen and why she needed to go. But looking at Susana's innocence, far more than anyone ought to decently retain in fazenda life, she couldn't say the words. If the words remained unspoken, maybe they, too, would fade. And eventually she would forget the horror of it, of knowing that the man in the Carnival mask was Julio Simon, of knowing that she shared DNA with that creature. Knowing that she was as capable of cruelty.

That was the point, she surmised. That she was every bit the same monster. That she couldn't resist the rewards he held out to her when they came to power in the fazenda, when their fazenda could call more shots in the world than she wanted to think about.

For a long time they had exploited their position as the sole suppliers of rain forest medicinals to the rest of the world, and no one would turn their back on proven medicines. Even if it meant bankruptcy, people were willing to pay. And Brazil was one of the world's major exporters of food. The rivers and the plains of the Planalto, the vast and wild interior, had bowed to cultivation and productivity. And there was power, clean hydroelectric power, almost enough to supply the entire continent. Hydroelectric that satisfied Geneva's strictest air requirements. Food. Medicine. Power. They had everything.

Now Julio Simon wanted to control the air itself. Almost all of the world's greatest oxygen-cleaning and recycling plant, the Brazilian rain forest, was under the direct control of the Forestation Ministry, which was practically interchangeable with the five fazendas the Ministry had created. From being a solution to the Ministry's problem, the fazendas had become the Ministry, then the power behind the military that had taken charge of the country itself. Now Julio Simon was questioning why their power had to stop at some surveyor's lines. After all, the Portuguese hadn't felt that way when they had first landed on Brazilian shores.

Why not? The north was falling apart under the weight of its own decadence and waste. They were dependent on the rain forests as they had never been on any single resource. It would be very easy to relocate the center of world opinion from Geneva and Paris and New York to Rio and Brasilia.

Why not? Zaide mused. There was no reason for them to look to the north for anything anymore. Brasilia had more than enough talent, enough energy, enough of the essentials and the people.

Maybe Julio Simon was not crazy. Maybe he was a visionary. Zaide couldn't lay the thought aside while she dressed and picked up the vert from the garage.

Twelve

B Y the time she stashed the vert in the Vielho-Markowicz company lot and caught a cab over to South 109, she had the outline of a plan. Julio Simon was one of the creative thinkers, that was something she could not deny. He was also a monster; she could not deny that either. Which meant that, having the germ of the idea, it was not her job to implement it. And to rid the world of her cousin, whose genetic similarity to her own genome terrified her.

And so she didn't notice the city much as the cab sped by the barren streets. She didn't even untint the windows for a view of the unbroken winter sky. It was the end of July. Winter would be over soon and the rains would begin again. Only a few weeks away. She wondered idly if anything would be the same when spring came. Like the spring of the Forestation Riots.

She remembered that October very well. She was still in the village school then, already training to work for the fazenda but not yet a member of the family. Their teacher Dona Emilia had told the class about it, how some malcontents from the city had spoiled everything for everyone and tried to burn the rain forest. They had succeeded only in killing the new growth in the cerrado, because of the bravery of the fazenda workers and the excellence of Brazilian technology.

She had thought the story simplistic but believable. Malcontents were like that, never leaving well enough alone, not able to accept that they had far more than they would under any other system. Of course, with only violence in the streets, there was nothing to be done but call in the army. And the people should be glad that at least the murder and pillage in the streets was over.

Then Zaide had arrived at the big house, where no one talked about the great fire or the riots that had followed. Where everyone was very pleased at how the generals were running things. Though, of course, at some point there would have to be elections again. But before that happened, the fazendas had the perfect opportunity to consolidate their holdings, to cinch their monopolies, to set everything in place for the U.N. courts so that a coming democracy would not erode the giant gains they made under the generals.

Zaide understood that perfectly well. Nor was she surprised at the attitude at the big house. They did stand to gain quite dramatically. But she was not prepared when she learned who had devised the plan for forest fire and intervention policy.

Julio Simon had just been rewarded with the Wave for his brilliant scheme. He was the favored one among the cousins. Susana had told her to watch him very carefully. "For myself," Susana had said late one night while they stayed up and ate candies in bed, "I would never cross him. I think that too much of our future depends on his rise. And I think that already Uncle Victor has chosen him to succeed as CEO. If you support him he could have a lot to offer you down the line."

Zaide had thought about that. She admired Julio Simon's ruthless brilliance, but it frightened her at the same time. She wasn't certain if she could really trust him, or if he would turn on her as well when it was time to collect on the debt.

She was so immersed in the past that she was surprised when she arrived and the cab dropped her. She paid with cold centavos and entered the neighborhood again. It hadn't changed. Indeed, even the people looked the same, as if they had frozen the night before and just come alive again for her benefit. The one difference was that this time Paulo was waiting for her.

He sat on a bench scribbling on a go-screen, staring at the words, crossing them out and writing something else. He was not wearing his painted coat. Instead he wore the full black pants she had first seen him in, and a loose soft shirt of the same color, which fell over the trousers to almost tunic length. His hair was tied back. She walked toward him slowly and was glad when he looked up and smiled. He shoved the go-screen into his bag and got up to greet her.

They ate in Beirut, an old, elegant establishment that had been one of the reasons 109 had become so famous. Zaide raised her eyebrows as he escorted her in.

"Oh, it's from the run yesterday," he said softly. "We might not make dinheiro as such from a burn, but there are people down here in 109 who are very happy that two loads of highwire went up. They like to show their appreciation,"

Zaide knew she was supposed to be impressed, and it was working. They dined on parsley salad and lamb, and then Paulo ordered an assortment of pastries that were soaked in honey. It was not like any food served on the fazenda. It was completely alien and completely lavish at the same time. Zaide was charmed.

They rode the bus back to Paulo's supermanzana in 713. This time she noted the number of the neighborhood block. It was as depressing as she remembered it. He took her back to the office. It was still terribly early; no one would be around for hours. So they had sex on the green carpet again until the night was deeply settled. Then they got dressed and joined the procession of the lost in the neighborhood.

The barzinho was brighter than she remembered, or maybe it was merely that there was less smoke. Several portable lamps were fixed to the pillars, and loops of fairy lights strung between them gave the area a glamour that was somehow embedded in its hopelessness as well as its brazen arrogance. Tonight, in the center, a wooden floor had been set up, sort of like a portable stage. So far the place was quiet and not very full. None of the working girls and their pimps would be down until business dropped off much closer to dawn. She saw some of the more respectable poor—Old Hector making book in the corner, the unemployed men too tired to remain angry for long, the *pivetes* who hung around the edges of the lights like animals afraid to get too close to the fire. Someone turned on a box, and rhythm filled the empty spaces.

From the shadows several young men emerged. They were dressed like Paulo and had the same delicate movements. One she even recognized from the *capoeira* circle at the Saint Anthony's Day celebration. Paulo smiled at her and she nodded. He wanted to play. She wanted to watch again, to see if somehow the gestalt she had experienced at the festival would return. If the *capoeira* itself would inform her still-nebulous plans.

The music mixed with the dancers. There were three bowmen and the drum, and even the girls joined in the singing. The *capoeiristas* stood in the *roda*, the circle, and swayed lightly, catching the beat of the drums. There was a tenseness about them, and suddenly the few people who were drinking paid attention. Zaide saw two older men lay bet money on the table. One of the elders went over and joined the singers, clapping his hands to the slow beat.

This was not exhibition, as the dance at the festival was. This was the real *capoeira*, not choreographed but lived, played. They called the matches *jogo*, and it was the master with the middle bow, called a *berimbau*, who controlled the rhythm and type of *jogo* in each pairing.

The master of this *roda* was immensely tall and very black. He had the defined gymnast's muscles of any *capoeirista*, and Zaide did not doubt that he could execute the most difficult moves of the form. He seemed to notice Paulo in particular and smiled at him broadly. That was when Zaide realized that for all his pure African-ebony skin, his eyes were a startling parrot-green.

She was shocked momentarily and then assumed that he

must have had lens implants. Which seemed strange in general. Usually the surgeons liked to keep people looking as normal as possible. The priests constantly agitated against anything they considered "mutilation," and this inhuman green could well qualify. Although that was perhaps why someone from the favela could afford these implants, they were less than perfect specimens.

The drumbeat built and the bows wailed until it seemed that the foundation pillars holding the building above them must be vibrating. Zaide didn't see the signal from the master, but two men broke free toward the center of the circle. One dropped back, supporting himself on one arm and arched, while the other whirled in a slow kick. The lower man pivoted his legs around overhead and held one thigh against his ear. Then he rotated his legs over his head and back to the floor and came up standing while his opponent swayed back and forth sharply, clapping to the music. A third joined them, whirling around, circling them both with a series of flying kicks as high as his shoulders. The original two each retreated, melting into the perimeter of the fighting circle, while a fourth opponent came forth to dance with the kicking man.

Zaide was on the edge of her seat. This was a contest, hotly played, but she couldn't see how it was pure combat. She didn't quite understand how some of the moves at angles unnatural to the human body could be used to fight. Two others had now taken the center. Their dance was more elaborate, one doing a dive to the floor while the other knocked the air with his skull.

The beat was strong. It shaped the moment, molding the dancers as they fought. Now there was no pretense of any dance at all, except that *capoeira* played with skill and power could not be called anything but dance.

The slow-motion underwater quality of movement was, Zaide realized, deceptive. The two participants created a circle, a single kinetic whole where all the elements combined in focus, in power, in constantly shifting line. Once perceived, the pattern changed, flowed into something else, something that imitated the idea but never repeated it. Subtle shades of tone became dominant and faded before they could be captured.

And yet the participants never touched each other. They rarely came close enough to be in any danger; most often they seemed to have little to do with each other. And yet, although she could not understand how the pieces fit together, there was an internal consistency that she recognized.

Then, in a single drop-kick it was done, one of the combatants hitting his head against the boards when he lost his balance standing on one hand. Blood spewing out his nose. It was just one more element. Pain.

Pain made her think of Julio Simon, made her reconsider her ideas. They were drifting in her mind the way the *capoeira* dancers recreated the universe to their pattern.

And then the word itself exploded in her head. *Capoeira* was not just the word for the martial dance, but for the scrublands themselves. The bush country that in more typical Portuguese was called the *cerrado*, the country that surrounded the city.

She didn't quite know what to make of the image that suddenly superimposed itself over her vision, but the two together fought and merged with the sound of the bows, like the fighters on the stage. She caught a glimpse of everything fused, complete, perfectly balanced, and then it swirled away in the relentless motion of the universe. She was so focused on her own vision that she didn't notice that Francisco Pope had sat down on an upended box next to her.

Paulo had come to the center. Without the mask, she could see his face was calm, almost beatific. And when he dove to the floor in an elegant back flip, he was positively transcendent. Every gesture was the beginning of the next sequence, the graceful consummation of the last. There were no demarcations, no pauses, no single moment in the whole which could be taken out of context, captured, held.

"He's good," Francisco said. "Even the old-timers say he's good, and not just for a white boy."

She didn't need Francisco Pope to tell her that. She could see it, even though she knew little of *capoeira*. His opponent was good too, but didn't have quite the edge of elegance, the counter-timing that made Paulo's performance something that stood apart.

Paulo took his opponent out elegantly. He merely took command over the space in the ring, leaving his opponent no room to move, to counter, to escape. Finally there remained no choice but to break through the wall of bodies swaying to the rhythm of the drum and tambourine.

As Paulo resumed his place on the circumference of the *capoeira* circle, Zaide turned to Pope. "I know something that may be of use to you," she said. "The security chief of the Vielho-Markowicz will be with the CEO at the Cathedral on Assumption Day. He has planned some kind of attack on Cadea, I think. But it would be a very good opportunity for something."

"For what?" Pope sounded bored. "Kidnapping isn't exactly easy in front of the entire city, you know."

Zaide shrugged. "I was thinking about revenge," she said softly. "You did business with Iraci das Chagas, didn't you? He killed her."

Pope narrowed his eyes, studying her. "Iraci das Chagas sold highwire. She was scum. He did me a favor getting rid of her, okay?"

Zaide wanted very badly to slam her hand against the fifty-gallon drum that served as their table and tell him exactly what he was doing wrong, the way she would do with lower-level employees on the fazenda. But this was not the fazenda. Suddenly the garish lights and the *capoeira* and the smell of stale *pinga* made the place absurd and alien to her, and she couldn't remember why she was here at all.

Then she centered herself. It was important never to lose control. Sonia Leah had taught her the trick, taking three very deep breaths and draining her body of words as the air left her lungs. It took a little time. Often the pause was read as something dangerous, and that was useful too.

"If you're not interested, it isn't my business," she said coolly. "I just thought that you might be intrigued by the possibilities. Cadea has been targeted by Vielho-Markowicz and they have been using favela tribes. I thought you might like to let the other cadres know about that, that they are being used in a fazenda war that has nothing at all to do with you. You know, your tribes are going to fight all the battles and come away without any of the goods."

Pope stared at her. His steel-colored eyes were as cold and sharp as his favorite blade. "Who the hell are you?" he asked, fury only temporarily held in check. "What the hell are you doing here screwing around with us? With Paulo?"

Zaide met his gaze for almost a full minute before she had to drop her eyes. "Sometimes I have access to certain information," she said softly. The drums were slowing now, the rhythms returning to normal. The dancers in the *capoeira* circle were shimmering with sweat under the gaudy pink and green and orange lights.

"Do you believe in fate?" Francisco asked, throwing her completely off balance.

"I never thought about it," Zaide replied. "I don't think so, not really. Why?"

"Because Paulo thinks you are something out of his fate," Pope replied darkly. "He saw a girl who looked exactly like you—he said it had to be your twin to be so close—die on the day he met you. But I don't believe in fate. I don't believe it's any more than a case of mistaken identity. Maybe a startling resemblance. I've seen that more than once. And he had only met her an hour before she died."

"Why are you telling me this?" Zaide asked, confused.

"I want to warn you. If you betray us, you're dead. You might turn Paulo's head. I want you to know you can't turn mine."

Zaide thought about that for a minute. "I didn't ask you to trust me. I gave you information freely to use. Because I think if you find me trustworthy, you will accept that I can help you."

Francisco looked her over carefully. The *capoeira* was ending and one of the girls who had arrived only minutes before was passing a tray of aguardente among the dancers. The musicians, except for the master, had changed their beat and now it was only a simple samba. Two of the girls who had been singing now jumped on the wooden platform and took their full skirts in their hands. Paulo was already in a conversation with the green-eyed man as he accepted a glass.

"Why do you want to help us?" Pope sneered. "Because you like condescending to favela rats who can satisfy you more than those soft slobs in your corporations?"

"No," Zaide answered, and she was surprised that she was neither angry at his insinuation or particularly affected by his obvious dislike of her. "I have my own agenda. And maybe Paulo is right, there is fate between us. Besides, with what I told you, maybe you don't want to get involved. The Serpentes are going to be there and they are very angry at you for burning the highwire shipment. They could be looking to hurt you. And they will definitely be going. So, no, I was wrong, you probably would be better off staying home."

Pope's face turned stark white in fury. "I know what you are," he said softly. "And if for one second I have any reason to distrust you, I'll tell Paulo. You can't imagine what he'd do if you betrayed him. You don't even want to imagine it."

"Do you really think I'm here because it's boring at home and your cadres are better fucks than the cousins?" she asked in the south-city dialect, practically spitting the words.

Francisco looked at her as if he were trying to decide that question. Zaide waited for him to answer, to drive his fist through the rusted surface of the metal drum. Instead he noticed Paulo coming, and showed as much discipline in containing his anger as Zaide had ever seen among her cousins.

Paulo approached the table holding two glasses in his left hand and drinking from the one in his right. He set them down carefully as he sat on the upturned box next to Zaide. The drink smelled raw, home-brewed, fermented sugar cane that was too strong and sweet and burned like napalm going down.

He raised his glass. "To Bakunin."

Francisco and Zaide raised theirs as well. Pope gave Zaide a wry look as they drank to the cadre.

The music got stronger and changed to a bright samba that matched the colored lights over the stage, which had conveniently become a dance floor. Some of the younger whores were dancing gaily, showing off for the customers and having as close to a good time as they had ever experienced. Steel, already drunk, staggered through the light walls toward the bar. "Drinks for everyone," he announced. "The whole house, the very best. For those little girls over there dancing and all the men and Hector, good Hector—give him a double. Vasco de Gama paid three-to-one today on the point spread. The first time I ever bet on a Rio team, you know that? My parents were from Rio so I always lay my dinheiro on São Paulo. Well, so Steel wins on the soccer scores and everybody drinks."

He was cheered, raised his glass to salute the assemblage, and turned back to his own drinking. The girls giggled. "There's one man who has friends," someone shouted.

Paulo and Francisco winced almost in unison. Zaide didn't notice. She was far too lost in the one bit of information Francisco had given her. Paulo had seen a girl who looked like her die.

A girl who looked exactly like her, according to Pope. He didn't believe it. She knew it was true. The genetic rejects, another one of her selves that had been a backwash when the final genome scans were done. She thought of herself as one of the *pivetes*, thrown out on the street in the satellite cities, useless to the fazendas that had made them. They were no different than any of the other street children, really. Zaide was pleased that she had survived in that environment. Few of the *pivetes* ever made it past twelve, according to government statistics.

But she had. And she had joined a cadre and she had died on a run. For highwire. Suddenly Zaide remembered Paulo asking if she could use a blowgun. It was one of the first things the children learned in the Vielho-Markowicz, and all of them were expected to become quite good. Zaide had been exceptional. So, obviously, had been her other selves.

She felt deprived that she had never met them. Until this moment they existed for her only in theory. They were not real, not women who lived and breathed and fought the way she did. But that must be who Paulo had met and seen die. On the same day as the festival.

Maybe it was not just coincidence. Maybe there was something to the idea of fate. Or a miracle. Oh, not a big miracle like Lourdes, but a miracle all the same. One of the small inconsistencies of daily life that happen because the universe is more organic and complex than any mechanistic model would make it. Zaide could accept that. It made a certain amount of sense. And there had to be something to explain the miracles that existed in the moment and were recorded so that everyone knew about them.

Like the Miracle of the Ice when the city was founded. It was one of the most famous stories about the founding of Brasilia, and had been one of Zaide's favorites. On the day the builders broke ground for the Catetinho, the first residential palace for the President, they brought out specially saved bottles of good whiskey to pass around. But they had no ice. It was in spring, at the end of October when the cloudscapes were at their most beautiful. And there was a sudden hailstorm, here in the interior of Brazil where there was never any snow or ice or hail, where it was never cold and in late October was moving toward summer. There was a hailstorm. It lasted all of fifteen minutes while the workers ran out in the falling ice screaming, "It's a miracle."

No, not a very big miracle. But still a miracle, an occurrence not within the probabilities of the universal pattern.

But it happened. Sometimes the miracles were small things that no one would even notice. Sometimes they made the universe itself seem like a sentient being.

Zaide knew it was not. This was only the playing out of the mathematical patterns that sometimes varied wildly and sometimes seemed unpredictable but had their own internal logic.

Like the *capoeira* played out, a small bit of pressure in one place would bring a great crashing climax later, when the chain of events that had looked implausible had begun to look inevitable. Only she had to nudge the pattern in the right place.

Pope gave Zaide a calculated look, then turned to Paulo. "I hear that the Serps are getting the data on Cadea from the Vielho-Markowicz. That we're all just being used in a fazenda fight. And I hear that the security chief for the Vielho-Markowicz is going to be at the Assumption Day Mass at the Cathedral."

Paulo's expression darkened and his hand tightened around his glass. "I'd like to slice them open and then grill them with palm oil and serve them up for Sunday dinner."

"Maybe that wouldn't be such a bad idea," Zaide said noncommittally.

The anger left Paulo's body. He left the glass on the metal drum and embraced Zaide as if she were the only thing he cared about in the world.

Zaide kissed his neck. Then her eyes met Pope's over Paulo's shoulder. He was clearly warning her. And she, she showed him she was not afraid.

Thirteen

S HE woke up in a different world. She remembered going into the clinic, lying down on the gurney and being strapped in. She remembered her head being very clear.

Now there was no clarity at all. Inside and around the pain there was a pull, as if her mind were being sucked away into some overwhelming tide. She could not resist it, although she desperately wanted to resist, wanted to stay anchored in her own skull in her own place.

Through her own fear she could feel the phrines from the secondary going into overload, the psychotropics penetrating and realigning the chemistry, peeling her resistance back one stubborn layer at a time. She knew the drugs, she knew the codes, and suddenly it seemed very wrong that the implants could have that kind of power over her. She was sentient, damn it.

And the drugs reminded her gently that she was programmed by them as much as anything else was programmed. That she couldn't help but respond, that she would be happier if she accepted that fact. Deep in the recess of racial memory, or maybe through the beginning of the brightly lit penetration she perceived in her skull, she was aware that this was precisely what people called fate. It was a very, very old idea, and she could rest in it and ride the Wave that was coming, the datastream that would so soon pour through those windows in her perception that grew more transparent. She felt like a small observer in a room. The walls were smooth and curved and ivory white, and there were two enormous round openings that were gloriously open to the outside. She could walk through those great arches, and the scene outside was inviting. The sky glistened and the grass looked soft. The breeze blew fresh, ruffling the grass, bringing a hint of the spring scent into her. Inside the room that was her skull.

And outside, the breeze that tempted so delicately was a strong wind that could turn into a dust devil or a gale. She knew that, but the knowing felt very abstract. And so she walked out her own eyes into the gentle invitation of the Wave.

There was only indigo, shining infinitely, forever. The indigo was thick, like old-fashioned ink, and her awareness was suspended through it. She was not cohesive.

And then she felt the movement. The whole indigo mass, the ocean that seemed to go on through forever, penetrating the city and the cerrado and all the minds that merged into this singular entity, all of it shifted. Flowed. Little eddies and whirls sprang up, became violent, affected large regions of the Wave before they died.

Only that was not right, either. That meant there was some time sequence involved and there was not. Or rather, the cause and the effect existed at the same time, and so neither functioned as it did in the big world.

She could sense all of it happening as if it were inside her. Nothing meant anything here, just as there was no linear logic. There was only fluid form that heaved, restless and aware.

She concentrated for a moment and felt a flex in the Wave. It was her own contraction of thought that created that movement, only the whirlpools and sinks and currents it started had always been there and had not been changed by her presence. Although she had created them.

Fear glittered through her. Causality and logic did not work in the Wave. All the basic assumptions of how things worked were suspended. Like the concept of *up* being useless without gravity, all the philosophies in the universe did not function here. Without a frame of reference to hang on to, she was completely a victim of the quanta flow.

Reference. Framework. She tried to think, but words did not function better in this space than time did. Suddenly in her frustration she imagined Julio Simon in the Wave, laughing at her.

That image stayed, solidified. Julio Simon. But it was not her cousin, only the pattern her cousin had created in the ceaseless pulsation of the quantum sea. His shadow, as it were.

The image did not become truly dense. Inside the form of Julio Simon she could see other patterns forming and breaking. She was curious. And her desire made the fluid formations huge, so that they filled the entire ocean, surrounding her on every side.

They were beautiful, creating themselves in their own image. She had no idea of scale. All the templates rotated and reproduced themselves over and over again, larger, smaller—invariable and eternal dimensions that could trap her in their organic growth.

It reminded her of the rain forest, growing, living, constantly expanding and yet so very fragile.

Around her the paradigm shifted, responsive to her thought although she had entered this pattern when she was first immersed in the datastream. This pattern was the rain forest. It was eternal, delicate, growing and expanding forever, and forever being cut down. This pattern belonged to her, to the family, to the fazenda.

Suddenly, joyfully, she understood. And in her understanding the shimmering around her quivered, reflecting her true entrance into that thing which was itself. The patterns were real, the mathematical models of reality that were complex and never the same and in some abstract way alive. Intrinsically organic, as if the particle universe and the stars and the rain forest all followed the same archetypal architecture, which was somehow recreated as the basis for every structure.

Her comprehension changed the pattern, made the colors around her brighter and more pure. She was dancing to the eternal quantum rhythm like the rhythm of the drums. Their vibration made her one with them, completely submerged in the universal heartbeat.

Then she realized where she had seen this all before, the kaleidoscope of movement and rhythm all tied together into a fluid whole. The *capoeira* was one more manifestation of the Wave. Through the dance of patterns inside her she made out the figure of an ancient woman wearing a red head scarf. She had heard of that somewhere, and in the Wave the knowledge washed gently through her cohesive awareness. This was a priestess of the old *candomble*, the ancient African religion the slaves had brought to Brazil and had never quite changed. It was part of the power flux of the Wave, along with the fazenda families and the government and the pressing mass energy of the population overall.

Nor was this an individual in reality. Rather, this was a position, a representation of force, just as the *capoeira* illustrated the way force moved in a chaotic structure. Like the Wave.

It was chaotic, organized with a complexity as organic as the whole universe. It was the whole universe, quantum existence being undifferentiated through spacetime. But she, Zaide Soledad Vielho-Markowicz, while here, also had another existence. Another sense of self, of power. Most of all, she had choice, although there was nothing to choose— everything had already been. The pattern was finished. And yet Zaide felt nibbling around the edge of her identity, and yet she was an entity and could in some way move within the quantum sea.

Zaide started, her consciousness suddenly coherent in the eternity of the indigo ocean. As awareness created her existence, it also created her separation from the whole and she could feel herself being ejected by the dancing subparticle world.

She tried to hang on, tried to get back, but she was no longer diffuse enough to interpermeate the Wave. It could not accept her. She was walled out, and there was pain. Real physical anguish that would not go away, and her consciousness would not sink into black oblivion and blot out the pain.

Then, through infinite time, *although there was no time; everything existed at once and cause and effect happened together in the same place*, through the nonexistence of time, she awoke.

The Bakunin office was almost quiet. The music was turned off, and the barzinho under the building wasn't open yet, so there was no noise in the street. Only Steel's loud snoring broke the calm. Nem Brito was carefully checking their ammunition supplies. "We'll need more darts soon," he said very softly.

Pope nodded, distracted. He was waiting for Sylvia, and he hadn't decided yet what he should do about the information. Rather, he knew he should talk to Paulo and he didn't want to. Paulo was too involved with the girl to distrust her, Francisco thought. Either that, or he was too impressed with this business of fate, which Francisco found infuriating.

But that wasn't the real reason he was upset, and he knew it. Francisco didn't trust Dr. Valdemar. There was something about the highwire addicts on the street, the Changelings half-done roaming the favelas, the *pivetes* picked up and gone. There were rumors of their being used for some strange and painful experiments. Nem Brito worked with them sometimes, and he knew about Nem Brito's past.

When he had recruited him, Nem Brito had first resisted. "I do not belong with you," he'd said, and his face had twisted with pain. Nem Brito was mixed Indian and Portuguese, true Brazilian, with morning-coffee-colored skin and heavy dark hair that fell near his waist, and a half-angry, half-sly expression. Now that expression was gone and there was only revealed honesty. Francisco was willing to put down dinheiro that he had been raised by the Indian part of the family.

Francisco had only shrugged. "I think you do belong," he said simply. "I've seen you around the neighborhood, seen you fading into shadows. You're good. You're very good."

Nem Brito had only winced and tried to walk away.

"I'll buy you a *pinga* if you'll just talk to me," Francisco had tempted him, hoping silently that Steel had been lucky with the soccer scores that day.

Two drinks later Nem Brito was a little more forthcoming. "I come from Rio, you know," he said softly. Francisco nodded, though it would have been hard to overlook the carioca accent. "I was one of the children who lived on the beach there. It is much worse than here. In Rio the rich go out and buy licenses to go shooting for sport on the beach. They drive down in open sandverts and fire. For sport. Although we were only living there, it was not what we wanted to be, believe me. But there were worse things than the hunts.

"I was a fetch. For a phrine lab. They sometimes need living people to produce certain chemicals, or at least that's cheaper than cloning partials."

"They were illegals, then," Francisco prompted.

Nem Brito shook his head. "Legals too. It saved a good bit of cash. I brought them in. I got fifty centavos for every one I lured down. It was easy. All I had to do was promise them a meal and I had half the beach ready to follow."

"But you came here," Francisco said.

"I got too old for it," Nem Brito answered. "And too many people wanted me dead. And in Rio that is a very easy thing to do. Brasilia—no one would ever look for me in Brasilia. Even if you were dying in Rio, you would go maybe to Recife or São Paulo or even Salvador. But no one would ever think of coming to Brasilia. So I am safe here."

Francisco had ordered them both another glass. "Paulo and I, we're building a very different kind of cadre this time. Not even like the Jaguars. We want to do more than take a little turf. We have plans, big plans. And we need people who are smart and street. You're both. The past is done. If you want to join us, you will make us very happy, Nem Brito. I think you are just the kind of person we need."

So Nem Brito had joined them. Now he spent a good deal of time with Dr. Valdemar and Paulo in the professor's illegal lab. Sometimes Francisco wondered if Nem Brito had gone back to his old occupation as a lure, though Francisco had tried to dismiss all the whispers as just so much gossip. After all, there wasn't much else to do in the southern supermanzanas except visit and chatter, and there wasn't much to talk about. Nothing happened, nothing changed. So there was bound to be gossip. He didn't believe anything he heard.

So he told himself. If only Paulo hadn't been so set on Changing, there wouldn't have been any problem. But Paulo had.

Francisco didn't understand it at all. He could not imagine any circumstance, except possibly given the alternative of death, where he would choose to change his essential human nature. Laurindo the snake-Change didn't impress him. What could a snake-change do, anyway? Except hiss a lot, which wasn't really very impressive at all.

But what Paulo wanted, the altered DNA to slowly restructure his implants, making him something not human at all . . . Something that was made only to destroy what had destroyed him. The old priestess would call it *Chango*, but Francisco knew the real name. Vengeance. Rage. It was not worth his body, it was not worth his pleasures and his pain.

Paulo had described what Dr. Valdemar had told him. First he would become chemically hypersensitive, and there was no research that could predict how long this would last. Even the smallest amounts of drugs would act unpredictably, which was something Paulo considered a benefit. The idea made Francisco slightly ill. He wanted to know exactly what something did and how, before he used it. He wanted to be in control.

But, then, that was always the difference between them. Francisco Pope always was in control, of himself, of his environment. Even through events where he had no power whatever, he retained a sense of at least regulating his own reactions.

And thus he had been inspired to create Bakunin. To completely control one's own circumstances, he believed, meant that no artificial laws should limit the possibilities. Laws like the Forestation Acts, for example. Destroy all the artifice, and natural law would emerge. The most capable, the strongest, the best and the worst, would survive. Weed out the weak, the incompetents, like the old pioneer society before them.

Strange to think that only seventy years ago the Planalto had been pure frontier, a place for the misfits and the outlaws to create themselves. Now there was no place free at all. Except the rain forest itself.

And no one could live there. Even the Indians of Amazonas thought the dark forest too dangerous. It was like a cavern where no sun penetrated the high canopy and the sun could not be seen, where anyone wandering too far from the riverbank camps would be lost. The Indians believed that these lost people were victims of evil forest spirits, or maybe became such themselves. Francisco had never been very clear on that. He had, however, been quite convinced that the rain forest was not a place for people to live. Especially not alone.

Then he had had a vision. Not like the vision of São Juan Bosco, who had seen the capital of the New World here on the Planalto. Nothing like that. He had only seen no one setting limits on his life, on anyone's life. Because he was better than all the limits anyone had ever set, he was able to do more, if only there hadn't been the Forestation Acts and the troubles and the military deciding that it had to intervene. He was better than that.

But what he wanted he thought was straightforward and simple and necessary. He had no complaint about life being unfair or unkind. This was its job; he didn't argue it. No, he just wanted a chance to try everything without anyone telling him no.

Paulo Sylvia had always been the polar opposite. Paulo believed in fate, believed in destruction and Kali, more from pain than any intellectual scruples. From what Francisco had observed, his best friend had very few. Those he adhered to, though, were utterly unassailable. Paulo would never betray a friend, he would defend those he accepted without any thought of cost. But outside the very small circle of those he considered his friends and family, he felt no responsibility whatever.

Francisco wondered where the new girl fit, whether she'd become one of the inner circle this quickly. Probably not. More likely she was just one more of the women who followed Paulo slavishly and weren't at all put off by the fact that his only interest in them was sex.

Only she was a fazenda trainee. He would bet money on it. Money was worthless; he would bet blood, he would bet a round at the barzinho later that night. Where Paulo had found her Francisco couldn't figure. He didn't really care. It was impossible to believe that Paulo didn't know who she was, and it was equally impossible to believe that he did.

Francisco picked up the Teflon knife Paulo had left on the desk and embedded it in the splintered wood over and over, his frustration driving the blade harder each time. He was so immersed in his anger that he didn't notice Paulo come in until a handful of phrines landed on the desk.

Francisco's head jerked up. "What the hell are those?" he demanded sharply.

Paulo only smiled. "I did some work today in the lab. I got a half klick of phrines and enough old centavos to pay for dinner and drinks all around tonight."

"Let Steel pay," Nem Brito said from the back. "He's got the money anyway."

Dislike passed like a shadow over Sylvia's face and then

was gone. "Well, anyway we'll be able to pay off Laurindo. And there should be plenty left for us."

"It's probably better if we deal with Jorge down at 109, have him sell our surplus and then pay Laurindo in cash," Francisco countered. "I don't want him asking about another source."

Paulo shrugged. Either way. Only he didn't like the way Francisco was acting, all tense and twitchy, the thin knife flipping in his hands like it was alive. The knife was the one he had given Paulo, and Paulo always felt a special attachment to it. As if the knife knew it had a life of its own, independent of its owner. He knew that was ridiculous, but at moments like this he could believe it far too easily.

"You're bored," he said to Francisco, knowing that was only part of the truth. "Let's do something."

"There isn't anything fun going on," Nem Brito volunteered.

"So we'll do something," Paulo said. "Come on, let's get out of here. Why don't we go out to Cuidad Libre?"

Francisco looked at him as if he were demented. "What the hell is there to do in Cuidad Libre?"

"I don't know. It's just not here, it's something different," Paulo protested.

"Maybe we should go to the Gilberto Salomao, or the sports complex," Nem Brito suggested.

"For what?" Francisco spat. "A game of tennis, maybe?"

Paulo closed his eyes for a moment. He had forgotten. Francisco had been a very good tennis player once. Back in the days when they had their club memberships and wore clothes imported from France. It seemed like a dreamtime past, and it hurt when he thought about how little time had really passed. Two years, just barely, had gone. No time at all, and yet plenty of time for him to see all his hopes gone.

No, that hadn't taken two years. It had taken two minutes, as much time as it took for the President to sign the legislation, as much time as it took for the generals to address the country, as much time as it took to run a bayonet through his mother's lungs. Hardly any time at all to make the world change, and it would not go back.

"So we'll go to the Gilberto Salomao and sell the phrines on the street to the verties and use the spare change to play the arcades," Nem Brito said as if the decision was made. "I suppose we ought to wake up Steel." Then he grimaced. Nem Brito didn't particularly like Steel any more than the others did. On the other hand, they'd all leeched off Steel more than he found comfortable, and paying for a few arcade games was worth the price. At least Steel would be plugged in and they wouldn't have to deal with his company.

"Yeah," Paulo agreed. "It's been a long time since we've been down there. And we can get a much better price ourselves than if we're selling to Jorge. He takes a healthy commission."

Francisco didn't voice his agreement, but he rose and put on his painted coat. The bottom was bordered with conch patterns, and across the back was the Great Pyramid with the giant snakes coming down the edges and the sun over it all, glorious and proud and colored with a thin leaf overlay of real gold. And, standing on the summit of the pyramid, facing the sun in worship, was a single priest in feathered robes holding a bleeding heart up in offering. The feathers were real, each snipped off the tip of the large parrot feathers that would have been used for such a robe, and glued to the coat, then stitched over with silk thread. It was very hard, fine work and Francisco had paid a lot to have it done.

Francisco led the way out to where their bikes were chained and then up the Exio Rodovairio Sul.

The Gilberto Salomao Commercial District was at the edge of the southern residential area. Once it had been an elegant place to spend an evening, with beer gardens and restaurants and bakeries and a cinema-in-the-round. It had lost some of its economic base but not its attraction, and although several of the bakeries had become games arcades and the beer gardens sold more phrines at their tables than brew, it was still popular with the entire city. Indeed, the verties who lived in the South Lake Mansion District and were too scared to go down to 109 could do their slumming and drug-buying here where there was still a patina of undeserved respectability.

They locked their powerbikes in a single bikebox and Francisco thumbchecked it. Then they hit the street.

Unlike the residential areas of Brasilia, the commercial district had been planned for nightlife. Only the planners had not quite had this in mind when they had created their egalitarian socialist city of the future. The future had come and it was not egalitarian; it was not socialist and it was not organized and well-ordered and Newtonian and neat. At least that's what Francisco thought whenever he was in the Gilberto Salomao. The verties, adolescents from the South Lake Mansion District, were out in droves. Francisco stared at them with loathing. They were rich and untouched by the Forestation Acts, by the military pacification patrols, by the curfew and the Sentinels of the Night who roamed in packs and broke in and carried off people in the dark. And even with elections announced for September, the Sentinels hadn't slackened their pace. Indeed, they seemed more active than ever, as if they needed to get in their fun before the new democracy made them illegal once again.

The verties didn't think about these things. They were far more concerned with whether or not they were going to get new verts for graduation and wearing the absolutely latest styles. Verties wore uniforms as rigid as the troopers—all their clothes from the right shops, all the same brands.

Suddenly Francisco realized that once he had tried to copy their style. He had not come from that level of wealth and he had too much talent to be satisfied by vertie goals, but during the days when he had played all comers at the Minas Tennis Club he had aspired to their ranks. Only for one summer, he told himself, only when he was very young. But they were without concerns, the verties, and that was why he hated them.

Suddenly he thought about Zaide, and he realized that he

respected her more than any of the verties on parade. Not only because of her own qualities, but because, even to him, it was obvious that the fazenda trainees were expected to produce something. They were supposed to work, and there were stories about what happened if they didn't. Even if she could buy and sell all the verties put together out of her pocket money, Zaide had a better grasp of reality than these spoiled scions of the upper middle class.

Francisco watched Paulo approach a gaggle of adolescents all dressed in the same shade of sea-green, and dripping jewelry. He talked to them for a few moments in a low voice. Francisco and Nem Brito waited far enough away not to appear threatening.

The teenagers disappeared into one of the arcades. Paulo stayed where he was, his eyes twitching over the street. Nem Brito and Francisco walked apart, slowly, down the block on opposite sides. Obviously this was not going to be a simple transaction. They waited until they saw the green-clad kids meet with Paulo again. This time they met up at a newsfax, like strangers who just happened to catch the same headline on the readout scan.

When Paulo rejoined them, he looked somewhere between furious and bemused. "They wanted to buy phrines on credit," he said, disbelieving. "They were too stupid to figure out that no one is going to sell on credit. Cold centavos or nothing. So they had to get change. I couldn't believe it. On the other hand I got over a hundred each."

The three of them burst out laughing all together.

"You got yourself a real crew of morons there," Nem Brito said.

And Francisco asked, "How many did you sell?"

Paulo smiled. "Ten. So we still have most of the stash left and a thousand centavos in cold dinheiro. You know, I could enjoy this if it wasn't so easy."

He dug the coins out of the deep pockets of his coat, enough coins to make the snake scales that wound over the pockets bulge. He gave handfuls to both Nem Brito and Francisco. "Come on, let's play."

They didn't select the nearest arcade. There was a group of well-scrubbed verties in sea-green playing one of the idiot games near the door. They passed and went down the street, past the beer garden and the Arab bakery, past the well-lit game emporium, to a small dark door with only a small, unlit sign. It said THE MAGIC SHOPPE. The three of them went inside.

Paulo had discovered this place only last year. It fascinated him. There were tricks to learn and buy, all kinds of gadgets, and a regular arcade out back in a game garden that served beer from an adjoining bar. Well, not quite regular games. This place didn't have Triton Warrior and SeaScape, which were popular in the vertie arcades. Only there were no verties out back, though the place was not empty. Most of the players at the link tables wore long, painted coats. Under the multicolored lights it was hard to make out the various designs, many taken from the *candomble* rituals or the ancient Inca legends.

There was a good chance that a number of these players came from the satellite cities. There might even be Serps among the players, although no one Paulo recognized straight off.

Not that he looked really hard. He headed straight for his favorite game and was pleased to see it was available. Changeling, it was, a VR rig coded with the various Changeling possibilities. For someone with a secondary, like Paulo, the virtual reality was even more cohesive with a full phrine link. This part was legal since it was his own phrine stimulated, nothing artificially induced at all.

Anyway, for as much time as he had money to buy he could have the body, the capabilities he should have. He dropped the coins into the slot and touched the icons for his choices. Snakeman didn't interest him, nor did underwater adaptation. He selected soldier and historic/fantasy monster together. Then on the next menu he selected Anglo-Celt (there was just a touch of Irish in his blood, along with the Portuguese and German, and just a little Indian somewhere) and asked for high conflict. Then under the free options he selected a literary work that he had played out several times before but still held his imagination.

His selections done, he got into the VR gear, the electrode patch over his own secondary, the helmet and gloves and sensory chair. By the time he had switched on each of the independent sensory inputs, the main system had written his character and adventure. There was a moment of dark silence and then he stepped into the body and experience that should, by rights, have been his.

He was Grendel. That was his private name for his dream. Paulo Sylvia knew he was a monster. He was something evil, twisted by fate and circumstance and by his own perverse desires. He didn't want to help the world, he didn't want to save humanity. Most of what he had seen of humanity hadn't impressed him much. And because of that, he knew he was a monster, a thing that did not belong anywhere. Except with his friends who were all as monstrous as himself.

The body created by the VR was not human, and shaped by Paulo's imagination it became the personification of the monster in complete detail. He was pleased with the leather hide, the warts and yellowish color in his eyes; he was pleased with his claws and strength and agility and resiliency. He had internal breathing tanks; he had double magnolines instead of nerves, and those were strong enough to create a shock when he clapped his hands.

The game opened like it always did, like he knew it had to. In the feast. There was the hero, puny, insubstantial. He had eliminated them all before. He was not worried by this insignificant thing, not worried in the least.

He was far more worried about the Queen, his mother. She was much more dangerous than some slight human. And he loved her and he hated her at the same time and he wasn't sure the feelings weren't all the same thing.

Paulo was content. He had played this game before. He waited to see the image of the Queen before him, more hideous than even her son, as it had been every other time he had paid out to play this scenario. And, exactly on cue, she appeared.

But she was not Grendel's dam, not what he had chosen at all. Draped in glimmering translucent black veils, she looked far too human—white skin and black hair like a fairy-tale princess.

The processor must have gotten it wrong, set him in the wrong scenario. That was the only explanation—there was some bleed from the fairy-tale fantasies made for children and dreamers. Then the Queen lifted her face and he recognized her. There was no mistake. It was Zaide who was in front of him, and he could not mistake the wicked conviction in her velvet mad eyes.

He wanted to run. No one he knew had ever showed up in a VR before. It must be reading it off his secondary, but why her? why now? It frightened him severely. He had never confronted Francisco in VR, had never fought Steel or Laurindo in the hero role and eliminated them as he had often wished to do. No matter how he had tried to cast the story, it had always come out the same. The faces had never changed.

And then he realized that he couldn't let the human kill her. Always before he had been saddened, partly because she was dead and partly because he hadn't done it himself. This time he had to rewrite the script and he was lost. It was wrong. The story, the very set reality of the story, had always been a comfort to him.

Paulo Sylvia was a monster. Paulo Sylvia was a fighter and everyone was afraid. Someone would stop Paulo Sylvia sometime, someone would recognize him and destroy him the way everything else in his life had been obliterated. And then it would all be over, the pain would finally end, burned out by the dying.

He played it every chance he could, whenever there was

enough dinheiro to drop coins into the machine, and fuel for
the powerbike to get up here.

She was looking at him, waiting. In reality he thought she
would probably suggest a plan. But this was not reality; it
was only virtual reality and he had to supply the creative energy himself.

"Perhaps," he found himself saying to this Zaide monster-
Queen, "if you could go there and seduce them. I think this
hero would not be able to cut off your head. They worship
beautiful women there, and you could distract him. And then
I'll sneak in while he is alone, listening to you, and between
the two of us we can finish him very easily."

The Zaide figure before him laughed in agreement, and
held up her hands. They were tipped with claws far longer
than his and seemed to be made of honed steel.

Now the game was not predictable. Maybe for the first
time he would survive. He might even win.

He had never considered winning before. That was not an
option. Nor did he appreciate false hope, not even in a game.
The game was just practice for life, for the end. Because
while he had never considered anything like winning, he had
always planned to go down hard, to go down a legend.

No, he had never even remotely considered winning before. Suddenly the thought pleased him greatly.

Fourteen

FRANCISCO watched while Nem Brito chose a game, and then returned to the comforting shadows of the magic shop proper. He enjoyed poking around, watching the little demonstrations the salesman gave when customers came in. He would even perform for Francisco, doing a trick with three brightly colored silk handkerchiefs. Francisco had seen it before.

He should go and play. He didn't know why he didn't want to. He knew Paulo's favorite game and how long he'd be at it. And Nem Brito was happy just to hang around and be part of them. Although what he was part of, Francisco knew, he didn't really comprehend. No, Nem Brito saw them as just one more cadre, a street tribe like the others. A little better packed for brains, perhaps, or maybe just with some upscale education that had suited them to nothing at all that was left.

Just then Francisco didn't really care anymore. He took the dinheiro and let it settle in his palm. There was a lot of it. He got up and left the magic shop, went across the street to the dance club where the verties hung.

Here were neon lights, pretenders to revelry, prettified versions of the fairy lights of the barzinho. Here the drinks were served in fine glasses and topped with paper umbrellas and no one ordered ordinary *pinga*. No, here all the verties were dressed in their finest and sipping fruit *batidas*, pretending that they were somewhere a little more menacing than the front porch of the Minas Tennis Club.

Pounding music filled the background, music that Francisco found repulsive. The beat was loud and the chairs vibrated, but it lacked the overwhelming organic interference of the *axe* drums or the samba beat. Those insisted, seduced, overpowered and became the body, the pulse in everyone's neck, everyone the same. This was merely an overlay that could be ignored as easily as danced, and what they were calling dancing here was bloodless gyration without the grace or sensuality or danger of true dance.

He didn't care. He ordered a beer and watched the scene around him, wondered if one of the vertie girls in some shade of pineapple and pink would dance with him.

He looked at all of them carefully, the blondes and the dusky ones, the innocent and the ones who were just as innocent but thought they were worldly. He picked one finally, a girl with tangled dark curls and a full mouth and body. She wore the same outfit that every other female in the establishment wore, only in slightly more subdued shades of blue and lavender. She hesitated a moment, tried to size Francisco up. And then, very cautiously, she agreed to dance.

He lost track of time dancing with first this vertie, and then with another, who wore heavy layers of iridescent lipstick that glittered red and pink and purple and silver under the neon and matched her optic dazzler earrings. Which by rights, she admitted freely, should have been discarded last season. Only she hated to part with them; they were a birthday present from her godfather and she hoped he didn't think the less of her for it.

"Damn, you couldn't leave a message or anything where you were going to be. It took us half the night to find you here," Paulo said loudly, one of his oversized hands clamping down firmly on Francisco's shoulder.

"And a vertie girl?" Nem Brito asked, an eyebrow raised. "I thought you would have had more taste than that."

The girl looked over the newcomers carefully and hesitated making a decision. Not that it was easy. The cadre were all attractive and menacing and radiated pure street. The girl took her time, confident that she was in control. She chose Paulo, crossing the two feet that separated them and arching her body against him as she made her choice.

Paulo leaned down, nuzzled her neck and found her ear. "You should have stayed with my friend," he whispered. "I don't like people who treat my friends like shit."

The girl jumped away from him as if she had been struck, then actually stuck out her tongue. Nem Brito laughed.

"Come on, let's go. I smell too much Mansion on the breath here," Paulo said, trying to half-drag Francisco with him.

"What's the matter?" Francisco said sharply. "I'm having a good time, okay? Go amuse yourselves. Or go home if you want."

"You're the one who locked the bikes," Nem Brito reminded him gently.

Paulo and Nem Brito pulled him gently away from the girl with the out-of-fashion dazzler earrings. "Hey, Francisco, I never thought I'd see you with one of those," Paulo said smiling. "I just thought you might need some excuse to get away."

"Oh? And you don't need any excuse to get away from your little rich girl, do you? You're the only one who likes them soft and well-fed."

"What?" Paulo was clearly confused.

Francisco smiled innocently. "You mean you never suspected? Your Zaide has got to be Mansion District at least. Look at the way she talks, the way she moves—look at what she knows. Have you ever figured out that she doesn't know about highwire?"

Paulo shook his head. "The Serps don't know either. Does that make them South Lake Mansion verties too? I don't get it."

Francisco sighed and walked out the door. There was no way he could stay in this place and explain to Paulo. The music was starting to really upset him anyway. Besides, he enjoyed the girls, but he knew perfectly well that they would go home to their safe estates with their outgate guardians and their overseeing families. And that they wouldn't dare take the likes of him back to their daddies, and they really didn't care. The girl with the dazzlers made that quite clear. So had the one in the subdued dress, wearing such colors only because her cousin had died a month ago and it was considered proper for someone of her class to show that form of respect.

It bothered Francisco that he hadn't remembered that custom, although he knew that his mother had worn no bright colors after her older brother had died of a heart attack at the age of forty-two. It had been called a tragedy, back when they lived in the northern half of the city and were respectable.

They were back in the night. Now that true dark had come, the Gilberto Salomao seemed even more festive, a party going on forever if only they could find the key to the fun. But the three young men in long, painted coats stood under the edge of the trees that had been wrapped in tiny white sparklers. "Italian-style" it was called, according to the girl with the out-of-fashion earrings, and there was no reason to disbelieve her.

"What about Zaide?" Paulo wasted no time.

"Okay, maybe she's not upper class," Francisco said. "But listen to her talk, look at her, will you? She doesn't understand anything about highwire and she knows way too much about the Cadea and the Vielho-Markowicz. Way too much."

"What do you mean, way too much?" Paulo asked, curiosity overcoming his defensive instinct.

"She didn't tell you about the Cadea and the Serps?" Francisco asked ingenuously. "She told *me* that the Serps were being used in a fazenda war to undermine the Cadea. And that it was the Vielho-Markowicz who were using them. Which is how the Serps were getting their data."

"So?" Paulo asked.

"How the hell did she know that?" Francisco demanded. "Then she said that if we wanted to get back at them, the

CEO and the head of Vielho-Markowicz Security would be at the cathedral for Mass on the Feast of the Assumption."

"You think she's a vertie?" Nem Brito asked softly.

Both Paulo and Francisco turned to look at him. He was generally quiet while they told all the stories and walked away with drunken proud swaggers. Nem Brito always remained quiet, a shadow behind them, never quite noticed except when he was gone.

"No," Pope answered quickly. "No vertie. Not stupid enough. And she doesn't talk about fashion all the time. So she's not one of them."

Then Paulo began to chuckle softly. "Francisco, your paranoia is a thing of art, you know. How does she know? Why not? Actually, if you think about it for half a minute it makes perfectly good sense, the Vielho-Markowicz against the Cadea. The Cadea are the only fazenda large enough to really challenge the Vielho-Markowicz since the merger. You read the papers, you know that. And as for Assumption Day, who isn't at the Cathedral on Assumption Day? Actually, I like her thinking. She's smarter than I thought, and I like that."

Nem Brito shrugged. Francisco Pope shrugged. There wasn't much he could say. He had a hunch, a feeling about Zaide. But Paulo would never listen. He never listened at all when it came to women, and there were times when it made Francisco more than a little crazy.

"You know," Paulo said softly, "maybe hitting the major fazenda on Assumption Day isn't such a bad idea. In a crowd like that they couldn't bring a deathmech in, and we could probably get away if we're organized enough."

Francisco was ready to explode. "It's a terrible idea. What the hell do we need with Cadea or Vielho-Markowicz? We're not some off-the-alley kidnappers out to finance our personal life styles with a snatch."

"Why not?" Nem Brito asked.

But Francisco could not answer. Facing Nem Brito, looking over his cadre's shoulder, he could see someone approaching slowly. Someone large.

The someone large wasted no time joining them. "Why did you all leave me like that?" Steel asked, his voice sounding hurt and childish. "You always do that."

"You always get drunk and pass out and we're not about to carry you every place," Paulo retorted sharply. "If you woke up in time for things you wouldn't have to ask."

Paulo drew away carefully. He disliked Steel more than either Nem Brito or Francisco did. Francisco thought that at least Steel had his uses, but Paulo couldn't help imagining what it would be like to highwire him.

Highwiring anyone was pretty nasty. The drug took its time lodging in the spinal column and slowly eating away at the nervous system. In the end, addicts looked like victims of diseases that had long been eliminated. According to reports, they felt no pain. They were in bliss. They were somewhere else, happyland-out while their bodies decayed.

The drug had originally been developed for people with secondaries, to lock into the phrine flush and destroy it so the individual burned on his own chemistry. Only the stuff turned anyone with secondaries into a vegetable. One dose in a person with a secondary, and the phrines went on full open and never shut down. The artificial internal chemistry went into high overdrive and ate the victim alive from the inside out. Not very pretty.

Dr. Valdemar had told Paulo all about it when he had given Paulo the mid-stage adrenal adjustment in payment for producing experimental specimens. The second step of the change Paulo wanted so badly, although not exactly the change he wanted most of all. Dr. Valdemar had explained that without fazenda tools Paulo could not be adapted to the Wave, no matter how much he would like to help. If anyone belonged in the Wave it was Paulo, Dr. Valdemar agreed. He was too smart and altogether too crazy for the real world. He was exactly what the Wave needed. And to Paulo the Wave was the only thing that made sense when everything else didn't.

Of all the Changelings possible, he had come to the conclusion that he needed to become a Waverider. Or the craziness and the knowing would kill him. Sometimes his own perceptions were too much to bear. Once upon a time the Wave had been a place for the brilliant insane. When he was institutionalized for the first time, the psychiatric director had said it was his only hope. That was all a fairy tale now.

But because that was not possible he had chosen second best, and Dr. Valdemar had been only too happy to try and accommodate him. To become the monster of his dreams, to be who he believed he was instead of what he could be, he needed far more than the first steps. But it was a beginning, and Dr. Valdemar had done a good job. Once he had been the most desired specialist for this kind of work. Paulo was fortunate; he could have gone to a backdoor quack and been butchered for his dinheiro. A lot of people were.

But Dr. Valdemar went further. He warned Paulo of the dangers, of the highwire. "You know," Dr. Valdemar said in his musing, otherworldly voice, "there is no reason to make or sell highwire. It is perhaps somewhat pleasant for the addicts, but why is there so much in the city? Why highwire instead of cocaine and opium? Those are traditional here; cocaine is easy to get. Why would anyone manufacture a new drug?"

It was a Dr. Valdemar kind of question, vague and unanswered. Nor did Dr. Valdemar care to get an answer. It was something political, something unpleasant, something that was squirming and messy and could not be contained in the body of a report with good quantitative analysis.

But the question had been a Chinese puzzle for Paulo. Nights when he couldn't sleep anyway he thought about it, twisted it in his mind, wondering. The fazendas produced highwire, ostensibly as an animal anesthetic for quality-testing pharmaceuticals. It was then supposedly stolen in large quantities and the amounts that made it to the supermanzanas were far more than any fifty fazendas could use. That much Paulo knew from Dr. Valdemar and Laurindo combined.

So obviously the fazendas were making the drug for street use, and making it cheaper than the old standards like cocaine. Which meant that it was easy to manufacture and that it was just straight profit, a thing Paulo found very easy to understand and hard to believe. Or there was a reason behind the action.

This appealed far more to his well-developed paranoia. And knowing that it particularly affected those with secondaries was somewhat appealing. Paulo enjoyed being in high-risk groups.

But armed even with that much knowledge, Francisco and Paulo had decided that highwire was one of their prime targets. If it was something that was useful to the fazendas, then it was something they needed to attack. On the street, who knew who had secondaries?

For Paulo it was merely self-preservation. For Francisco it was closer to an ethical campaign than a pragmatic decision. Not that Francisco hated drugs, or even the violence of the fazendas or what people on highwire did. It was more that he hated what highwire made people become. Anger didn't frighten Francisco Pope. Being vacant, removed from awareness like his mother, scared him more than he could ever acknowledge. So he took care of his mother and he tried to eliminate all the highwire he could.

In the hours near dawn when even most of the favela slept, when he heard Paulo's steady breathing and knew that his friend was asleep, then Francisco wondered if Dona Elena was really just in shock or an addict. He tried to catch her.

Once, he tore up the apartment looking for a stash. He hadn't been able to find anything, which only meant that he might be looking in all the wrong places, all the wrong ways. Dona Elena had always been very canny until the revolt and their subsequent descent in the world. Her retreat from reality, living in a strange combination of fantasy and memory, could easily be mental illness. And Francisco knew it could just as easily be highwire.

And he hoped it was the drug. That, if he could find it, if he could eliminate it, she could beat it. There was nothing at all he could do about willful madness. He hated admitting that.

The anger was not quite enough to satisfy Francisco Pope. So he let it ride, and followed Steel into one of the more typical arcades in the Gilberto Salomao, thinking all the while of what it would be like to substitute highwire for Steel's usual phrines and watch him die on the green carpet back home.

Watching Steel chat pleasantly with Nem Brito, Francisco hung back. Paulo joined him, fell into step. They had been friends since they were old enough to hit each other over the head with toy verts in their sandbox days. Days when their fathers worked together and they all had verts. Each knew when the other had something to discuss.

"If you want to go through the setup on Assumption Day in the Cathedral I think you're insane, that girl has got your judgment," Francisco warned his friend.

"I agree," Paulo said softly. "I believe Zaide, I trust her. But I won't commit us to an action based on her data. Not yet. But that's not until August anyway. That's a month away. Maybe we could do something first. Maybe Zaide could give us something useful on the Vielho-Markowicz."

"That isn't what we need," Francisco mused. "What we need is a way into the Wave. I suppose you didn't ask Dr. Valdemar about that tonight, did you?"

Paulo began to play with the stick in his belt. That wasn't a good sign. "I *did* ask, right? Remember? Or you think I haven't begged a million times, on my knees if I had to, for that Change? But I suppose you're too bored tonight to bother remembering that."

Francisco didn't like it when Paulo used that acid tone of voice. He liked it even less when he realized he deserved it.

The frustration and anger and boredom all combined and contrasted sharply with the commercial gaiety around him.

A gaggle of verties in iridescent butterfly-blue hesitated in front of the arcade. Their voices cut through the dark and Francisco and Paulo both winced at the jagged presumptuousness in their tones. They couldn't hear the words exactly, which Francisco thought was just as well. He forgot he had been having a pleasant time with the girl with the dazzler earrings. Now, looking at this new bunch, he wanted only to kick one of those well-fed faces in.

Instead he took a fifty-centavo coin from his pocket and threw it hard against the pink neon beer sign two doors down. The neon tube exploded violently, a miniature nuke in the pleasure strip. The verties huddled together and looked terribly frightened.

Francisco gave them an intimidating stare and adjusted his coat on his shoulders. The rage had bled off a little with the neon gas. Paulo had faded back into the shadows between a closed bakery and the lights. Francisco felt a slight pressure on his arm, Paulo directing him into the dark. With their brilliant coats it wasn't always easy to keep out of sight. This was a good niche. But Paulo had always been talented that way.

Then the owner or manager of the beer hall came out the door screaming, demanding from the verties whether they had done it, or had seen what had happened. The four or five of them against the arcade display wall all shook their heads vigorously and protested that they knew nothing at all.

The owner didn't stop for a second. "I'm calling the police and hauling you all off to court. Bunch of no-good spoilt brats, I know your kind. This is your idea of a good time, isn't it? And you think that money will just cover it all up and you can go away and keep on busting up honest people's establishments."

It looked like he had more to say, but the words were breaking up in the owner's frustration. The verties all looked very properly scared. Francisco could hear Paulo's low-pitched chuckle soft near his ear.

Then the bar owner must have caught the pale coats in the dark. He turned toward them. "And what about you, south scum? I'll have you locked away so fast, your own shadow won't be able to follow you. What are you doing there, any-way?"

Francisco stepped out from the sheltering bakery door. "We were trying to express our affections, but if you're go-ing to fight and blow up neon signs, it's going to be too noisy. Come on, Paulo."

They emerged together, both tall and looking large and mean in their favela rags. Francisco couldn't tell if the dead silence was shock or horror or offended sensibilities. The pleasure the verties' discomfort brought him was making up for his earlier boredom. This was finally getting to be at least a little amusing.

Paulo played along, trailing at Francisco's sleeve and keeping his face down as if he were ashamed. Indeed, he was quite red. Only Francisco knew it was from holding back laughter. They made it to the bikeboxes and collapsed be-hind them, stuffing their sleeves into their mouths to muffle their convulsions.

A boot swung over the bikebox. Francisco's hand was on his knife before he had stopped chuckling. Paulo pressed himself against the box, and his oversized hands shot up and captured the boot, pulling its owner over the box and down. It was Nem Brito.

"You gave us a real scare," Francisco chided.

"That was really funny," Nem Brito said, completely un-ruffled by his cadre's greeting. "That stuff with the verties and the neon sign. Now can we get moving? I left Steel im-pressing some adolescent pretribal types in the Lighthouse Arcade."

Paulo grinned.

"Look," Francisco reminded him, "at least we don't have to see it."

"So open the box and let's go home," Nem Brito said. "I think we've done about all the fun there is here tonight. And I don't want to wait and be paraded as Steel's cadre, you know?"

But as they walked their bikes over the Gilberto Salomao, they saw other white and painted longcoats in the distance. In the dark they couldn't make out the designs.

"Serps?" Nem Brito asked in a whisper.

Paulo shrugged. But the other cadre, whoever they were, watched from the shadows. Only when they had mounted the bikes and turned the power on, lighting the tail blaze, did the others begin to drift in their direction.

Fifteen

FRANCISCO raised a hand, and all three snapped the connection on their bikes. Paulo had his knife in his hand. Nem Brito stroked his dart gun against his collar. Francisco stood up, his hands empty.

Paulo didn't recognize the approaching cadre as Serps. Their coats were painted with jaguar motifs. One was spotted all over like the coat of the animal. The others were more usual copies of Indian designs done in greens and yellows, Jaguar Tribe colors.

Very slowly Paulo replaced his Teflon knife in his boot. Jaguar Tribe was far higher status than the Serps and had a rep that any other cadre would give blood to own. No one who wasn't a member would dare paint jaguar motifs on a coat. And if Paulo's sources among the Serps were correct, the one in the spotted coat should be their warlord.

One of the lieutenants, a very tall man with onyx-black skin and parrot-green eyes, was familiar. Paulo knew he was a master *capoeirista*, that they had played a *jogo* more than once, but he couldn't remember his name. The tall man studied him and seemed to recognize him, but didn't seem at all perturbed. He gave Paulo a secretive half-smile to which Paulo responded politely. He wished he could remember the man's name. Not to seemed very impolite.

The three Jaguars approached with their hands held well outside their pockets. They had come to parley. Paulo wondered how the cadre had known where to find them. Or maybe it was fate, like everything else.

"You are Bakunin?" the leader asked. Paulo thought he seemed terribly normal at this distance. Not noticeably taller than himself or Francisco, not unusually old or scarred. He had a nice face, Paulo thought. And then remembered that he was most likely a consummate actor.

His voice was remarkable only in that he sounded like a newscaster. None of the favela accent hardened the edges of his speech, and his Portuguese was educated-sounding and polite. But of course, there was no reason not to be polite yet.

"Yes," Francisco answered evenly. "Paulo and I share the leadership." He indicated Paulo, who nodded to identify himself further. "And this is Nem Brito, one of our most trusted lieutenants."

There was a long minute of silence. Paulo thought if they wanted something they should make it clear they wanted to talk. But it seemed as if they weren't certain. And the tension built.

"This place is full of verties and other South Lake garbage," Paulo said finally, breaking the impasse. "Nobody respectable here at all. We were just leaving. If you would like to join us at the barzinho in South 713, you would be very welcome."

"South 713," the leader repeated. Then he smiled and held out his hand. "My name is Aluizio and I am very glad to meet you. I have heard about you from the Serps. They are not very happy right now. I salute you."

Aluizio shook hands with the three of them quite warmly, and then so did his two companions. "Yes, indeed, I have heard some complaints about you in certain quarters," Aluizio continued, smiling widely. "I thought maybe it was time we all got to know each other."

"But how did you know we'd be here?" Nem Brito asked from the back, ignoring Francisco's warning look.

Aluizio's face became composed, almost angelic. "The priestess told us. The gods spoke in the *axe*, and the *ogun* of Oxala, who is our patron, said that we were to go directly to the Gilberto Salomao and speak to the friends Oxala has provided. Although as a rule we would not come here. Usually the company smells too much of dinheiro for our taste. But everything Oxala has ever directed us to do has been to our benefit, so I would not question the word of the god."

Paulo had the urge to roll his eyes. He was certain Francisco was feeling the same way. He also knew they couldn't afford the flippancy. These guys ran the Jaguars and they believed in the Yoruba gods, and after all they had met up here, hadn't they? Which meant that Paulo liked it rather less.

"If you don't have bikes we can take the bus," Francisco said. "We can leave the bikes here in the box overnight."

Paulo knew this meeting was important, but he hadn't realized that Francisco was that impressed. His powerbike was the one thing Francisco owned that he really cared about. Leaving it overnight would be a major sacrifice.

"No, we have bikes. Come, we'll ride together," Aluizio said confidently, gaiety at the edge of his words.

Paulo liked the Jaguar Tribe leader immediately, and that disturbed him. There was something magical about Aluizio, something that could only be called charismatic.

They rode down the Exio Rodoviario Sul in formation, the old and weary powerbikes glittering under the street lights and hissing ominously in unison. They did not go to the barzinho. Instead, Francisco ushered their guests up to the office and dispatched Nem Brito below to buy *pinga* and fried manioc, and Paulo went with him to borrow a few boxes to sit on. Entertaining guests, especially such distinguished guests, required a few comforts that when they were alone they could do without.

Once Aluizio and his cadre were settled in the chairs and a huge plate of fresh manioc was sitting in the middle of the desk with a vial of toothpicks, also borrowed from below, they all relaxed. Aluizio took one of the chunks of manioc and then began to talk.

"I do not know how much you here in the city know about what happens out in the satellite cities. We know you have had an alliance with the Serpentes and have made them look like the fools they are. You are efficient. You are even elegant in your execution. This is something I and my cadre admire. And I think we should explore our natural alliance. Perhaps we will come into some data we can share or use."

Paulo nodded in appreciation. "But I don't understand why," he admitted bluntly. "The Jaguars are the most dangerous tribe in the whole region. I can't understand why you would want to parley with us. I find it very confusing."

Francisco shot him a glance that meant "shut up." Paulo chose to ignore it. "I mean, you are a major force, you don't need us."

Aluizio set his glass delicately on the desk. His eyes were as dark as Paulo's and they burned, but not with Paulo's rage. Only desire seemed to fill the Jaguar commander's small frame. This close in good light, Paulo could see that he was mixed black and Indian and white, but the Indian seemed to prevail slightly in his coloring and build. His straight black hair was pure Indian, his nose absolutely Portuguese and his mouth completely Yoruba. The harmonious mix of races was part of his magical appeal.

He was truly Brazilian, Paulo thought, and regretted once again his very white skin. Well, at least he didn't have red hair like Francisco, who didn't look Brazilian at all. In the days when they could afford nice restaurants, people had often spoken English or German to Francisco, taking him for a tourist. At least no one had ever done that to Paulo.

"I am glad you understand that we are friends, and I am happy that you have expressed your concern," he said, looking at Francisco. Obviously he had not missed Francisco's look, either. "And you are right, we are strong enough that we don't need any help to pull runs on the corps and make some dinheiro. Maybe snatch a willing young lady and relieve her father of some excess bank account when things get boring. But we are not in the city itself, and if we are ever going to be anything more than a tribe, we need all of us together."

This time the silence was stretched like the crossbow. They all understood and yet no one could say anything, not immediately. Jaguars and Bakunin both believed that they were alone with their vision. Neither Francisco nor Aluizio seemed certain that they were pleased to find that others had dreamed the same revelation. It was Paulo who stood, stretched, took a piece of the cooling manioc neatly on a toothpick. He stared at the wall while he spoke, as if his words were written there and he was only reading.

"What we need is the Wave. Without it, all we can do is take down the façade of the structure. We have to get inside to affect the thing itself. And it doesn't matter how many of us there are and how good we are. Or we're all just dreaming."

The hurt colored his voice. The part of him that had given up hope wanted to go on, talk about how to tear everything apart and who cares how it came back together? He most likely wouldn't see it anyway.

"But you have the fazenda connections," Aluizio protested. "The Vielho-Markowicz girl, isn't she a Waverider?"

Paulo froze. "What girl?" he asked slowly.

Aluizio shrugged. "Why else would I want to talk to any cadre as insignificant as Bakunin?" he asked ingenuously. "You have that girl with the green vert running with you. Everyone knows. Joao saw her at the *capoeira* circle the other night."

Suddenly Paulo felt it all over again. The green-eyed man who had been the master of the *roda* in the barzinho that night, had been there studying him, had even come over and made some conversation. Joao, yes, they had called him "Dr. Joao" for the way he talked about philosophy and the universe as if he had been a professor at the University. In fact, one of the other *capoeiristas* had suggested, there was no reason not to suppose he was Dr. Joao in reality. Now the name clicked into place with the event.

Which meant that Aluizio knew all along where they were headed, which superquadra was their home. Maybe he had even looked for them at the barzinho earlier that night, and only when they had not appeared had they gone looking. Or maybe they had followed Steel. That seemed the most likely, and it was one more piece of evidence Paulo filed against the man.

Hating Steel was much easier than thinking about Zaide. Under his breath Paulo swore he'd cut her if he ever saw her again. Which wasn't likely, he reminded himself. He hadn't seen her in over a week, and she knew where they were if she wanted to find him.

The jackal doesn't betray his friends. But he usually wasn't betrayed either. Paulo Sylvia wanted to do some damage, to break and destroy things to drain out the rage.

A hand engulfed his shoulder. It was not Francisco or Nem Brito—they knew better than to get near him when the rage was this close to the surface. But the hand was larger than his own and black and very calm. Dr. Joao, whose very presence even as a potential enemy, was sedate and quiet as the sea. Something of the Jaguar cadre's immense assurance was communicated, and Paulo felt himself relax and breathe deeply. The only other time he could remember being so peaceful was when Dr. Valdemar had given him the anesthesia before installing the secondary.

"I saw her the night I was master of the *roda* here," Dr. Joao said. His voice was soft and as educated as his name, and full of authority. Paulo noticed that even Aluizio regarded him with a respect bordering on awe. "I saw her, and Oxala spoke to me. He said, 'That girl is the key.' He said, 'If you wish to defeat Exu Tiriri, then she will be your ally. Her friends are your allies.' This was the word of the god."

It took all of Paulo's control and all of Dr. Joao's calm for Paulo not to strike out. The mention of Oxala here, in this place where nothing that irrational or stupid was ever mentioned, put him off balance.

Besides which, he had spoken to Dr. Joao. And the man might just have had a fine way of speaking and not teach something like classical literature at the University, but

Paulo had expected better. At least he had illusions that Dr. Joao was an intellectual, a man of reason. Now he saw that the green-eyed man was no different from any cadre member in the southern neighborhoods.

He felt betrayed, although rationally he knew it was only his own fantasies that had betrayed him. Still, he had to repress the desire to bodily throw Dr. Joao and Aluizio and the third Jaguar out of the Bakunin office. Immediately.

That would not be polite. Nor politic. So he leashed his fury and tried to contain it. He regretted the *pinga* he had drunk earlier. It made concentration difficult, and he needed to think clearly. He felt trapped and that made him panicky. He knew the phrines and the *pinga* were affecting his emotions, running him through a series of hairpin turns too fast.

"How do you know Zaide is Vielho-Markowicz?" Paulo heard Francisco ask. Not that it mattered. As soon as Dr. Joao had said it, Paulo recognized it as truth. "Besides this revelation from Oxala, that is." Francisco revised his question without the sneering undertone Paulo knew he himself would be unable to mask.

Francisco was very good at being cold in these situations. Maybe that was why they were such a good team, Paulo reflected. Francisco was always as icy as his eyes. And Paulo was constantly living in drama, in passion, everything fraught with meaning and consequence and symbolic weight. Francisco cut through to the bones of reality and kept things simple and clean.

"We will need some evidence to confront her." Francisco even managed not to insult the Jaguar's beliefs. Paulo was impressed.

"Oh, that's easy," Aluizio said cheerfully. "We have spotted her with the green vert with the Vielho-Markowicz logo on the door. After the *capoeira*, Dr. Joao followed her when she left the barzhino. It was very very late, he said, but he waited and followed the cab she took. And she went back to the Vielho-Markowicz headquarters in the Northern Commercial District. She used the fingerlock and it opened right up in the middle of the night."

"So now all we have to find out is whether she is really with us or if she's using us," Francisco said, his eyes slicing Paulo.

Paulo opened the door gently and walked out. He was not going to let anyone bait him, not in front of Aluizio when it meant so much. The Jaguars might not need Bakunin, and if they decided that they didn't, then he and Francisco and the rest of their cadre would disappear into the favela like any of the street rats in the capital. On their own turf the Jags were the law. And off their turf they still demanded respect, and held enough power to get it.

He walked out into the warm winter night. The sounds of poor men drinking echoed under the building. The strange multiple colors of the fairy lights reflected raggedly along the cracked pavement in a few places, just enough to be disturbing. He had been through too much that night, too many changes, too many ideas. Between the phrines and the *pinga* he was overwhelmed to start.

He wanted to go someplace restful, where he could sort out the jumbled events and data and make a connection. He couldn't go back to the Pope apartment on the sixth floor without Francisco. Not that he wouldn't be welcomed, but Dona Elena would ask questions and he didn't know what Francisco had told her.

Besides, he wanted to lay it all out with Dr. Valdemar. The old professor was sharp and logical and didn't care much about cadres or politics or any of the things that Bakunin and the Jaguars and the fazenda group all found so important. No, Dr. Valdemar was more interested in other things. Paulo liked the way his mind ran. If he lived long enough, Paulo thought, he would like to learn to think like that also.

He wanted to learn to be free. Francisco was free, he thought, and so was Aluizio. But he was not. He was somehow tied to reaction, to circumstance that denied him access to everything he wanted.

He turned around and looked up. There were no lights. There was no window in the closet Bakunin had taken over. The façade of the building was blank and proud of what it denied him. Underneath, it kept its occupants well-occupied with its tawdry little Gilberto Salomao.

Paulo suddenly felt as if he could not breathe. If he didn't get out of this life, he knew he couldn't contain the anger much longer. It was building inside him and he could feel it, and every time he thought he had found a release and it was gone, it only came back later, darker, more destructive. And it frightened him. If he didn't find a way to be free of it soon, he knew he would destroy everything he could find. Including Zaide and Aluizio and Bakunin. Including Francisco, who was closer than a brother. Including himself.

Sixteen

IN the moonlight the uniform residences of South 713 were no less depressing than they were by day. Although Paulo had turned away from the barzinho, he could hear the music even this far away. The drums were playing a samba beat now and he could hear drunken voices singing the way they sang to accompany the *capoeira* games. But he didn't want any part of the singing, the drinking. He didn't want to see the old men sitting on boxes, laughing and telling the same old stories over again, and he realized with bitterness that he was grateful that his father was dead. He didn't have to remember his father as one of them.

It was a full moon. He wanted to get away from the noise and the population of the city. He wanted the clean stark cerrado. He unlocked his powerbike and rode out of the city on the Belo Horizonte road.

It was not far until the city dropped behind him. The sky was brilliant with stars, where they were not washed out by the full moon. The cold light made the scrubland a study in tangled shadows. There were a few flat white rocks surrounded by stunted trees and brush. It was very dry now, and the dust, unsettled by the light breeze drifting across the road, was the only sound.

Silent and colorless—Paulo thought he could have been on some alien planet circling one of the stars that were splattered across the sky. He could have been at some point in the distant past, before humanity had taken this form, when insects were the highest form of life. He felt like an anomaly in the landscape.

He pulled the bike to the side of the road. He knew it was smarter not to leave the highway. There were poisonous snakes in the cerrado and there were giant termite hills. There was tough scrub covering the ground, so it was difficult to walk. Reasonable people did not go out of the city at night. Reasonable people did not go out into the cerrado at all.

Paulo pulled the bike to the edge of the road and laid it under a bushy shadow. He did worry about snakes, and wondered what he would do if one curled around the handlebars or threaded itself through the power lines. But he thought he remembered that snakes didn't like the night; it was too cold for them.

He did not go far off the road, only as far as a good flat-topped boulder on which to sit. He drew his feet up and covered himself with his coat, the pale canvas blending in with the stone in the moonlight.

Around him, alive, quivered the Wave. He knew it. Out here away from the people, the chatter and the noise, he could almost taste the energy crackling through the atmosphere. It was nascent in the virgin scrub, something that was not new but had always been and always would be there—just out of his grasp.

Pain went through him, desire sharp and glittering and laughing at him because he was forever outside. And here he did not keep on the anger but let the sadness seep through. Alone in this place he could face the disappointments that Francisco had tried to comfort and share. But Francisco had enough of his own disappointments.

Here he could spill out his rage and his sadness. No matter how big it got, no matter how searing his grief, it was nothing here against the ancient land, the endless sky. In the distant season of tornadoes and the summer rains his feelings were nothing at all compared to the power of the storms. The violence of summer comforted him. But even in the winter silence he was aware of that power, the underlying energy of the Wave, although no one would ever understand it. Or so Dr. Valdemar had told him.

In the city his insignificance was a constant torment. Here it was merely another fragment of reality. Under the vast uncaring sky Paulo Sylvia found comfort.

The moon and stars moved slightly. He hardly noticed. He was full of his own thoughts, his surroundings with their somber peace bringing him some sense of proportion. And so it was that at first he didn't notice the noise in the background. It was far away and familiar, droning softly on the road.

Finally his hearing connected to his brain and he realized he was hearing powerbikes. The soft rumbling that he barely noticed in the city seemed very loud.

He turned very slowly, being careful to keep his coat over his legs. He wanted to blend into the landscape, to remain unnoticed. And yet he felt curiously detached, as if what happened on the road did not touch him at all.

Three powerbikes glittered in the moonlight, pushing to speed on the deserted highway. They were riding in crisp formation, and even from this distance Paulo could tell the riders were wearing painted gaucho coats. He could even make out that the designs were familiar.

They were pushing speed, not so far as to burn the power lines, but just to the edge for the sheer joy of it. Paulo could feel it, watching them ride by, velocity held barely in check, control riding a wild machine. Riding the Wave. His face glowed with pleasure just watching them as he had watched the sky and the stunted trees.

They came closer and he was able to distinguish the patterns on the coat. The Jaguars riding home, triumphant. They had made contact with Bakunin, had sealed the end of the Serps and the beginning of something new.

Out here in the still-pristine wilderness, Paulo could touch the excitement of that newness. Although he and Francisco had talked about it often, for the first time he could actually see the future taking shape, a different shape than before, as if Fate had hesitated at a crossroads and Paulo Sylvia had the opportunity to suggest a path. The tribes could unite. With a vision like his and Francisco's and someone with the authority of Aluizio joining together, there was just the smallest possibility that they could nudge the progress of destiny away from the sinking hopelessness of the favela.

For that one moment in the clean cerrado night, hope was born. Paulo Sylvia felt it flicker inside him, tentative and vulnerable and just barely alive. For the first time in two years Paulo was young again, with the faith and aspiration that had been denied. It felt like pain.

And then another sound entered the scene. This one was well known and loud. It overwhelmed the landscape the way the bikes never could. Overhead, like the buzzards of the cerrado, two oversized security verts swung out of the starfield and came into position over the highway. Their floodlights blinded him for a moment, as they must have also blinded the riders on the ground. And then the light exploded.

He fell by reflex to the rock below and hugged it. Darkness surrounded him. He wasn't sure if something had hurt his eyes. Then he realized that it was only the absence of intense illumination. Slowly he rolled over so that he lay supine on the boulder and stared up at the sky.

The verts were gone. Or rather, they had turned off their signal lights and had blended into the sky. If he searched carefully, he could most likely find traces of their movement against the stars.

Instead he sat up and slid down from the rock. He was careful of his footing. On the road he could see the three powerbikes and their riders on their sides, scattered like broken toys. He wanted to run to them, but he picked his way carefully through the tough scrub, avoiding a huge termite hill that could have caused him a sprain at the least. It felt like forever before he got down to the road. None of them had moved.

In the clear moonlight he could identify them by their coats without seeing the faces. It was Aluizio and Dr. Joao and the Jaguar whose name he never had known. He didn't have to touch them to know they were dead. In the stillness of the night their stillness was absolute.

He went to the bodies and awkwardly tried to find a pulse in Aluizio's neck. The head lolled and he smelled a faint whiff of burning, all the more hideous for being so light on the breeze. Whoever was in those verts had fried the Jaguars' brains inside their skulls. Paulo had the sudden image of cracking open Aluizio's face and finding it full of ash.

He left Aluizio and the unnamed Jaguar to go to Dr. Joao. He touched the man's cheek, not yet cooled with death, and closed those eyes that were brighter and harder now that they were unoccupied. Implants for sure, though what they would do or why, was something he would never know. Dr. Joao's skin was softer than any adult's skin should be, like the finest underlayers of fur.

He should do something, go back to town, get the authorities, do something. But there was nothing at all to do that mattered. The dead didn't need his help, seemed perfectly sufficient unto themselves scattered on the empty road.

Paulo got his powerbike from under the tree and rode home down the center line. Any peace or healing he had received in the cerrado fused with his anger and crystallized into something like a gem.

When he returned to South 713, everything was exactly the way he had left it. But nothing was the same. Somehow the night had shifted, a small fraction of a degree changed in the course of the universe, which would compound itself into something completely different. Fate had spoken.

Paulo felt it but there was no excitement in him, no blinding rage. There was only the eternal empty cold, the moonlight, the security of a purpose.

It was her first family dinner in over a week. Zaide Soledad was not really certain that she was ready to sit up for so long, to try and eat and make conversation. She didn't even want to go to the trouble of getting properly dressed. Undergarments and hose and shoes all bound her and made her weary.

That was to be expected. She remembered when she had received her secondaries, how she had felt for days afterwards, and realized that her slowness was normal. Only she couldn't afford to be slow. Already she'd lost too much time against Julio Simon.

Susana, already dressed, held up clothes and chattered while Zaide rested. After sitting up for almost an hour she was exhausted again.

"You probably shouldn't go tonight," Susana said brightly. "It's still way early. Why don't you go back to bed and I'll send up a tray and you can rest."

Zaide closed her eyes. The thought was heaven. Slowly, she made herself shake her head. "I think I'd better get back as soon as possible," she said carefully. "No telling how much damage Julio Simon has already done."

"Damage?" Susana asked. "I don't think he's done any real damage. Uncle Victor ordered him to make it up to the Cadea, so he was going to take care of the street gangs that sabotaged the highwire shipments." Susana hesitated, studying two dresses. "I think you should wear the red silk," she said finally, hanging a sophisticated sheath on the canopy support of Zaide's bed. "The peach linen is too young, I think. Especially now. You have to make the point that you aren't a trainee anymore."

Zaide thought about that and licked her lips. "But if I look young and not very dangerous, then maybe Julio will see me that way," she mused.

Susana sighed, took the red dress and replaced it in the closet. "I suppose you're going to wear your hair down, too," her cousin said, disappointed.

"Absolutely," Zaide agreed. "With a bow."

Susana rolled her eyes, and for all her very adult dress, she looked like a child in her big sister's clothes. Zaide got up slowly from her chair and slipped on the dress. Then Susana helped her comb her hair and she was ready to face the family.

Zaide and Susana arrived just in time to take their places before dinner was served. The chicken, cooked in coconut milk and palm oil with just a touch of spice, was delicious. This surprised Zaide, that she had any taste for food at all. But she found she was starved and heaped her plate with rice and greens.

Her appetite did not go unnoticed. Sonia Leah smiled approvingly. "You must be recovered," Miguel Leal said. "After clinic food you're always hungry. But you have to listen to what Cousin Julio's been doing while you've been recuperating."

There was a moment of embarrassed silence. Then Julio swallowed and looked at her carefully, then at Uncle Victor. "I suppose it's not quite so interesting as Cousin Miguel makes it out to be," he said. "Merely that perhaps it would be better if the group that is responsible for all the Cadea losses was punished. After all, it would show our good faith to the Cadea. And they are difficult to deal with. Naturally, I never saw them as dependable allies in any event."

"Naturally," Zaide echoed, keeping her voice carefully neutral. "And so what have you done?"

"I have done very little," Julio answered. He took a roll and broke it carefully, then fastidiously buttered one half. He did not look at anyone, and his knife was the only implement moving. "I have been watching the groups rather carefully, as you may have imagined. Anyway, last night we caught three of them on the Belo Horizonte road and ashed them."

The food in Zaide's stomach lurched and solidified. She felt sick and cold as if there was a sudden chill in the room. "That's not very subtle," she said slowly. Not a good comeback, really, but it was better than the plain shock she felt.

"Oh, but that's the interesting part," Julio Simon said, his eyes locked with hers. "You see, the gang members we left, they weren't the ones who raided Cadea. No, that group is very small and not well established. No, we took out the leadership of one of the biggest gangs in the entire state. After they had been visiting our target group. And with the right words put into the right places, well, let them kill each other off. It makes our lives much simpler."

"And of course you put the right words into the right places," Sonia Leah said sharply.

"I believe so," Julio answered blandly.

Zaide couldn't look at the food anymore. She wanted to be out of there, she needed to be gone. But first she had to sit quietly through another discussion of the upcoming Alado soccer match, play with the guava paste and dry cheese for dessert, and then change her clothing. She could not possibly arrive in the residential superquadras of the favela dressed like a lost little rich girl.

Zaide Soledad was still shaky on her feet when she got out of the cab at South 713. She hoped that was the right number, that she had remembered it accurately. The fact that the buildings looked familiar meant nothing; every place in Brasilia looked like everyplace else. And she had never been there by day, had never made out the graffiti splashed over the front of the residential structures. In fact if it weren't for the glitter of multicolored lights indicating the barzinho, she wouldn't know which building to enter. The six in this neighborhood all looked identical in the dark. Exactly the way they were planned to be, useful and egalitarian and all the things that had never happened the way they had been planned.

Very few things, she reflected, came out the way they were planned. For example, she had not planned to come back here. Not ever. And here she was.

And not only because of Julio's new, sickening deception. She realized as she sat at the table that she hated him more because they were made from the same DNA. And that was another reason that she had to come back here. Julio Simon was her own evil. Only she could destroy him. The cadre she knew as Bakunin was strangely clean, innocent in a way she didn't understand.

There was something about these people that drew her. It was not just Paulo alone, she acknowledged. It wasn't even so much each of them as individuals. But there was something about the way they behaved together, towards each other and even towards her that made her return. There was a kind of loyalty that she had never experienced on the fazenda, although of course the family should behave like any other. That's why they were adopted in the first place.

But there were things that confused her, and they were like the scab on her hand that she picked at and played with and tore until the skin scarred. She couldn't let it alone, even when she knew she ought to, even when she told herself firmly to forget the thing. Her fingers seemed to have a will of their own and they somehow made their way obsessively to the hardened flesh. She didn't know that she had pulled the scab off until Susana had commented on the blood staining her cuff.

In the same way, she didn't remember changing into the black split skirt and blouse and high boots, couldn't fathom how the address had floated from the deep recesses of her brain. She didn't have any recollection of ordering the vert or going to the garage to pick it up, flying over kilometers of cerrado and parking it, getting into the cab. Nothing registered at all. And now she was here.

She hoped she wasn't too late. The fairy lights beneath the building beckoned, but somehow Zaide was repulsed. She didn't want to go to that public place. Following instinct, she walked up the steps instead. What was once a securely locked building was now open to the elements. She went in, turned, looked for the black lettering she remembered. When she had been there before, there had been no lock.

She stood in front of the door for a moment, and then knocked. There was no answer. She knocked louder, until her knuckles ached. And then she tried the door and it gave easily. She opened it and stepped in and found herself facing a crossbow bolt loaded and ready in a black pistol that looked all the more dangerous for being in miniature. The pistol was leveled at her throat and the finger on the trigger was Paulo Sylvia's.

Seventeen

THEY stood frozen, both of them confused. Finally Paulo dropped the weapon and stepped aside. He had been alone in the Bakunin office, Zaide saw. She closed the door behind her.

Something was different. The sexuality that glistened between them was still there, more taut and voracious than ever. And yet there was a new element. Paulo was holding himself back, wary, as if he didn't trust her.

"I'm sorry," she began softly. "I know I was away, it couldn't be helped. I wasn't well. That's over. But I have some information that you need."

He studied her silently and she knew he wasn't sure whether to believe her or not. Though he had lowered the crossbow pistol, it still rested in his hand, and Zaide knew he was fast.

"You weren't well." He echoed her words but changed the inflection to show he wasn't certain. "How do you know what we need? Maybe another Cadea executive you'd like me to take out to increase your influence in the family, isn't that more like it?"

Zaide said nothing. She felt as if he'd kicked her in the ribs with his steel-toed boots. She looked down, away, at the desk, which was covered with pale pink and yellow printout. It was messy, expansive, the way Paulo would leave the desk.

"No," she said and her voice was very small. She turned

and sat down at the desk. Then, very deliberately, she closed her eyes.

Paulo came and stood behind her, his large hands caressing her jaw, then moving down her throat. There was a veiled threat under the sensuality, physical strength held back only by choice. And he could chose not to hold back; those immense hands could so easily break her neck.

"Why did you come back?" he asked from behind her, his hands dropping from her shoulders, in retreat. "Or did you think we were so stupid we wouldn't catch on to your game?"

"Because I had to," she said, and there was something naked about the way she spoke that shocked her. "Because . . . Let me tell you a story." She closed her eyes. "When I was very little there were seven S-series experiments. That's what we were, not children, not people, just potential trainees if we proved out. Anyway, there was one boy in our series. Amilton Sergio was his name, and he picked on the other kids in the nursery. He was a bully. Like Julio Simon, I guess, only maybe not quite so calculating or so careful. Anyway, he smashed plates and threw our dinners on the floor. He was S-series, of course. Anyway, one day Julio Simon came in to watch us all, his little siblings as we are, and he saw Amilton. And I remember him saying to the rest of us, 'Why do you let him do that?' And I asked him, 'What are we supposed to do?' and Julio Simon just shrugged. Then he told us either we would be dead or Amilton would be. That was the only way things could end. And if Amilton Sergio could survive our hatred and destroy us, then he would have earned his place in the family.

"I thought about that a lot, about earning a place in the family. I must have been about seven at the time. I knew that everything had to be earned. So I thought about it a lot. Later they said that I was the smartest of the series batch, although they were afraid that I didn't have enough of the S-series aggressiveness. My cousin Susana is the perfect example of that, lots of ability but not aggressive. But that was later.

"Anyway, that night when the nurse was gone, I went to Amilton's bed and told him I had something special to show him. Something that I'd hidden from everyone else, but he was so special that Julio Simon said I should show him. So he followed me up to the attic steps and through the trunks to the small gable outside. He didn't want to climb out the window. He wanted to know what was so special out the window.

"So I told him there was a nest of baby parrots. And even Amilton knew that parrots are very expensive and if we could capture them and sedate them enough to sell, they would bring a good price. A whole nest full— Of course, I didn't know how many babies a parrot has at once. But you see, it was the bottom line. That counted more than anything. So I told him I had found the nest but I was too scared to climb out on the gable to get the birds, and that if he did it, then they were his birds, if he'd give me a fifteen percent cut. We argued for a while and agreed on seven.

"He climbed out on the roof. And I pushed him off."

"And?" Paulo asked. "Did they ever find out?"

Zaide smiled. "They knew the next morning when they found Amilton Sergio with a broken neck on the porch steps. He was still alive then, and he said it was me. So he was quietly disposed of and I was sent to the village. My future was assured, even if I wasn't a member of the family yet. I would always belong to the fazenda, I would always have work. And the other little S-series were packed off to become *pivetes* down here."

Paulo shook his head. The crossbow pistol was still in his reach and the top of his Teflon knife was visible in the strap of his boot.

"I still don't know what that means to me," he said finally. "So you're tough. Maybe you fazenda types are tougher than we are, maybe that's why you're in charge. But I don't have to like it. I don't have to put up with being on the bottom of the pile."

"I came back because I don't want you dead," she said

heavily. "Julio Simon is trying to make you look responsible for some gang murders. He didn't say who. But he's making damn sure that the wrong people know all the wrong things. I think the Serps are going to be gunning for you. I think that you need to be prepared."

Zaide's face was as dry as the cerrado in winter. There were no true deserts in Brazil, no place that was not abundantly full of life, no place so inimical to humans that there was no purchase to cling to. Only in the heart of the fazendas was it so dry that there was no room for tears. Finally she realized that she didn't have the concepts along with the words to explain. Only that there was something here that mattered more than Sonia Leah's sacred bottom line.

And Paulo was closed to her. Even with the rapport between them, she had no idea what he was thinking, and that frightened her. "Prepared for what?" he said finally, and his voice was heaving with contempt. "For the Serps to come break down the door and ash us all? With your Julio Simon's guns? How do I know you aren't running for him? It would make a hell of a lot more sense."

There was venom in his tone and it stung her. There was nothing she could do but leave. She had delivered her message. It had been stupid to come, to think that whatever it was she was looking for was hidden here. This was only a bare, ugly room in a favela, furnished with castoffs. The people, as well as the carpeting, were things that no one wanted any longer.

She was a fool and Sonia Leah was right. Julio Simon was right. Everyone looked at the bottom line. Everyone, in the end, took care of themselves. There was no such thing as heroism, only stupidity.

Tears filled her eyes, blurred her vision. She hadn't realized how desperately she wanted something more until now when it was time to give up and go. Time to cut her losses. She'd had some fun. The stories would be a delicious scandal someday—Zaide Soledad's affair with a favela savage in a painted canvas coat and a knife in his boot. Time to return to reality, to finally accept that her desires did not exist outside her own head. She put her hand on the knob and opened the door.

"Wait," Paulo said softly. He pulled out the black knife and held her gaze steadily. "You weren't afraid. You knew I could hurt you if I wanted to, and you weren't afraid."

"I thought that you wouldn't hurt a friend. Maybe I was wrong. Maybe I'm not a friend," Zaide said bitterly.

Paulo shook his head. "There are a lot of things I'd do, but I don't betray my friends." He took a breath and looked at the matte-black Teflon blade. "When Francisco gave this to me on my birthday we talked about starting a cadre. Not like the tribes in the satellite cities or the gangs in Rio. But there are a lot of us on the street. I just don't have anything to lose. I don't care much anymore, because there isn't anything I can have that I want. Except people.

"Anyway, Francisco and I created Bakunin for us. All of us. To unite the tribes. To have power. Maybe only to make people like you afraid at night, but that's some power at least. That's something. To make sure the fazendas remember, that the government remembers. To haunt them.

"Because no one can make you free. Freedom is something you must have inside you before you go gunning. The only way to be free is to act that way.

"Anyway, Francisco and I, we started Bakunin. When Steel and Nem Brito joined, we all marked the wall in blood. Everyone who's been part of us."

Zaide blinked. "You mean you think that if I'm silly enough to go along with some blood ceremony you'll trust me? That's absurd."

Paulo smiled and shrugged. Then he rotated the knife so that it was held firmly down, instead of out, in his right hand. His left he clenched in a fist and stretched backward so that the violet lines under the skin in his wrist were clear. He cut deeply, without hesitation, not slicing the arteries like some schoolchild playing at suicide, but neatly severing a vein so that blood welled up and flowed over his skin, his fist, down the inside of his arm.

The blood held Zaide. Intellectually she considered it childish, but she could not deny the primitive fascination. Opening your own skin, inducing pain to make a point, she had not been prepared for the visceral power of if. The raw sexuality of it. The hubris. The act seemed to magnify Paulo, making him stronger and more proud, more like Achilles and Hector and Ulysses, who defied the gods and paid but were not defeated.

It was as if he had shown her that he was secretly one of them, and was asking her to join him. She could not refuse.

The knife was warm and heavy. She took it and held it the way Paulo had. Her own flesh seemed distant, unreal, and she cut and watched the blood well up as if it were happening in some dream. As if it were happening in the Wave.

Then she blotted her wrist against the wall, on a patch among other rust-stained smears. She had not thought about those streaks before, having assumed they were simply part of the ambiance. There was a certain satisfaction in knowing that her mark was up on the wall with the rest of them, that it would remain there as part of whatever Bakunin was or would become.

Paulo took the knife and gently wiped the blade on the inside of his canvas coat. It left a dark smudge. He sheathed the knife and then took Zaide's wounded wrist and kissed it, lapped up the remaining blood with his tongue, which tickled on her skin.

"Does that make you trust me?" she asked teasingly.

Paulo smiled at her. "No," he answered. "But it means you are part of Bakunin. So now if you betray us, at least you know that you are part of it. And it's not just about ritual, anyway. Every cadre has a blood wall. Call it a DNA identification file of the membership."

For some reason that made her laugh.

"So tell me more about what this Julio Simon of yours is planning," Paulo said. "And tell me, what was this medical thing that meant you couldn't come? Francisco said that he thought you were a Waverider. He thinks we need it."

She heard the bitterness in his voice and it made her sad. "Did you want the interface?" she asked gently. "Because, you know, the fazendas are very careful about who they adopt. Who's permitted in. It's not like a place where you are discrete and the data are discrete like a library. It's more like you are merged with it and everyone else who's ever been a part of the Wave, as if you're actually creating it while you're in it along with everyone else.

"It isn't being in another phase of reality so much as simply becoming conscious of what there always is. We all function on the quantum level all the time. We aren't any different from any other matter in the universe. And, really, I don't understand why the families keep it all so private anyway. It isn't like the magic key to power or anything."

Hunger burned in his face, stark desire frustrated. She could see that he hated her for the experience he could not have. He hated her, and yet her value rose in his estimation as well. She was the thing that Francisco had been looking for all along, the key to the fazenda wall.

"Don't tell me," he said, his voice husky and low. "Tell that to Francisco. I don't want to know."

She held him, then, horribly aware of the inequality. There was nothing she could do to change that. There was no way she could give him what he wanted and what she had. The anonymity of the festivals was lost, the masks that kept them all safe from their differences were gone.

"I had the secondaries in a little over two years ago," Paulo said quietly. "I'd already failed the psych on the Changeling program, but I thought I could get in as a spacer. I scored second, internationally, on the intelligence and intuitive reasoning cuts. It was almost a sure thing. They didn't worry about the psych that much, too many cultures. And I thought I'd maybe end up in training in the U.S. or maybe Geneva for orbitals. I was waiting to hear, when the Forestation Riots came along. And of course after that it was impossible. Besides, no one could find me even if the United Nations hadn't intervened to keep the peace. And after that I couldn't go, anyway."

Although it had not been U.N. forces that had backed up the government in Brasilia, intervention by the U.N. had been necessary in Rio, where the mobs looted the whole downtown and rioted for days, where the beaches became a campground for the angry and an amphibious landing base for the foreigners.

They couldn't afford to let the riots go on. The fazenda families made it all too clear when they organized the call for help. They couldn't afford to change the Forestation Acts, and they were too scared to try. In the end the fazenda families won again.

The foreigners only knew that the rain forest had to be protected. They couldn't know by what means. Or so Dona Elena had said in the first days, when she was still a journalist and not a basket case.

The fact that the U.N. peacekeeping forces had backed up the government and increased the fazendas' power had impressed Paulo. He counted his majority from that realization. Before that time he had gone on innocently, thinking that ability and drive and sheer creative force would carry him. That once he left the stifling stratification of Brazil he could do anything, be anything. That somehow the rest of the world was more free.

When the U.N. forces hit Ipanema Beach, his illusions were shattered forever. He had prayed that they would rectify things, march into the interior, take Brasilia, try the newly formed Ministry of Forestation for inhumanity and return the Sylvia family to their rightful position. And then he would leave, off to the training program to ride the Wave far away, to become part of the larger world. Maybe the larger universe.

He had believed all those things. And when he found out he was wrong, it was worse than betrayal by a friend. It was the end of his childhood. It was the end of his dreams, and life no longer had much value beyond hate.

The hate had burned and warmed him, kept him alive. It had become intrinsic to his definition. But now, with Zaide, it had turned on him like Exu Tiriri, laughing as he was caught. He hated what had produced her. He wished he could hate her, too, but she had returned to him and he couldn't.

Zaide felt his conflict sharper than the stinging on her wrist where she had made the cut. It had never occurred to her before how it would feel to live every day wanting something that was out of reach. Impossible.

The silence was illusion. The door to the office crashed down, tearing the hinges from the molding.

Paulo had the crossbow pistol aimed and ready before the first of their attackers came through the door. He didn't bother with the niceties of identification. The crossbow bolt homed on the expanse of canvas and stained it with blood.

The crossbow pistol was powerful and accurate. And it took too long to reload. Serps came through the door, dart guns and knives ready, surrounding them. One relieved Paulo of his Teflon knife, relishing the heft of it in a series of movements. They kept him covered with the dart guns, not daring to come too close. Zaide they didn't seem to consider a threat, but one of the large Serps held her hands behind her and breathed on her neck. Zaide recoiled. It must have been over a week since her captor had bathed.

"Aie, I think Julio Simon will like this little catch, his dear little cousin leading us right to the target," one of the Serps said, giggling.

Paulo looked at Zaide with disbelief. She understood all too clearly that Julio Simon had set her up. And the whole thing made her furious. The hot fetid stench of the Serp holding her was sickening. She didn't even need to think.

She stomped backwards on her captor's instep with her full weight. As he howled off balance and released her hands, she jabbed her elbow back into his ribs. He screamed again.

The three Serps covering Paulo turned their attention to Zaide. One of them, a woman, had a blowgun to her lips. Paulo dove to his hands and catapulted in a dance movement, his legs sweeping hers from under her. The soldier slammed into the green carpet and her blowgun skidded from her hands across the floor.

Paulo did not stop. He could not had he wanted to——the momentum and thrust of action was flowing through him. He swung around on one arm, his legs windmilling wildly into the attacker who had spoken earlier.

Zaide went after the Serp soldier's blowgun. It had landed against the wall, and in the mêlée she was forgotten. There was only the one loaded dart. Zaide aimed and fired at the Serp who had been the leader and whom Paulo had brought down.

Outside there was stunning noise, yelling and screaming and singing all together with the unrelenting drums. The rhythms filled Zaide with strength. She was invincible, one with the drumming and the power that engulfed her, which was exactly like moving through the Wave.

While Paulo kicked one Serp in the doorway, another dashed at him from the side. Zaide saw it all too clearly, suspended in time. No cause, no effect, no speed at all. Thought was clear and very precise. She could see it all before she knew what to do.

The blowgun in her hand was a long, thick, hollow wooden tube. She cracked it over the head of the Serp going after Paulo as he passed her, unaware of her existence.

It was over abruptly. She was alone with those who had fallen in the attack, and as they stirred in pain she suddenly wondered if they would get up and go for her again. The shouts and noise from beyond the office seemed to surround her. She stepped over the Serp Paulo had shot in the doorway and went into the hall. There was no one there, and it was almost quiet until she went outside.

Down on the ground, the patch of bare land before the residence was the aftermath of a full-scale victory. There were young men and women lying on the ground and others playing drums and tambourines. The old men with their jars of *pinga* and the little whores who knew all the songs, were out there in what looked like a *roda* from hell. Behind the dancing *capoeiristas* multicolored fairy lights sparkled like stars, and their faces were masks of shadows twisted in victory and rage.

Carnival in the apocalypse, Zaide thought. Then she saw Francisco's brilliant red hair in the crowd, Paulo standing next to him. They were the only ones not moving, not dancing, not drinking and singing and celebrating victory over their own kind. Not taking lengths of rope or dead wire and tying the attackers to the concrete pilings that held the building above the ground.

Francisco looked up frankly at Zaide, who stood on the top step of the building. She met his gaze but could not read it. As she walked down the steps to join them, someone thrust a glass into her hand. She took it, nodded thanks carefully, and continued until she had reached the space of calm where Francisco stood.

"So?" was all he said. But she saw the concealed distrust in Paulo and the tautness in the way Francisco spoke, and she saw it all as clearly as she had in the Wave.

"I wonder why he didn't give them an asher," Zaide said carelessly.

"Probably because he didn't want them to hurt you." Paulo practically spit out the words.

"I don't know," Zaide said, and she turned from Francisco to Paulo. "But if anyone hates Julio Simon, I do, and with a damned bit more reason than you do."

Then Francisco shocked her by laughing. "She's got you there, Paulo," he said between deep, generous peals.

Steel came up to the three of them and spoke directly to Francisco. "They're all Serps, all right," he said. "And we've got most of them restrained."

"What about the ones in the office?" Zaide asked sharply. "Or are you going to let them slink back out of the city, too?"

Francisco smiled unpleasantly. Nem Brito appeared from behind one of the singing girls and shook his head. "Let them go," he counseled softy. "We might be able to use them later."

"No," Paulo countermanded.

In the middle of the argument and the party three verts appeared overhead, their high-power searchlights bleaching out the Carnival atmosphere. The verts hovered, whining, and then slowly they descended.

A door on the largest vert opened and Julio Simon himself appeared in the hatchway. He smiled at Zaide Soledad, and his smile was one of pure contempt. "I must thank you for your assistance, cousin," he yelled over the noise of the verts, which were at rest but still under power. "But isn't it time to admit that I won?"

Security troops, wearing the Vielho-Markowicz logo and carrying ashers, came out of the other two verts. There was nothing anyone could do against an asher. Nothing at all. But it was Julio Simon himself with his shard gun who made the capture and escorted them aboard the vert.

Zaide watched as they ascended. Below it looked like the aftermath of a party in a Bosch version of the pit. The drum still played, the rhythms echoing through the hull of the vert. There was power in the drums, and promise. She tried not to think of Paulo and Francisco, Steel and Nem Brito, bound and taken to Julio Simon's personal retreat. Instead she thought about the pulsating energy of the drums, the energies of the quantum world which both were and were not around her. Where this always was and never was. Where the outcome was known and where Fate had never been born and where all the screaming protests and fears of Zaide Soledad were so much chaff in the particle wind.

Eighteen

IT was close to dawn when they arrived back at the fazenda. No one was out to greet her cousin's victory. Only the chorus of parrots and the faintest false blue at the horizon cut through the sleeping dark. Julio Simon gave the orders. Zaide was escorted to her room, where Susana waited with a handful of bright pink phrines and a glass of orange juice.

She wanted to scream, to wake up. It was disjointed like a dream, like something that was the invention of subconsciousness and not the real world. "Lie down in the net," Susana said softly, and then Zaide felt the effects of the phrines opening the secondaries, calming and relaxing, a different sensation than she had had before. The net in her shimmered and merged and she was trapped in it, locked, panicked without a body for reference. Not like that first time, when she was gently guided. This time the Wave overtook her and she couldn't break free.

She was every place. There was no identity, no focus, only various intensities and configurations that were all fractile and beautiful. Zaide Soledad did not exist. There was only the net in the Wave, the quantum ride through a reality that did not care at all about anything in the world she had left.

But she cared. She knew. And she remembered.

The memory focused her attention on a very small complex in the Vielho-Markowicz territory. Once she gave it attention she found she was there, in the structure of the circuitry. Locks, millions of locks and passwords, all guarded and walled in with defenders at every gate. Security complex. She recognized the paranoia and the dark that was Julio Simon. There was no living presence at this level, there was no intelligence. There was only function and design.

Locks and circuits and guards. Zaide Soledad passed most of the guards easily. She was family, and besides, they weren't expecting her. They had been created in case of outside intrusion from the Ministry or the Cadea or maybe some unnamed group at the University who were more intent on research than on effect. This was how Julio Simon thought. He did not worry about his cousin stepping into his own territory, taking it for granted that in the end his priorities benefited them both.

There was no amusement here, but Zaide Soledad, whatever identity she retained, was amused. Julio Simon could not defend against what he could not conceive. And in his wildest imaginings Zaide knew that it would never occur to him that someone from the family might want to slip his locks in the Security Outpost.

The system was quite simple inside the Wave. With the correct credentials, she passed into the heart of the Security files, all open to her and at her disposal. She had been Julio Simon's first choice for a partner, after all. They had similar gene scans, they were both S-series and much the same. And so it wasn't so much like breaking in as entering a place where she was assumed to need access and that access was freely given.

The center of it all was the single geometric figure, like a crystal, which was the seed of everything else. It replicated and multiplied and twisted itself into an infinity of direction in a single bound plane. She rode the lines down, going on forever, time and space merged and forgotten, no longer even existing except as a shred of a dream.

She went into the locks themselves, the photocircuitry that ran through the whole complex. She keyed the sequences, diverting energy from the main systems and highjacking it across unintended spaces. Not entirely easy work, but straightforward.

She had no awareness of the people themselves, could not hear or see them. Even the concept of friend meant nothing. Zaide Soledad and Julio Simon and Paulo Sylvia and Francisco Pope did not exist. Nothing was left of hope and pain and beginnings and ends, not even memory. Only energymattermovementinfinity existed.

And then even that went away and there was the infinity of nothing at all.

Zaide awoke to Susana arriving with a dinner tray. Outside the plum-colored chintz curtains it was newly dark. Her head hurt and she was thirsty. Susana had provided a large glass of *guarana*, wet and sweet to replenish her body, along with the grilled fish and rice.

"What happened?" Zaide moaned.

Susana settled the tray across Zaide's lap, then pulled up one of the fancifully upholstered boudoir chairs and sat down. "Well, Julio Simon captured his rebels and you're down one or so," Susana explained. "But since he had to walk in himself and you were there, he didn't do as well as he hoped and Uncle Victor seems to think that you're about equal. Sonia Leah is reserving judgment."

"I meant, how long have we been here and where are Paulo and the others and what has Julio done to them?" Zaide asked briskly. Half her fish was eaten and she felt more alive.

Susana shrugged. "It's only just after dinner. Tonight there is a pianist from São Paulo, Cousin Anna. She is playing in the parlor tonight in about half an hour if you're up to it. She's playing an all-Liszt program."

Zaide looked at Susana as if her cousin must be out of her mind. "You think I really want to go hear a Liszt concert now? When Julio Simon's been gaining behind my back?" Susana would understand that. But Zaide was also worried about her friends, and that was a new feeling for her. She didn't understand why it was all so urgent, why she needed to reassure herself that Julio Simon had not destroyed Paulo, had not turned him into a lump of terrorized insane flesh.

Susana nodded resolutely. "I needed a good excuse to get out of listening to that stuff," she said, half-smiling. "If you could use me along."

Zaide half-panicked. "Why?" she blurted out. "You could get in bad trouble."

Susana raised her eyes to the window and Zaide saw they were as cold as Sonia Leah's heart. "One of you will win. And whoever does will rise fairly high in the fazenda. Julio Simon already owes me for giving you the phrines this morning. But you'll owe me a lot more, Zaide. I want to leave the fazenda. I want to go to Rio or to the research facility in São Paulo."

Bottom line. Zaide appreciated that. Looking into Susana's face, she knew that her cousin was barely enduring the fazenda, the hierarchy, the training. And soon Susana wouldn't be able to take it anymore and she would break like all the more fragile S-series did, that instability they all shared, that made them brilliant and made them insane.

Just like her. Zaide smiled thinly. She, too, was insane. If she was reasonable, she wouldn't even consider springing Bakunin from Julio Simon's jail. If she were Sonia Leah, she would have cut her losses long ago. But she was S-series and more prone to take a risk than many of them and too stubborn to get out when things looked bad.

"Good," Susana said firmly. "Then let's get moving while everyone's listening to Liszt. If we move fast enough, we'll be in time for cake at the end."

Zaide blinked. She hadn't expected Susana to be so ready, with a plan already laid out. Not that it was much of a plan, Susana agreed. But as Zaide dressed in plain dark green to blend in with the night, Susana explained how she had picked up the vert Zaide had left in town and brought it in auto and hidden it out behind the field house. Easy enough to get to, and not a place Julio Simon would think to look.

They left the room and went down the stairs to the deserted porch. Everyone was already gathering in the warm light of the main parlor. Zaide remembered all the times she had sat in the warm yellow light of the old-fashioned chandeliers, the elegantly scrolled wooden furniture upholstered in shades of gold and bronze with the softest hint of moss-green and verdigris. The piano was an antique, mirror-bright wood in one corner of the room, usually dressed in a gold-fringed silk tapestry with a vase of orchids and palm fronds on top. Tonight, of course, the piano would be open and the scarf draped over a side table, where the aunts and uncles would pick up their glasses of champagne.

Everyone would sit absolutely silent during the recital, sipping at a glass, perhaps, and wishing they were anywhere else. Zaide could not manage to regret missing this musical evening. She had been through too many others.

She stole out into the dark, Susana at her side. They paused at the games cabana on the side of the tennis courts, where Zaide picked up her blowgun and tucked a Teflon knife into her boot. Just like Paulo.

Susana smiled approval, then showed Zaide that she was carrying one of the security shock wands in her low boot. Zaide was both confused and impressed with her choice. They were heavy-duty weapons and even family had to be processed and printed to be issued one.

Susana saw the confusion on Zaide's face, and made her round eyes childlike and wide. "I'm in a Security internship rotation," she said softly. "Everyone seemed to think it was a good idea for me."

Zaide said nothing, but reminded herself that Susana was more of a force than she realized. Maybe because Susana didn't care so much about the family politics, Zaide reflected, her cousin had always seemed weak and easy to manipulate. Everything is the same if you don't care. She would have to be more careful of Susana in the future.

The prisoners were being held in Julio Simon's field house, which was equipped for such guests. The holding area, designed so that family members could conduct interrogations at their leisure and without the admittedly minor restrictions of the official inquiries downtown, was on bioscan code. Family members, naturally, had no trouble getting in. Or getting what they wanted.

Zaide held back while Susana went directly to the guard on duty in front of the monitors. Being family, she set off none of the alarms. Zaide followed, and while Susana talked, she watched the prisoners on the monitors.

The cells were arranged four around a central desk, which presumably was for the interrogator. The cells were clean and had decent facilities. They were certainly better than anything Zaide had encountered in the southern sector of the city. The traditional bars made up one wall, and the doors were secured with old-fashioned mechanical locks. Zaide started. She hadn't thought about mechanicals. She couldn't have touched them in the Wave. She would have to find something that would break the mechanism.

She dropped her eyes from the reading boards with their unblinking steady progress of colors. Everything the same, no changes at all. And then she noticed the guard's shock wand lying on the ledge under the monitor panel. That should do it for the mechanical locks.

There were supposedly bioscan sensors and electrical fields as well. She had thought she had taken care of these in the Wave, but from what she could see, according to the monitor position they were all functioning. Fluorescent green and gray lines lay flat across the board. Zaide wondered briefly if she had in fact done anything at all in the Wave, or if she had simply been dreaming. Or maybe the Wave itself was a kind of dream, a subjective reality that never affected the objective world.

She would have to assume that she had in fact turned off the remote security fields. And if she was wrong, then she would have to think of something else. But part of her mind was convinced that she wasn't wrong, couldn't be wrong, that she had made some change in the systems and made certain that they wouldn't be found out.

Only then did she look at the individuals, displayed in multiple images on the large screens around the guard's desk. Nem Brito, Steel, Pope and Paulo. All four were taking their captivity differently. Pope was pacing like an animal, his eyes on everything at once. Nem Brito had withdrawn into himself, completely self-contained. Steel talked at everyone, talked about anything that meant nothing, trying to keep his spirits up, trying to convince himself that the situation was not as hopeless as he knew it was. And Paulo sat perfectly still with his eyes closed and his hands on his knees as if only the tension in his arms and face kept him from exploding.

Susana talked to the guard easily, small talk about the fazenda and the Security roster and Julio Simon's possible promotion. "Maybe these prisoners will clinch it," she said, smiling. "Actually, we came down to talk to them for a bit, if that's not too much trouble."

Zaide rolled her eyes. Sometimes she simply could not believe how naive Susana was. But somehow the guard didn't find Susana silly.

"I wish I could let you through," he said, and the regret in his voice sounded real. "But Senhor Julio Simon said that no one was to go back there."

"Oh, I'm sure he didn't mean family," Susana said, completely oblivious.

"I assume he didn't," the guard replied carefully. "But he didn't say *except* family and I wouldn't want to lose my job."

Susana made a sympathetic hum in her throat and nodded. The guard's face was pleading. He wasn't watching Zaide at all.

Zaide was a little perturbed that the guard took no note of the fact that his shock wand was within easy reach, and was not attached to his person at all. It probably wasn't comfortable attached to his belt if he sat for long periods. Somehow she didn't think Julio Simon would accept that as an excuse.

Zaide didn't even turn it on. While Susana started on yet

another tack, Zaide snatched the wand and cracked it over the guard's head.

"You didn't have to do that," Susana hissed. "I would have convinced him . . ."

But Zaide was already through the door and into the holding area. She went straight to Paulo's cell and pointed the wand at the old-fashioned mechanical lock hoping she hadn't destroyed the weapon's delicate calibration when she'd put it to use more crude than it was designed to handle.

The flash wavered a little through the tones, but she clipped the setting up higher and it held. The lock shattered. She went on to the next, Nem Brito, not thinking at all. She was on automatic. She didn't even notice Paulo get up, join her, search for a weapon of his own.

"What are you doing here?" he asked as the lock on Pope's cage went.

"What does it look like I'm doing?" she snapped. "Having a tea party? Pass the chocolate cookies, please."

Paulo grinned. He bent down and pulled out the knife in Zaide's boot, hefted it lightly in his fingers. He took the door, pulled Susana through quickly while Zaide used the wand on the last lock.

This time the sonics wailed through an octave before settling into the right white. Steel made a face.

"Don't run it down to the limit," Paulo ordered harshly. "We need it. Kick it, Steel."

Steel slammed one boot into the bars and the lock gave. "Let's move," Zaide said briskly, leading the way through the door and into the monitor room. "There's a vert behind the athletic house to your left. It's already set for autopilot with coordinates to 109." A lone alarm went off in their ears.

Susana turned, took the guard's rolling chair and slammed Steel in the ribs. Then, not pausing, she pulled out her own wand and pointed it at all of them. Including Zaide. Susana met her cousin's eyes, shrugged, and threw the controls over the blue zone.

Paulo lunged, the Teflon knife held loosely in his right

hand. He moved slowly to the side, around and under an imaginary opponent, as he came on. Susana tried to keep the wand on him, but even on broad stroke she couldn't anticipate his moves. They were too slow, counter-intuitive, low, not the street-style attack she had been taught to defend against.

Steel and Nem Brito were already running. Pope pulled Zaide's hand. "He's got her," Pope hissed. "Come on. Now."

Pope tried to draw her away but Zaide couldn't leave. She couldn't move. She saw the *capoeira*, this time played deadly. Susana could die.

Then Zaide realized that Susana had been perfectly willing to kill her. The bottom line. Family values, after all. She'd been a fool to trust Susana and she knew it. And she also knew that if Susana hurt Paulo, her cousin would pay for it.

But Susana had been more a fool than she. Her cousin was so busy concentrating on Paulo that she hadn't bothered with Zaide. Zaide took the opening and slipped around the corner and rolled under the desk of the guard's station. When she came up she was facing Paulo and Susana's back was toward her.

Then Paulo gestured with his left hand for her to leave. Susana raised the wand and pointed it at Paulo. Zaide, behind her cousin, saw her adjust the setting from blue to red.

There was no hesitation, there was no thought. Zaide lifted the defective wand in her own hand and fired. She had forgotten that the setting was already at full. She had forgotten that the thing was unreliable. There was only the opportunity and she took it.

Susana crumpled, hit from behind with a wavering blast from Zaide's wand. She didn't know whether Susana was dead or just unconscious, and she froze with the fear that came after the action. And the guards who arrived found Zaide standing over her cousin's body, a wand aimed at an escaping prisoner.

In the frieze Paulo slowly raised his hands. He met

Zaide's eyes and nodded almost imperceptibly. She wanted to open full fire on the guards—they wouldn't expect it—but they were already covering Paulo. No matter which one she got first, he was dead meat. Not her plan at all.

And from the way Paulo gestured so carefully, he was going to play it out. Maybe he wasn't even sure she really was on his side, that she had honestly intended to free them all, but he was going to play it out anyway. He was going to pretend that she had made the capture, and the look on his face said she'd better go along.

She threw down the wand and stalked out, unwilling to watch them lock Paulo back up. Unwilling for him to see her cry. Strange how much it hurt. No one had ever protected her before.

She walked alone in the dark through the orchid garden to the artificial waterfall near the edge of the forest. It was her special place in the compound, and in the middle of the night no one would disturb her there. The scent of the flowers and the steady music of the falls weren't as restful as she remembered. There was only the gaping knowledge of failure.

She didn't know if her initial impulse to free the cadre was because she couldn't stand to see them at Julio's mercy, or because she wanted to raise the stakes against Julio in her own vendetta, or whether she was simply seduced by the recklessness of it all. Or if she really loved Paulo. That was something she considered and from which she recoiled, and she didn't dare even think the word again. But his playing along, covering for her, protecting her, that cost something.

Bottom line, she should leave him alone. She should have the sangfroid to walk away, let cousin Julio do what he would. Bottom line. She'd gain position in the family, spoiling all the plans Julio Simon had bragged about over so many dinners. All her background, all her experience, screamed at her to leave it alone.

But she couldn't. The solemn look on Paulo's face when he had raised his hands, creating the charade, haunted her.

He had not been angry or defeated; he hadn't even had the time to consider the decision. But he hadn't been resigned.

He had played by his own rules, and he expected her to play by them too. He expected revenge. Guaranteed.

And he had a right to expect it, she realized slowly. He had bought that right. And she had an obligation to try and set him free. It was the only protection and the only wealth the favela had.

She would set him free. Or she would pay them back. How, precisely, she didn't know.

Nineteen

TAKING phrines because she could not sleep might have been a mistake. Or maybe more of Susana's treachery. But perhaps, she thought as dark sleep closed in, perhaps the phrines made no difference at all. Perhaps this was payback for the day.

Because in the night there were dreams. They were in the barzinho in 713, only it was not beneath a building—it was a fragment in the Wave. She was there with Paulo and Francisco and a very black man with unnaturally green eyes who was the *mestre* of the *capoeira*.

They were playing—she knew it was *capoeira*—but it was like nothing Paulo had ever shown her. All the players used wands like sticks in a *maculele* dance, only the wands were all on and their vibration was like the musical bow, the *berimbau* that controlled the game. A woman came through the *roda*, an ancient woman wearing the red of a *candomble* priestess. Her face was maybe a hundred years old, but she danced through the circle lithe and strong like a young girl. She danced grimly, her feet pounding the earth a calling to the gods, her hands raised in supplication, her deep back-bends and cartwheels the cavorting energies of the possession she believed in.

Then the old priestess called Zaide to the center of the *roda*, and the master played out the rhythm that defined and controlled the *jogo*. Somehow Zaide understood the rhythm, the game, and she was horrified. But she could not resist.

She danced with the woman, whirling and stamping like any ignorant interior brat in the *candomble*.

Paulo joined them and they danced around him. His movements were things that Zaide had seen him do before, standing on a single bent arm while holding a leg over his shoulder, but this time the whole gesture was filled with pain. It was only *capoeira*, but somehow the familiar moves had become exaggerated and twisted so that they resembled the damned writhing in flames.

She had seen this tableau before, paintings in a gallery, in the village church she had never attended. Images multiplied, and she saw things she had never seen before, things that were broken down into the nowness of the Wave.

All of this was in the Wave, was part of it. The recognition shocked her. The Wave was a datastream, a quantum-level interface structure that had been created to serve the needs of the masters.

Only it had become the master. Stupid and small, the minds that had thought they could twist the Wave to their own purposes. It was itself, it had always been and had always interfaced with the lives of women and men. It was them as much as their flesh and their fears.

In her dream the Wave itself laughed at her. Laughed at the very thought of Creation. It was itself, it had always existed except that there was no past. There was no future. There was only now. And people should have been content to access where they belonged instead of coming directly down into what was and what was not.

The laughter echoed through waking. It made her uneasy, disoriented. She had to think for a moment why she was so worried today, why the urgency was on her.

But then she remembered, she cursed the hours she had slept. She dressed quickly, professionally, and went down to breakfast. She was not hungry but the family would notice if she was late, and of all mornings, she dared not be late on this one. Still, no one questioned her as she took coffee and a pastry from the sideboard.

Julio Simon was there. His face was slightly gray and there were violet stains under his eyes. Zaide was suddenly afraid. She hoped in despair that he had not been up all night "taking care" of his prisoner. Paulo could be dying by now, hideously mutilated while she had slept. The two bites she had eaten turned solid in her stomach and even the remaining coffee threatened to make her ill.

But Julio did not turn to her and gloat the way she expected him to. Instead he stared at his hands as he cut the guava on his plate precisely with his fork and knife. Zaide was certain that he had no more wish to eat than she herself did.

Zaide was even more surprised when Susana appeared. She had thought her cousin was dead, and assumed that at the least she would have spent the day in the infirmary, but Susana was dressed very professionally in a pale violet suit and matching shoes, her hair pinned in a knot and her face perfectly made up. Zaide blinked. She had never seen Susana looking so powerful, so polished, so ready to assume command.

Susana gave Zaide a hard, sardonic smile. Then she poured herself a cup of coffee from the silver pot on the sideboard and turned to chat with Sonia Leah.

Zaide swallowed hard. Sonia Leah and Susana as allies? She hadn't thought that the head of the Finance Department had even bothered to acknowledge Susana. Susana wasn't Sonia Leah's usual protégée, too unpredictable, not serious enough, irresponsible. Unless Zaide was wrong.

Everything shifted. Suddenly Zaide wondered whether the cousin who had gotten her into scrapes and had introduced her to the world of festivals and Brasilia and irresponsible habits had been doing so as part of a campaign.

As the whole thing became clear in Zaide's mind, she wanted to shoot herself for having been so blind and trusting. And she was impressed with Susana's audacity. It wasn't everyone who could plot a scheme that intricate and pull it off. Even Julio Simon couldn't have been so duplicitous.

Zaide left most of her pastry and an untouched cup of stone-cold coffee and quit the dining room. Instead of reporting directly to the Marketing office for the day's assignment, she wandered out on the lawn and to the garage. There she called up the valet and ordered a vert to go into the rain forest. Alone.

The system queried whether she would like to be accompanied. If not a family member, one of the harvesters would be happy to go along. The valet didn't like her solitary request, although it informed her politely that perhaps she should reconsider, or perhaps report to the infirmary for a physical. It didn't approve of her going alone, of anyone ever being alone. Alone was a signal of illness in humans. She slammed a hand against the screen in frustration. Then, calmed somewhat, she informed the valet this was merely driving practice. Solo practice it accepted.

She flew to the waterfall deep in the rain forest. Landing was difficult on the small expanse of flat rock near the pool below. There was barely room for the skids, and one of them hung over into the foliage. She got out and paid no attention as the massive ferns tugged at her hem and heavy moisture clung to the fine linen of her jacket. The heavy loam underfoot sucked at her light Italian heels, pulling them from her feet at every step.

The forest was loud, much louder than the fazenda dining room. It reminded her of the barzinho, parrots screeching loudly in the trees, the roar of water on rock, falling from impossible heights. No, she thought, she was hardly alone here.

Besides, there were the ghosts.

Susana had shown her this place on one of their very first secret forays. She had trusted Susana without reservation. After all, her cousin was an S-series, had already stated a preference for R&D and for a big city posting. Susana had always presented herself as no threat to Zaide Soledad.

But then, Zaide reflected, how long had she known

Susana? She had only been brought up to the big house in the last year. After the first cut of selection and the first batch of rejects to be dumped in the city were gone, the remaining candidates moved from the nursery to primary school. While the nursery and the candidates' school were both on the fazenda in the workers' village, they were still many kilometers from the big house. Sometimes elder cousins would come and visit, but the children never went to the main house headquarters. That was only for the very few.

Besides, their teachers reminded them constantly that they were already set for life, they were in a very good position on the fazenda. They would always have work and a place to live in the village. They were the fortunate ones.

Susana had been two years ahead of her and so she had barely known her cousin before coming to the big house. When she arrived she found that she had been assigned a room with Susana, whose previous roommate had been sent to head the Accounting Division of the Recife branch.

After living in the dorm with all the girls in her stage, sharing a room with Susana seemed very lonely. She had missed the pillow fights and the late-night whispers and the smuggled sweets hidden under the bedclothes for weeks until there was enough for a clandestine party. She had almost cried the first night and wished there were a few others in the room.

But Susana had been fun and kind and had helped her out so much during the first days as she adjusted to life in the big house. Now that seemed like a lifetime ago, although Zaide knew it was really only a year and a half. Susana had helped her pick out her first dinner dresses and had told her how to talk to Sonia Leah, and Uncle Victor, who was like a god in the candidates' school.

And then Zaide realized that Susana had acted exactly the way they had all been taught to act. The bottom line always came first. Susana had been in competition with her from the first, the way they were both competing with Julio Simon, the way they all competed for approval from Sonia Leah and Uncle Victor.

She couldn't hate Susana for having acted in her own best interests. Her seemingly too-soft cousin had merely proven herself worthy of respect. Zaide knew that she might have done the same thing.

The water rushed over the falls, and the cool mist sparkled on her face and hands. It glittered in her black hair like jewels. Zaide realized that she was crying. Strange. She would have thought that she would be more upset about Paulo than about Susana. But her cousin's actions were hard for her to accept. Especially all the time they had spent together, when Susana always acted as if she weren't interested in the higher echelons of management. Zaide thought she knew Susana as well as anyone knew anyone. And she had been dead wrong.

Bottom line. They were alone. Much as the valet and the people of the village considered being alone a sign of sickness, the inhabitants of the big house were always alone. They had no choice.

Susana was merely what the fazenda had made her. And Zaide herself suddenly saw quite clearly that she wouldn't have even been aware that other options existed before she had known Paulo and Francisco. Before she had become a member of Bakunin herself.

She kicked off her shoes and dropped her jacket from her shoulders. She stepped onto one of the flat rocks in the water and let the cold rush of water wash away her tears.

It was just one more test, one more thing she had learned. The icy shock of water cooled her anger and her despair.

She could not trust Susana, the closest friend she had. And yet she knew she could trust Paulo, and that he trusted her. She owed him something for that trust, she realized. She had to get him out. If there was anything left of Paulo after Julio Simon had spent even a few hours with him.

She shook herself off like a puppy and scrambled back to land. She was anxious to return, and every second away from the house and from the Security office weighed on her.

Mud formed on her feet and she had to scrape it off on the step of the vert. She tore her hose on the metal and felt like she'd taken off a layer of skin. The pain was good, payment for the time away.

It seemed to take forever to return, although the ride couldn't be more than two hours with the vert full out at max. She had to slow down a little on approaching the house, or someone would ask uncomfortable questions. Finally she got the vert checked in with the valet and she was ready.

There was no plan in her head, nothing except the need to get to Paulo *now*, get him away from Julio Simon. She started to march over in the direction of Security. Her bruised feet made her remember that she was soaking wet and not presentable.

She begrudged the time, and so it took a moment to decide. She sprinted back to the house, toweled her hair quickly and changed into an ice-blue suit, leaving her wet clothes in a heap in the middle of the floor.

She had to keep from running, pace herself to a brisk walk across the lawn and down past the row of trees to the Security field house. A guard sat at the reception desk in the front. "Yes, Senhor Julio Simon did say that you might come," the guard said easily. "He left orders that he is with the prisoner and they are not to be disturbed. However, if you wish to question the prisoner yourself, you may return this evening after Senhor Julio is finished."

Zaide wanted to fling the door open anyway. Stop Julio Simon from whatever he was doing. The guard was relaxed, not expecting anything.

And then she turned and marched out. She couldn't stop Julio Simon. He would be armed. And he would not hesitate to use whatever he had on her. She was responsible for making him an enemy, and she wasn't prepared to kill him here. She was unarmed and this was his territory.

No matter how badly she wanted to go in, no matter how her imagination twisted and warped whatever was going on in the silence behind that smooth apricot door, there was nothing she could do. Nothing that would help. Nothing that would stop Julio Simon, that would free Paulo.

She thought of Paulo and she moaned a little and bent over slightly, even though she was outside and in full view of the house. Paulo. With Julio Simon. Iraci. The tape. God.

She felt like she'd been slammed into concrete. How she managed to make her feet move on the white path was beyond her. All Zaide knew was when she made it through the door. She couldn't stay here. But her room was no good either, full of Susana's presence. She climbed the wide stairs, passed the first two landings that contained the cousins' rooms and utilities.

There was a door here and the stairs narrowed. Zaide kept going, past the servants' quarters and on up to the attic. Here it smelled of warm sunlight and old dry forgotten things. She pulled herself over to a chair and collapsed.

Pain washed through her. She thought of Paulo's ice-white skin torn and flayed, new scars laid like latticework over his back and thighs.

She thought of the things she had read and learned when she was in the village school studying history. About a time before, when Brazil was a military dictatorship and there were assassination squads and the police taught courses in torture. Of ancient brittle films taken in classrooms, men with buckets over their heads that echoed their screams. How the films showed demonstration victims in front of entire lecture halls, naked, their feet in plastic basins of ice water and electrodes taped to their armpits and genitals. How the lecturer pressed the controls and the victim writhed and screamed and how all the uniformed men in the audience took notes.

She dry-heaved and shuddered. Fragments of memory fused with Julio Simon, with Paulo. She remembered pain, and the past contorted her body and then let her go. Slowly she came back to the attic and wondered numbly if Paulo would even be alive come evening.

The light slanted obliquely through the attic windows, casting heavy shadows between the shafts of light. Suddenly Zaide realized that the chair on which she was seated was decorated with bright gold paint and a crown on the top. Once this had served as a throne for the puppet plays she had heard of but did not remember.

There was other scenery, too, a painted fairy-tale castle and what appeared to be an enchanted garden. A paper-hung sculptured tree stood alone against the lingering light. Shiny enameled fruit hung from it, mangoes and coconuts and guavas and oranges, apples and pears. There were feathered birds on its branches, parrots in red and green and stunning blue, all of them studded with glass jewels and painted crowns. There was even an ornate cage hanging from the tree and in it was a stuffed white cockatoo with paste diamonds sparkling through its plumage.

Once someone had created beauty and pleasure with these, here on this fazenda. Zaide reached out to touch a bright green pear. As her finger brushed it, it fell from the tree and split open on the bare floor. The pieces heaved on the floor and then turned over by themselves. Inside had been a maggots' nest, dozens of flat white worms now struggling to hold on to their never-living host.

Zaide recoiled. She couldn't lift the door beam fast enough, couldn't get down the stairs and away any more quickly than she did, although she wished she could. There was only her room for refuge now, the room she shared with Susana. There was no choice, she had to go.

Susana was dressing for dinner when Zaide came in. Susana looked as if the night before had never happened. She had a bright aqua dress laid out on her bed.

"I wondered when you were coming," Susana commented as if nothing had changed. "You worked pretty late today. You'd better hurry if you're not going to be late for dinner. You'd better put up your hair—you don't have time to curl it."

Zaide watched Susana dress. Her cousin behaved the

same way she had behaved every night since Zaide had moved into the big house. Zaide had to admit to herself that she was impressed. She pulled a dress out of the closet and threw her jacket and skirt on the bed.

"No, don't wear that," Susana said. "I don't know why you even bought it—that shade of blue is terrible on you. Wear the pink and gray print."

Zaide acquiesced, stunned that Susana was still dressing her. Although she had to admit that the pink and gray was one of her best.

"You mean, after last night, after I tried to buzz you . . ." Zaide stammered.

Susana turned and smiled with perfect innocence. "But you were just protecting your interests. It makes perfect sense. You don't think I'd hold something like that against you, do you?" Then Susana laughed.

"Now hurry up," Susana chided briskly. "We're having my favorite tonight, *vatapá*. I don't want to be late."

Twenty

SHE barely touched the fish at dinner, and didn't make any pretense of eating the rice or beans or vegetables, although *vatapá* was one of her favorite dishes as well. Usually she couldn't resist the fish in its dark pepper and manioc flour sauce. She could hardly bear the conversation— hearing her cousins' well-modulated, educated voices around the table made her want to scream and pull their hair.

Especially when Sonia Leah praised her efforts in retaining the one prisoner they did have. "I know that Susana did her best to prevent the break. Julio Simon told me that you were instrumental in recapturing this Paulo person after she had been stunned by the captives. He said that he personally found you there covering him with your wand. But one thing I don't understand is how they got loose in the first place. And how you girls managed to get down there at the right time. Weren't you supposed to be practicing your vert landings then? I was sure I saw that on the day's schedule."

"We were on our way over to the garage when we thought about checking by the Security field house," Susana said smoothly in her high, wispy, little girl voice. "It was fortunate, I suppose." But she flashed a smile at Sonia Leah, who nodded with approval.

At least Julio Simon was quiet. Zaide didn't know if that was good or bad. He could be upset about the three prisoners who got away, or he could be pleased about the day spent questioning the one remaining. In any event Zaide was glad that he wasn't talking.

She played with her rice pudding at dessert, but didn't manage to eat more than a taste, and that was just for show. Julio Simon kept glancing over at her, and there was a question in his eyes that Zaide desperately wanted to avoid. She had never been more relieved when dessert was cleared and they were free to leave. She got up immediately and went upstairs before anyone could question her.

In her room she pulled off the dinner dress and kicked off the matching pink kid heels. She pulled on her most nondescript jeans, a dark button-down shirt and athletic shoes. There were things Paulo might need. Phrines, maybe, if he was in bad shape. She took one of the tiny envelopes Susana had left for her on the night table. He would need dinheiro. She had some cash, enough at least for him to make it to the favela and disappear for a few days if he was careful, and maybe longer if he had help.

Then she went into Susana's closet, pulled over the upholstered boudoir chair and stood on it to see the high shelf. Mostly there were scarves and purses. She felt around in the back and grabbed something hard and round like a truncheon. It was a wand.

So Susana hadn't returned it to Security. Which meant a number of things, Zaide thought, but the most important of all was that she had the wand now. And if she needed to, she could use it. She tied the thong on the handle end through her belt loops and went down the stairs.

She didn't care about being seen by any of the cousins as they dressed and set out for the evening's sporting event, a ride through the forest paths. Except for her shoes, she was perfectly dressed for an evening ride, and if someone commented that she needed to put on boots, she could always make a face. Everyone knew that Zaide had never been much of a horsewoman.

Still, she was pleased with the activity. Julio Simon was one of the family's best riders and he was only too pleased to show off his skill. And while it was probably difficult for him to tear himself away from his prisoner long enough for a ride with the cousins, Zaide didn't doubt that he would go. Julio Simon had a reputation for his riding.

So did Susana. Suddenly Zaide wondered whether she was really an S-series at all. Genetically she should be very comparable to the others, but the three of them were terribly different.

Or maybe not so different. Susana had turned out to have an appetite for the family games and was remarkably good at them.

She passed three of the younger trainees around Manuel Leal. No S-series in the bunch, she noted. She waved and walked through the door as if she were on her way to the stables. She took that path instead of cutting over the lawn in case anyone was watching or following. She was early, the ride wasn't due to begin for forty-five minutes at least. But that gave her the margin she needed, and for anyone who wondered, it would just look as if she were going out to the horses early. Knowing how long it took Zaide to saddle a mount, no one would even notice.

She actually went in to the stables, walked through, and out the back door, and from there doubled around behind the picnic grove to the back of the Security field house. She ran around to the front so the guard wouldn't be alarmed at her coming in by any other door, but she slipped in quickly. The lengthening shadows covered her from anyone watching from the path, she hoped. It was too late for that now.

She flashed her friendliest smile at the guard, a hard-looking woman several years older than herself. The guard's face didn't lose its sour cast.

"I'm Zaide from the big house," Zaide said with forced cheerfulness. "I was told that if I wanted to question the prisoner privately I could do so when Senhor Julio Simon was finished for the day."

If anything, the woman looked even more sullen. Zaide pressed her hand against the ID plate and she knew the guard had no choice. She was a member of the family; the guard didn't have the authority to keep her out.

"Dona Zaide," the guard said, grudging the honorific. "Yes, there's a note there that you expressed interest. You may have fifteen minutes. I'll be here if you need any assistance," she added, with a look that told Zaide no one had better ask for anything more tonight.

"I shouldn't, thank you." Zaide remained unfailingly polite. It was part of her training. "However, I would like half an hour and with the monitors off. I'll be able to activate the intercom if I need you."

The guard's expression went from sullen to suspicious. "It's against procedure," she informed Zaide.

"Well, then, we'll just have to change procedure this time," she said with forced cheer.

The guard looked as if she were ready to kill Zaide, but there was the simple fact that the family could do whatever they wanted. This was something both women knew, and face-to-face there was nothing the guard could do but back down.

"It's for your own protection, Dona Zaide," the guard protested feebly, making one last attempt to thwart her.

Zaide fought to keep her voice light and even. She had something more important to do than antagonize the guard. "I'm aware of that, and I thank you. But I do need some private information about the street gangs, and I think he'll talk more freely if he knows no one else is watching. Since I have seen my cousin Julio Simon this evening, I am quite certain that I can obtain the data I need."

The guard pursed her mouth at this confidence about the family politics. Clearly she did not approve. But there was nothing she could do. She switched off the bank of monitors and then stepped from behind the station to unlock the door leading to the holding cells. Zaide thanked her again before going inside.

The lock she'd blasted off the cage yesterday had not been repaired. A length of chain secured with a padlock took its place.

Then Paulo turned on the bunk and faced her. She drew in

a breath and tried not to gag. The blood clotted on his clothes and the broken fingers were bad enough. But it was his burned-out eyes that made her want to turn away.

The smell of the burning lingered and made her choke. She forced herself to look, coldly this time. There was no way she would ever, ever forget his ruined face. It would keep her awake nights for the rest of her life.

She went up to the bars and pressed her cheek against the steel. "It's Zaide," she whispered.

He tried to hide his face with his battered hands, unwieldy mitts that covered the worst wounds, where his eyes had been. "Can't go," he whispered. "Burning. Burning." Then he inhaled sharply. Zaide thought it was a sob.

"What do you want?" she asked softly, but she already knew the answer. *Revenge, guaranteed. Blood oath and revenge.*

"Can you come to the bars?" she asked. "I can't get any closer."

She couldn't watch while he dragged himself across the two meters of concrete floor to her voice. She knelt down and touched his hair, his neck, the places where there was no damage yet. "What can I do for you?" she asked again.

"Highwire," he said.

She could tell that the words were hurting him, that speech was only more pain. "Do you want highwire?" she asked quickly.

"No. He gave me. Burning. Secondaries, burning. Don't want . . . to be . . . carrot." Paulo managed to get the words out between ragged breaths.

The secondaries. She remembered. Paulo had the secondaries. Fear mixed with pain in her body, at the sites of her own secondaries. Worse was the thought of what was left after the drug had done its job.

She ran her fingers through his hair and felt him trembling underneath. "Julio Simon is dead," she whispered, leaning down. "As of this second he is dead, and I promise you I will humiliate him first. I will make him suffer, more than just physically. I promise you."

"Him. Not me," Paulo said. "I want it over please."

She knew, had known from the first what she had come here to do. She held him through the bars, trying not to cry. She had done her best, had done better than any favela girl would have managed. But it wasn't enough.

She could feel the tremors in the cords of his neck, the spasms that wouldn't end. She'd seen the training clips from the experiments early on. The phrines burned out and then attacked the brain. Once the shaking started it wouldn't end, not for a very long time, but nothing could be done. The victims eventually began to drool, and it made her think of rabies.

But Julio would make it last as long as he could. As the higher functions went, it would be easy for him to make Paulo betray his friends. And then, once his intelligence was gone and dead, he could still feel pain. Julio Simon would keep him alive for a long, long time.

And that would be the most painful torment of all. She could not let him suffer that. Should not let him suffer at all, not when it was in her power to stop it. But she couldn't, not without his unambiguous demand. Which he had given, as close to begging as he had ever been.

"I have a wand," she said gently.

"Please," he whispered. And then he turned his face in her hands and kissed her palm.

She took the wand off her belt loop and turned it on. As he heard the soft energy hum, Paulo relaxed against her hand. Her knees pushed through the bars. She caressed his neck gently before touching the wand to his temple with the setting on red.

Twenty-one

THE big house was quiet when Zaide Soledad got back. The cousins had not yet returned from their ride. Only an hour had gone by. And hour and a lifetime.

She did not go up to her room. Instead, she went into the parlor and sat down in one of the satin-upholstered wing chairs next to the piano. It was a commanding position. She held herself steady.

Anger boiled inside her, far too hot for her to trust. That was one thing she had learned from Sonia Leah, never to act from emotional bias. It was dangerous. It was stupid. It led to mistakes, and right now she couldn't afford any of those.

She waited. It seemed like eternity. It seemed like nothing at all. Grief was like the Wave, and time dissolved in it. She waited until Uncle Victor came in and faced her.

She knew he would come. She knew that there wouldn't be many people in the house now. She knew he would be curious, was watching for nuances in her little private war. That he was waiting to see who won.

"The prisoner is dead," she stated flatly. "I killed him. Julio Simon gave him highwire and he had secondaries."

Uncle Victor's warm eyes studied her. "It's your first, isn't it?" he asked gently. "It is Julio Simon's job—you should have left it to him."

Zaide blinked. She felt distanced from reality. Inside she felt something hideous and ugly and knew that she needed to let it burst from her and cry. But now it was still too tight and hidden, and she was grateful. She had to face Uncle Victor with discipline, not sloppy tears.

"Julio Simon enjoys suffering," she stated harshly. "I don't. I'd kill a horse in that much pain."

Uncle Victor put out his hand and Zaide took it. Gently he helped her from her chair. "The first one is always the most difficult," he said very softly. "I think it is wasteful to kill when it isn't necessary, but in this case I think you had no choice."

He continued to hold her hand as if she were a very little girl, and led her out of the parlor, past the Cousins' Room and the dining room and the breakfast room, into the over-sized white and terra-cotta kitchen. She was vaguely aware of the fact that she had never been here before, that this was territory more alien than the board room. She couldn't un-derstand why he was taking her here, except maybe to kill her where no one would mind the mess and the noise.

But Uncle Victor wouldn't have to worry about such things, her numb brain informed her. If he wanted her out of the way, there were easier methods. But thinking was too hard. Her mind was solid and inert, a great lump of useless clay. Besides, no matter what he did, she didn't really care. Not at all.

He settled her on one of the high wooden stools where Bebe served her assistants, and with his own hands made her a child's breakfast coffee. He took out a handful of beans picked fresh on the fazenda, one of their most important ex-ports, and threw them into a heavy hot iron skillet. When they were done, he ground them and brewed them with hot milk. In another pan he heated and whipped the cream with sugar, then mixed it with the weak coffee brewed with milk. He poured the mixture into a bright red mug and added a lit-tle cinnamon and placed it in front of her.

The comfort of the mingled smells and warm beverage went through her harder than any weapon. She cupped both her hands around the thick mug and drank like a child. The tears started to come. She didn't notice.

Uncle Victor patted her shoulder gently. "You have done very, very well, Zaide Soledad," he said, and his voice was sweet and low. "You are still very young, and Julio Simon has experience as well as ability. And if Sonia Leah and I could stop this thing now and send Julio Simon to head the office in Belém, we would. But you know better than that. There are limits on what any of us can do."

He turned away and paced across the room. Zaide heard his heels on the hard tile floor. "Even if we sent Julio Simon away," he continued, "even then, he would be in the Wave. And so for your own sake you must either make your peace with him or destroy him." He paused. "I should not tell you this. I hope you succeed."

Footsteps echoed sharply on the tile, and then the door swung closed. Zaide heard it only peripherally. The dam had broken and all she could do was cry. There was no future—even the next minutes seemed impossible. All she could do was cry into the steaming cup forever.

At least she was alone, in the one place where she would be left alone until morning. Even Julio Simon would never find her here. She folded her arms and lay her head on them and sobbed endlessly in the night.

It was verging on dawn when she left the house through the kitchen door. She could feel moisture thickening the air. Soon the dry winter would be over and the rains would begin. The day smelled new and the newness was alien. She was not ready to leave the shelter of the night, of her own grief. She could not face the family.

She went to the garage and ordered a vert. When it was delivered she wiped the order from the autovalet memory. She didn't want to make it too easy for Julio Simon to follow her. Although they would find the vert eventually, there was no reason for her to make it obvious. For a moment she wondered whether he had implanted a tracker below her skin, but she didn't think there would have been an opportunity for that.

Unless—the phrines. On her last trip to the city she had taken phrines that Susana had given her. There were tracer elements that could be incorporated, some that were permanent and others that were temporary. Julio Simon was smart enough to use a temp on her. Something that lasted too long would be detected if she had any reason to visit a doctor.

The best thing to do would be to have them analyzed, but there was no time for that. She had to suspect the worst, even if it meant giving up some serious dinheiro in street value. There was the tiny envelope with a supply in her back pocket. It had been provided by Susana. She wondered what her cousin had exacted as payment for that. She walked out to where the vert was parked, spilled the phrines on the ground next to the garage. Then she nudged a clod of moist earth over them with the side of her shoe. Let Julio Simon find that when he went looking.

There was very little traffic in the early hours. The few oversized commercial haulers that dominated the travel lanes were pushing top speed. Somehow she managed to get the vert into the pattern and locked in to city-incoming. It was not the most elegant or evasive way to go, but Zaide's thoughts were still muddled and slow. She thought the city grid could handle things much better than she could.

Besides, she already knew that she was going to ditch the vert at the fazenda headquarters and take a cab. Or something. The headquarters itself directed the parking maneuver and Zaide left it with the valet. Then she took the lift down and left the building. There was no need to stop in the ladies' lounge; she hadn't brought a change of clothes.

She didn't see a cab when she hit the commercial street. There were plenty of workers and students on powerbikes. It was still too early for the fazenda-based executives to be arriving, but the lower-level managers were being delivered in oversized corporate vehicles. The city was slowly coming to life.

Zaide began to walk from the Northern Commercial District down to the Esplanade. It was a miserably long walk, made more difficult by being uninviting. The streets were desolate, bare, faceless. It suited her mood exactly.

The Esplanade was full of government workers arriving at their ministries. She resented them, walking quickly from their parking lots, go-pads swinging from their shoulders in leather cases. They were all alive—to them, the day was new and things in the universe were being born again. For her, everything was frozen in that moment in the night when Paulo had died. Since then there was no time.

No future, no past, no cause. All and everything existed at once.

Her memory of the Wave only made her a little angry. She didn't have energy to be very angry since all her strength was focused on grief.

She stood in the most perfect spot in the city at the perfect moment. Straight down the grassy plaza she could see the sun rising between the two matched Towers of Congress, something so visceral and primitive and utterly beautiful that she could not fail to be moved. In September there would be elections again. Uncle Victor had agreed, and it had been announced. But even this victory only touched her with more pain. The world should not be trying to become, just when someone she cared about had died. When she had killed him.

Deliberately Zaide Soledad turned her back on the sunrise and walked instead to the bus terminal. She remembered the bus she had to take, had gone on it enough times to feel confident. This was no longer alien territory but merely one more insult to be endured, one more smile that hurt because there should be no smiles.

She avoided looking at anyone on the bus. Instead she watched out the windows as they took the Exio Rodoviario Sul past the trashed lawns and hedges that framed the uniform superquadras of Brasilia.

Seven-thirteen showed no signs of life. From the eager busyness of the Esplanade, ready to get up and produce the new Brazil, this part of town was still sleeping off the overindulgence of the night. The barzinho was closed and the fairy lights were off. The usual complement of young men and underage whores who stood guard over the staircase entrances of the buildings were all gone now. After a serious night of business they needed their morning's rest.

For a moment Zaide stood in the middle of the square, confused. All the buildings looked alike, and in the daylight they looked far worse than she had realized. Nighttime had cast a glamour over them, *pinga* and good friends and stories making the square a warm and welcoming place to be. Now she saw how many windows were broken, how many *guaraná* bottles were piled up over what had once been lawn but was now only a few ragged blades of brown grass in a scuffed red desert.

She walked around the buildings twice before she thought she recognized the right one. To make certain, she walked under the pilings. Deep in the center she could see lights strung around the massive pillars. She came out into the sunlight and ascended the stairs.

There had once been a security lock on the building, but the door opened at her touch. To the left, she remembered, down maybe two doors. She recognized the writing and tried the knob to what she thought was the Bakunin headquarters.

She had done this before. And last time it was Paulo who had stood behind the door with the crossbow pistol aimed at her ribs. For a moment she thought crazily that he was probably inside, that everything else had been some hideous joke and once she opened the door he would jump forward and scare her and scream "Surprise!" And then everyone would laugh. She believed that as she tried to open the door.

It was off the hinges, but wedged firmly into the opening. She could not move it. She pounded on the heavy steel.

"Paulo?" a voice yelled sleepily from inside.

"No, it's Zaide, let me in," she demanded.

There was no response. Zaide waited. She was certain whoever had answered her had gone back to sleep. Then Steel was standing there in loose striped *capoeira* pants, yawning. She could see his entire upper body was badly bruised. Julio Simon or one of the guards, for fun probably, had done a thorough job in the short time he had been a guest of the fazenda field house.

He didn't let her in to the office. "Where's Paulo?" he demanded.

Zaide looked at the linoleum tile on the corridor floor. "He's dead," she said very quietly. "Julio Simon used highwire on him, and he had secondaries, you know. Can I come in?"

Steel scowled. "Are you playing decoy again?" He almost spat the words.

Zaide turned heavily to leave. She felt as if the last shred of rationality she had clung to through these hours had become insubstantial and was dissolving. There was nothing at all left. She waited only to stop being, to stop hurting.

"Wait a minute, she got us out of there." A voice came from behind Steel. It was Nem Brito. "I think she deserves to come in at least."

Zaide didn't move until Nem Brito came out and fetched her inside. He held her arm to guide her and settled her in the corner. Then he propped a warm pillow behind her back and tucked a thin sleeping bag around her legs. "You look like you haven't had any sleep at all," he said.

She shook her head.

"I'd rather you went up and told Francisco about this," Steel said emphatically. "That sadist could be following her again. And how do we know she didn't mean to lead him here in the first place?"

Zaide raised her head from her knees. "I think the phrines he gave me had a tracer," she said mechanically. "I dumped them. All. Besides if he wanted to, they know where this place is now anyway. You probably shouldn't have come back here."

"Are you saying he doesn't want us?" Nem Brito asked mildly.

Zaide shrugged. "He would most likely wait until you

thought you were safe and then attack," she said flatly. "Staying here for any time isn't a good idea."

"Upstairs, then," Nem Brito suggested.

Steel shook his head as if Nem Brito were a less than bright schoolboy.

"Where, then?" Nem Brito asked.

Steel made a face.

"I'm taking her upstairs," Nem Brito announced firmly. "I don't care if you like it or not. And I don't think it'll matter too much anyway."

Zaide heard the words, but they registered only dimly on her consciousness. She was tired and the pillow behind her back felt good. The sleeping bag around her legs was soft and just warm enough to make her realize how tired she was. She had not expected anything to feel so comforting. Not that she thought she could sleep, but it would be nice to lie down and rest for a while. Not because it was possible, even for a second, to forget, but because the body had its own needs.

Her own body felt like a thing apart, a pet, and she resented the fact that she had to give in to its demands. She wanted to ignore it the way she always had, and go on. But her back protested, her legs refused to move. Her head felt stuffed with packing straw, and she was thinking about as effectively.

So she was too tired to protest when Nem Brito dragged her up by the arm. It made her shoulder sore. Then he and Steel pushed her out of the little office with the hideous green carpet, and back out into the hall.

They went to the end of the hallway and took the fire stairs up. The concrete walls were decorated with spray-painted slogans and pictograms that were hard to distinguish in the dull red light. The stairwell was lit only by red bulbs all the way up, and the eerie glow they cast made it hard to remember that outside it was bright daylight.

They went up and up and up. Zaide's legs felt heavy. She heard rustling on the floors above them and once caught a glimpse of a moving shadow and a door whispering shut, but she didn't see any people. She could feel the whole building around her watching, passing messages to each other so that by the time she reached the top floor everyone would know. But they were staying out of her sight, out of her way.

"At least there aren't any cannibals out now," Steel said, trying to raise general morale.

Nem Brito ignored him. Zaide had to concentrate on the climbing. Her thighs were trembling with the strain and she was breathing hard.

"*Vertie bitch,*" Steel whispered under his breath.

Zaide was so exhausted that she didn't notice. Or didn't realize that she was the person he was talking about. Or just didn't care.

Zaide guessed they were going to the top floor. She knew that the residential buildings were never more than six sto ries high. Still, that did not make the climb any less interminable.

When they finally reached the sixth floor, she found the hallway was no brighter than the stairs. Only red lights glowed in the fixtures, those that still had any lights at all. There weren't many. There was some writing on the walls here, too, but there wasn't enough light to read it or to make out the pictures clearly. They just blended in with the shadows.

She was breathing heavily, so it was hard to talk. But she couldn't help but gasp out, "Why red?" to Nem Brito.

He looked at her like he understood. "First people stole the white bulbs for their apartments. And then no one had jobs or got up in the morning. Anyway, the red makes it easier to adjust when you come in from the night or just wake up. You can see an enemy faster, you aren't blind. So whoever needs that much protection comes up with the dinheiro on each floor. It's turned out to be a good warning system, too. Anyone coming in with a flashlight, we know it's an enemy and we can see him coming from far away.

And would you believe, they still haven't learned to keep the light down."

Steel came up behind them both and laughed, shrill and superior. "But for me, you see, it doesn't matter at all," he informed them. "I got some super eyes when I went Changeling. It's about the only mod that's worth anything anymore. I did get some good eyes. I see best in infrared anyway, so these give the ones like me a real advantage."

Zaide ignored the uneducated construction and nodded, then turned to Nem Brito. "How many half-Changelings like him are there?" she asked softly, mostly to keep Nem Brito on her side and talking. To support him against Steel. Just like the fazenda.

"None of the others could be like him," Nem Brito whispered to her.

"More than people want to believe," Steel said, answering her question, and the bitterness came clearly through his tone. "Maybe about half a million walking around with pre-riot secondaries. Maybe about a quarter of those went the full way and Changed. The government Changed me. I got the eyes and the speed and all the hormone treatments young enough, too. I thought it was all set, I was going to be part of the Protection Teams. You remember them? It was a long time ago."

It wasn't so long ago, and Zaide remembered very clearly. The Protection Teams had replaced the police for a while, until the new dictatorship decided they were too dangerous and cut the whole lot of them. Secretly Zaide thought that maybe they really had been too dangerous, and besides mechs could do the job better.

Well, at least that job, she amended mentally. For no reason at all, she thought of Bebe in the kitchen. No one had ever managed to make a mech that replaced a real human cook. But that was an art, not merely a function.

They stopped suddenly in front of a door. Nem Brito knocked sharply, quickly, and paced until the door opened.

The woman facing them looked like one of the statues of a

martyred saint. Her hair was thick and silver-blond and fell over her shoulders like a veil. Her face had the lines of someone who had known pain and had made her peace with it. But her large, infinitely blue eyes were eternally drowned in the past.

Francisco Pope, Zaide thought, took after his mother. Except that she was soft and had surrendered, and he was unyielding. To Zaide, through her exhaustion, they looked like the same thing. Both Francisco and his mother were victims, she thought. The difference was that this woman knew it and refused to face it.

"Dona Elena, this is Zaide Soledad, a friend of ours." Nem Brito made the introduction that Steel disdained.

"We have to talk to Francisco, it's important," Steel said.

Dona Elena turned toward Zaide and smiled. "Would you like something to drink, a cafézinho perhaps?" the woman asked with the graciousness of a bygone age. "The boys are so rude, I am sorry you have to see them like this, forgetting their manners. Francisco is asleep. You are welcome to wait for him here."

Zaide accepted the strong coffee and the invitation into the living room. There was a sofa and two chairs that were scarred and worn, the pale blue and ivory damask upholstery threadbare and stained, but Zaide recognized that they had once been of fine quality. They contrasted strongly with a green painted door on cinder blocks that served as a coffee-table and had likewise been painted in kindergarten-bright colors.

Zaide settled on the edge of the sofa and crossed her ankles the way Sonia Leah always did. She sipped the coffee in silence until Francisco entered.

He looked as if he'd just been dragged out of bed. He wore a rumpled soccer team T-shirt and sweat pants, and his expression was faintly disoriented. But mostly Zaide was shocked by his eyes. For the first time, their clear crystal blue did not make her think of ice or steel. He looked warm, human, and hurt.

"Is it true about Paulo?" he asked.

She set the coffee cup on the table and nodded. "I tried," she said. "It was too late. But I promised him . . ." And then she felt the tears again and was surprised. She thought that she had none left, that she had cried all the tears in the world the night before.

Francisco took her hand very gently, and she saw her misery on his face. "What did you promise?" he asked softly.

"Revenge," she said. "It's not good enough, but it was the only thing left." Then she caught her breath. "I didn't come here to get your help or even your approval. I came here because I couldn't stay with them, and to warn you. Julio Simon knows where the office is, and even though he killed Paulo, he is still humiliated because the rest of you got away. It puts him in a very bad position."

"I have to go out for a while," he told her. "You look exhausted. Why don't you stay here and sleep? You should be safe enough here. My mother will look after you. We'll talk later."

He was very gentle with her as he showed her to the dark room he and Paulo had shared. He didn't turn on the light, but groped through a pile of clothes at the end of one of the beds for a black shirt and jeans. He picked up a pair of heavy boots from under the pile, and took the painted and feathered coat from off the hook inside the door.

"That one was Paulo's," he told her, indicating the far bed. "But you're welcome to either. I'll be gone for a while."

Zaide waited until he had closed the door quietly behind him before she lay on the bed he had pointed at as Paulo's. She was certain that she wouldn't be able to sleep, that the dull throbbing that wouldn't go away would lock her in consciousness. But the exhaustion overcame her and she collapsed.

Twenty-two

NEM Brito and Steel were waiting in the kitchen when Francisco emerged from the bathroom, now dressed for the day. He carried the painted coat slung over one shoulder.

"So what do we do now?" Nem Brito asked. "Where are we going to go now?"

Francisco looked at him curiously. "Paulo's dead," he said, rolling the words through his mouth, tasting them, hearing them as if they were strange and distant. "Paulo Sylvia is dead. And we don't have his body. We can't even bury him properly."

"Have some coffee," Steel said, turning around to offer Francisco a cup that had been sitting next to the stove. "Dona Elena is in the living room. I don't think she knows who we are anymore."

Francisco sipped the coffee. It was lukewarm and bitter, overbrewed. And there was no sugar in it. But he knew that it would at least get him awake, although he didn't want to be awake. He wanted this to be a dream and when he woke up Paulo would be alive, tossing in the bed across from his.

He gulped the coffee and forced himself to acknowledge reality. If this were a dream, then the coffee wouldn't be so bad. So Paulo was dead. Paulo had been his brother, his mirror for his whole life. Somehow Francisco felt as if he were dead, too, icy cold and without volition.

"Let's go," Steel said, taking the empty cup and putting it in the sink. "Let's get out of here."

"Where?" Nem Brito asked bitterly.

Steel shook his head. "The cemetery. Where else?"

They went down without saying goodbye to Dona Elena. The cemetery for the southern half of the city was close, but they took the powerbikes anyway. They went out to the back road between 713 and 913 and drove through the hospital sector into the spiral-shaped cemetery.

Francisco wondered if the conch spiral of the cemetery reflected the ancient Indian patterns for a reason. Even if Niemeyer believed he designed only for the future, he could not avoid the archetypes of the subconscious racial past. Bitterness filled Francisco that he could even think that way. He thought too much like a university student, that was the problem. He read too much, thought too much.

That had been Paulo's problem, too, he thought. They hadn't been able to stop thinking, to simply blend into the environment and live by its laws. Steel had done it, he thought, and Nem Brito. But he and Paulo had never been able to excise that part of themselves that refused to simply accept reality. That intelligence had never let him rest and had fueled Paolo's incessant rage.

He hardly noticed where they were among the graves. Nem Brito had led them into an older portion of the cemetery. There was supposed to be a cemetery on the northern side of the city as well, but it was still just a barren field, not yet in use. So Francisco was faintly pleased by the fact that the dead of Brasilia all lay together, rich and poor, fazenda and favela alike. Well, maybe not the fazenda families. They had their own private burial crypts on their own land. But only here was the democracy that the designers of the city had intended.

He didn't want to talk to Nem Brito or Steel. They were poor substitutes for his friend who was closer than a brother. Instead he wandered through the grave markers looking at the names and dates and wondering who these people had been in life.

Antonio Alejandro Vargas Machado, April 4, 1971–July

17, 2026, Beloved husband and father. Ana Luz de Oliveira Gonzaga, Sept. 21, 1991–Jan. 12, 1998, Blessed Virgin protect her. Luis Amilton Creuza Schwann, August 9, 1959–March 14, 2021.

None of them had lived to be old. He wondered what Paulo's stone would look like, just his name and the date. Twenty-two years old, Paulo wouldn't be out of place in this cemetery where far too may people were much too young.

How many people had he known who had died very young? There was Paulo and his whole family, and Francisco thought maybe he had been luckier to see them all dead than like Dona Elena. But a lot of people had died then during the disturbances, two of his teachers and his cousin Marcelo. It hadn't been a normal time, if any time was normal. Somehow, random, violent death at the hands of the terror squads and the Forestation Police, and later the peacekeeping forces, seemed more acceptable than in other times. Maybe because it was so common. Or maybe because it had all been so unreal.

It was the people who had died during the quiet times that haunted his memory now. There had been Davi Mansur, who had drowned in the lake the summer they had been ten. He hadn't thought about it at the time; he had dived in after Davi and tried to bring him in, but he hadn't been a good enough swimmer and Davi had been thrashing hard in the water. Paulo had run to get a lifeguard, but by the time an adult came to help, it was too late. Davi had been in their class, had lived upstairs from Paulo when they had all been middle class and lived in the northern part of the city.

Then there had been Humberto Lino and Birgitte Vermond, who had died of highwire in the room that had become the Bakunin office. Francisco had helped to pull their bodies out of there and send them decently to the cemetery. Humberto had been seventeen and Birgitte had been fifteen and pregnant. He had known both of them vaguely; Paulo had bought phrines from Humberto once. They hadn't been very good quality, but Laurindo had been off somewhere at the time. Paulo had slept with Birgitte before she had begun doing highwire every day, but then Paulo had slept with half the females in the superquadra, so maybe it didn't quite count.

Only Paulo had been terribly upset about their deaths. He had also been part of the group who helped bring them out of the stinking room, which had no plumbing, and lay them out decently. Francisco had been distant and saddened by it. The whole thing had made him think of important questions and philosophy. But Paulo had gone completely white and hadn't talked at all, not even when Francisco tried.

That night Steel had loaned Paulo enough dinheiro from his winnings to get falling down drunk, and Paulo had babbled through the early morning while Francisco had tried to sleep. He wondered now what Paulo had been trying to say and if he should have stayed up to listen.

He was so engrossed in his memories that he didn't hear Steel behind him. "What are we going to do with her?" Steel asked, and Francisco was so startled that he wheeled around and swung wildly. The momentum was too strong—he couldn't pull the punch. But Steel dropped gracefully under his blow in a move that Francisco recognized as *capoeira*. Steel did not get up; he simply sat down and crossed his legs and refused to look at Francisco.

Francisco stepped back, then sat down on the grass next to him. "I'm pretty jumpy," he admitted. "You shouldn't have startled me."

Steel shrugged. "It doesn't matter. I just want to know what we're going to do about Zaide? I know you're jumpy and you're probably not ready to make any decisions yet, but I think she could be a plant and I don't trust her. I think we ought to ditch her as soon as we can. I'm not even sure I liked taking her up to your place. I didn't think it was a good idea for her to know where your family is. But Nem Brito insisted and had already started and you know how soft he is on girls."

Francisco heard the words and what was behind the words. "You don't like her, do you? You never did."

"Why should I?" Steel asked. "She's from the other side of the lake, a vertie at least. You can't trust them. You can hardly talk to them. So far as I could see, she was just one more of Paulo's girls."

"You resented his girls," Francisco said softly.

"So did you," Steel pointed out, and Francisco winced internally as he recognized that it was true.

He sat without speaking, staring at the headstones without seeing the names and dates that marched along in silent rows. He wondered if they would recover the body, if in the next section of graves there would be a plain stone that read *Paulo Teodore Ramos Sylvia, September 7, 2006 July 24, 2028*

But Steel was there, waiting. Francisco could feel the nervous energy radiating from him, forcing his attention. It took him a moment to orient himself, to remember what they were talking about. Paulo's latest girlfriend, yes. "I think she could help us a great deal," Francisco said carefully. "And I'm fairly certain she isn't a vertie."

"You don't know, you can't be sure," Steel argued stubbornly. "And what if she's the one who led the Vielho-Markowicz to us in the first place? You can't think they just showed up out of nowhere."

Francisco shook his head. "If she was followed or if she led them, those are two very different things. And if she thinks she knows how they were able to follow her, and managed to give them the slip this time, then it's okay, I think. At least we should give her the benefit of the doubt, since she did manage to break us out of that prison in the first place."

"But she didn't break Paulo out and now he's dead," Steel protested. "And maybe that's the way they meant it all along."

"You, my friend, are paranoid," Francisco said.

"And I am still alive and a lot of other people aren't," Steel argued.

"Agreed," Francisco gave him. "But if what I think is true, then this Zaide could be very useful to us. For a plan I have."

"You always have plans," Steel groused. "You never tell them to me, only Paulo. Well, Paulo is dead, and if you think you can run everything alone, then you're crazy. Aluizio is dead, Dr. Joao is dead, but I intend to survive. That's what I want, Francisco Pope, I want to survive. I don't want some stranger staring at my tombstone and wondering why I died so young."

He waited for a reply, but when Francisco just kept on gazing at the headstones, Steel took a deep breath and plunged ahead. "And the Jaguars are going to demand blood, you know that, and they're going to hold us responsible. And the Serps already hate us. It's falling apart, Francisco. We had a dream, but we never really had a chance and now it's all falling apart. Because of this girl."

"And you want out before the whole thing crashes down," Francisco said.

"Yes."

"Then go. Disappear. Don't ever bother me again." Francisco dismissed him.

"Wait a minute," Steel protested. "You're not cutting me out like that. I won't permit it. Paulo wouldn't do it if he were alive. We'd yell, we'd fight, but he wouldn't just tell me to walk away."

Francisco was silent. A cortege came around the spiral road, and he could almost pretend that it was Paulo's funeral, which he would never see. Even though the cars were old and expensive and the people behaved with the elegance of the Southern Lake Mansion District, Francisco felt a sudden companionship. They were grieving. So was he.

So was Steel. Francisco knew enough to understand it. He didn't know how to make anything else work. Steel was right, the Jaguars would be out for blood or payment and the Serps hated them on sight.

All his dreams of pulling together the favela tribes and taking the streets were just that, dreams. And they always had been, he realized. The fantasies of an angry, hurt child.

But Francisco Pope had studied history and he remembered what he had learned. Most revolutions failed. There was a great deal of blood and rhetoric and then very soon everything was all the same again. His first instinct had been right, he had to get where the real power was and that was not on the streets.

He had to get into a position of power. To someplace where he could effect changes. He had to get into the Wave. He had known that for a long time. And he suspected very strongly that Zaide was a Waverider. She knew too much, she was in the right place. And if she was willing to help them, then maybe there was a chance.

"Just trust me," Francisco said heavily as Steel paced behind him. "Just for a little while, trust me. Or leave. It's entirely up to you. But one thing I can't do is be Paulo, and I can't bring him back."

South 109 seemed busier than usual, Francisco thought. There seemed to be more vendors out with tables of merchandise and there were lines at the more popular eating places. The crowd of loiterers also seemed a little thicker than he had expected. Normally he could scan everyone in the superquadra as he purchased a strawberry ice cream, but today there were layers and layers of people and they shifted constantly.

Not that he cared about seeing most of them. He was looking for one person in particular, a snake-Changeling phrine dealer. And he had dinheiro.

"Pretty busy today, isn't it?" He made petty conversation with the ice-cream vendor.

"Everyone wants to see the showdown," the vendor replied chattily. "Palmeiras against Flamengo. That's all anyone here has been talking about since Palmeiras made the finals. It's been nearly ten years since they've made the national standings and everyone wants to watch. The big-screen bars are all packed, I couldn't even get inside."

"What showdown, my friend?" Francisco asked. "I didn't know anything was supposed to happen here."

The vendor smiled broadly. He was missing an incisor and three bottom teeth.

"I can't believe that you aren't following the national championship soccer match! Those clubs have been rivals since before there was a Brasilia. If you're with us, then don't go into the World Cup bar—that place is packed with *them*. It should be over soon, actually. I'm waiting to hear the final score. I've got a lot of money riding in the soccer lottery this week."

"You're supporting the Palmeiras?" Francisco asked casually, noting the miniature green and white club flag fixed to the edge of the cart.

The ice-cream vendor smiled broadly and nodded. "But I couldn't get tickets today—it's the national championship match and they've been sold out for weeks. My son-in-law was going to take me, but someone broke into his house and robbed him. All my daughter's jewelry, their cash, and the tickets. And you know, they were upset about the tickets most." The man paused for a moment and stared at Francisco carefully. "You look familiar."

Francisco was surprised. Perhaps the vendor had seen him before—he often came down here—but it was strange to be recognized that way.

After some hesitation, the vendor said, "I know, you look a little like the posters that are around. Of course, no one would mistake you for the kidnapper, I'm sure. In the picture he doesn't have red hair, so there couldn't be any mistake. But there is a resemblance, I have to say."

"Posters?" Francisco demanded sharply. "What posters?"

"They're all over the place," the man answered disinterestedly. "They say that some company is looking for three prisoners who broke out and kidnapped some fazenda girl. There's pictures up on the trees and a reward."

Francisco paid for his ice cream and thanked the man before slipping into the crowd. Now he wasn't just looking for Laurindo. He was also looking for the poster.

He found one pasted to one of the cement pilings of a residential building. It was high-quality, and the reproduction was excellent. Nem Brito and Steel stared out into the crowd. They were unmistakable. He had been a little more fortunate. The poster had his name written large, but the picture was fuzzy and not in color.

He had to get out of there. His face was in front of every one, with a reward offered for his capture. He wondered why no one had accused him and hauled him off already. Maybe, he prayed, it was his coloring. Many people recognized his bright red hair but not his features. Maybe, just maybe . . .

He felt naked and vulnerable. He should turn and hide, get his powerbike out of the box and leave. Immediately. But he had to at least see what the rest of the poster said. He pulled out his handkerchief and pressed it over his face as if he had a bad cold and was about to cough. For verisimilitude, he made a few coughing sounds into the soft cotton. Then, his face as masked as he could manage, he turned his attention back to the poster.

Below their pictures was a paragraph of text and then three other pictures, as if they had been matched. The paragraph described the hunted men as murderers and kidnappers, who had abducted a young girl from the fazenda and murdered her companion. Her family was sick with grief, and they wanted her back. Any information as to her whereabouts or the apprehension of the kidnappers would be rewarded generously.

Then there were the photos. The first was a picture of the dead Jaguars on the Belo Horizonte road. That one had a clear shot of a buzzard picking out Dr. Joao's too-green eye. It looked almost posed. It was identified only as an incident in which the suspects were thought to have begun their killing spree.

Next to that was a picture of Zaide Soledad. It was a few years old and she looked very young. The school uniform she wore made her look gawky and adolescent and completely innocent. And in the next picture, identified as her companion, was Paulo—tortured and dead. The fury raced through Francisco. It was bad enough to have see this abomination. But to be accused of doing that, and to his best friend, it was unthinkable.

He tried to tear the poster off the concrete pillar, but it had been freshly secured and the edges were firm. And it was still the middle of dry winter, no rain to soak the offending page free.

In the background he heard a deep, hoarse roar emanating from the World Cup bar. One of the teams must have scored a goal.

"I suggest you leave here before someone recognizes you," a voice hissed softly in his ear. "The reward is ten thousand centavos, and even I would be tempted to turn you in."

Francisco turned slowly. It was Laurindo. Trust the dealer to find him when he had cash ready to go.

"Fine. You're the one I was looking for anyway. I need phrines and then we're out of here," Francisco said, his voice muffled by the handkerchief.

He began to walk briskly toward where his powerbike was locked. Never one to lose a sale, Laurindo followed him.

"You have dinheiro?" he asked quickly. "I can't take credit."

"Yes," Francisco replied.

"I've got horseshoes and orchid and Amazon Smash at a good price," Laurindo said, panting as he gave his spiel and tried to keep up with Francisco. "Very clean."

"I want the stuff the Waveriders use to regulate the

implants—I don't know what it's called," Francisco interrupted him. "And I want it lab quality."

"That'll cost you premium," Laurindo said.

"I'll pay. No problem." Francisco smiled at him. "Just get me the stuff."

"Where?" Laurindo asked.

Francisco smiled. "Be at the barzinho in 713 tonight, late. I'll send someone I can trust, someone whose face isn't plastered all over town." Francisco thought he detected a shadow of disappointment in Laurindo's expression. He tried to tell himself that he couldn't read the face of a snake-Change anyway, that his eyes had been built to be narrow and cold, that his nostrils always flared. It didn't matter. He didn't trust Laurindo now. He didn't know if Laurindo planned to betray him, but he couldn't take the chance that he might.

"What about some earnest money?" Laurindo asked as Francisco straddled the bike and strapped on his helmet.

Francisco thought about it. Given Laurindo's behavior, he had no choice but to cancel the deal, blow off the meeting. By late tonight he intended to be far away from Brasilia, on the road to Recife or Belo Horizonte, where there were no posters with his face all over town. But it probably wasn't a good idea to let Laurindo know that. And though they'd never done business like that before, this time he reached into his pocket and took out a handful of cash.

"Earnest enough for you?" he asked.

Laurindo thumbed through the bills and nodded. "Tonight at the barzinho. I'll be there."

As Francisco rode away, he heard another groan and then a cheer. Down at the corner he saw a couple of people in green and white shirts and hats waving little club flags. The Palmeiras of São Paulo in their green and whites had won the national championship for the first time in over twenty years.

On a powerbike it should have taken no more than ten minutes to be home, but the streets were crowded with celebrating soccer fans cavorting in the streets like it was Carnival. Streamers flew and large banners hung out the windows of several large buildings. Francisco remembered the last time he had thought about soccer, the year that the Brazilian team had been disqualified from the World Cup. He and Paulo had still been living in the northern sector then. They had strung black paper streamers all over their school. Downtown in the commercial sector even the fazenda headquarters had been draped in mourning, long black ribbons trailing from the windows. He hadn't noticed any soccer games much since then.

It took him more than half an hour to get back to 713. Even here the central area of the superquadra was full of men wearing Palmeiras green and white and drinking toasts to all the clubs in the league, those who lost as well as those who won. For if they had not lost against the favored team, then they might have won later on and thus take away this lovely victory. Francisco did not take off the helmet until he entered his mother's apartment.

Even six stories above the street he could hear the drunken celebration going on below. The apartment was quiet. Steel and Nem Brito were playing cards in the kitchen. Dona Elena sat in the living room staring at the blank wall, an open Bible in her lap. Her fingers twitched spasmodically across the page, but she was not reading. She wasn't even really there.

He wondered where Zaide was as he told Steel and Nem Brito about the posters and the reward. "They're everywhere," Francisco said finally. "We'd have to leave the Mato Grosso entirely," he said, musing. "They must have posted the satellite cities too."

"We could go to Rio," Steel said, and there was pleasure in his face. "We could live out on the beach, and the cariocas are all beautiful. We could go to the clubs every night and in the day we would lie out on the warm sand and drink *batidas* and *guaraña* and tease the tourists."

Nem Brito shook his head sadly. "You know what they do

to people who live on the beach?" he asked. "The verties get in a hunting vert and go shooting the *pivetes* on the beach for fun. It's quite a problem for the snatchers; they're trying to get it stopped, but they haven't had a whole lot of luck so far." Nem Brito looked down at his hands. He was a carioca and the soft accent had blurred but never been completely erased.

"I know someplace we can go," Zaide said, breaking into the conversation.

Francisco wheeled around. He hadn't heard her come in. She stood in the hallway wrapped in one of Dona Elena's fine silk and lace nightgowns. Her dark hair fell over half her face and bruised sleepy eyes. Suddenly Francisco saw her, not the fazenda Waverider he could use or some symbol of the Forestation Acts. She had fought hard and lost a lot and she was tired. But in her face he read the strength to go back to the battle. It had cost her a great deal and it would cost more, and she was willing to pay.

For the first time he respected her, understood what it was that had drawn Paulo. There was a fire in her that matched his, and pride. He found himself smiling at her and meaning it for the first time.

"Do I have to explain the situation, or did you hear me?" Francisco asked.

"In this place it would have been hard not to hear you," she replied. "Still. I know someplace we could go very easily and no one would ever look for you there."

Francisco looked at her. Nem Brito and even Steel were waiting.

"The fazenda," she said simply. "All we have to do is get over to the Northern Commercial District. I've got a vert there."

Steel rolled his eyes. "Great. And what do we do when we arrive at the fazenda? Walk into the big house and shake hands with your cousins?"

"Maybe that wouldn't be such a bad idea," Zaide threw back in his face. "But that wasn't the way I had it laid out, actually. What I planned was to place you either in the village, or in the attic. You wouldn't believe what there is in the attic at the big house. You could live there forever."

"And we just wait until you give the word? Great," Francisco protested.

Zaide shrugged. "The vert has enough fuel to get us to Rio or Belo Horizonte, if you like. Maybe we could get to São Paulo from there. But I thought you wanted to change things; I thought you wanted to challenge the Forestation Acts and the fazenda families. I didn't think you wanted to run." She flung the words in their faces.

"You don't risk anything," Steel said, his tone menacing and low. "You could even turn us over and collect the reward yourself. That would be great publicity, wouldn't it? Kidnap victim escapes and captures her kidnappers. It would make the families look like gods."

Zaide laughed. "You know, I'm glad you're not a cousin. You'd be worse than Julio Simon." She hesitated while Steel blinked and regained his composure. "You think just like he does—that's what he'd do and what he expects. And if it were just bottom line, I would do it, too. It would gain me some more respect in the family and I could depose him, get him sent to Belém for good. And there isn't much damage he could do from there."

She bit her lip and shook her head as if trying to shake off a bad dream. "But then what about Paulo? What about all of us?" She dropped her voice and her tone became suggestive. "I could give you all the power you ever wanted. It's easy to be radical when you don't have any power. What would you do if you had the resources of the Vielho-Markowicz? Or if you were in the Wave? Or if we backed one of you to run for Congress?"

Desire greater than anything he had ever imagined flared through Francisco Pope. He had always known that the Wave was the key, and the longing for it had destroyed Paulo. Now the temptation was beyond his ability to deny. "How?" he asked, and his voice was hoarse with longing.

"The operations are always done at the fazenda infirmary, which is a few kilometers from the big house in its own clearing. I think you could stay there in any case. No one is going to find you there, and the staff is not particularly concerned with family politics. If we ask them to look after someone, they do. The infirmary is generally considered off-limits in family wars." This time her smile was hard and glittering. "As for the Wave, I don't know. I can't promise. Only that the possibility exists. Maybe. If I play everything right."

"But you think you can get us out of the city and hide us in your infirmary, under Julio Simon's nose?" Francisco asked again. "That's twisted. It appeals to me."

Zaide smiled. "The only problem is getting out of here. We have to get to the Northern Commercial District. From there it's no problem. But if someone down in the street recognizes us and turns us in, we're in trouble. If Julio Simon gets us into his private little enclave, the only thing we could hope for would be a fast death."

The roar from the street was the only sound breaking the silence. Outside and well down, the words of the soccer anthem were indistinct but the tune was unmistakable. Francisco heard it and suddenly everything connected. "I can get us out of here," he said.

"How?" Nem Brito asked.

This time it was Francisco's turn. "Trust me," he told them. "Just trust me." His eyes met Zaide Soledad's, and they entered into an agreement that was no less binding for not being spoken.

Twenty-three

F INDING two green shirts and two white ones had not been difficult. A green marker had made the shirt a cheap soccer club advertisement, but that was not so unusual. People too poor to buy club shirts often made their own.

Zaide gave Steel enough dinheiro to buy club caps for all of them. His face was on the poster, but a mascot mask took care of that easily enough. He returned with the caps, a couple of flags, some streamers and noisemakers and another mask.

Dona Elena came into the kitchen and watched them put on the soccer club colors. "You know, when I was very young we used Carnival paints and did designs on our faces and hands, too," she said in a faraway voice. "And I used to make matching designs for your father and me. One year I made both of us into jaguars. It was very beautiful but we didn't win the prize. It was a very good prize that year, a new home audio system. But we didn't win."

Francisco's eyes met Zaide's. Fate had guided his mother into the kitchen for a reason. Francisco walked up and took his mother's hands. "Mama, do you still have the Carnival makeup crayons? Could you do that to us? Make us up the way you did in the past?"

Dona Elena giggled like a young girl and dashed out of the kitchen. She returned barely seconds later with a pack of greasepaint crayons in every brilliant color imaginable, including metallic gold and silver. She lit a cigarette and it dangled from her hand as she worked on them. Zaide was certain it was going to fall or burn down to her fingers, but somehow Dona Elena always managed to rescue it without looking. She was too busy with their faces.

The green paint-stick had been untouched when she opened the pack. First she did Francisco, painting lines horizontally across his eyes and cheekbones. Then she wrote the club name on his forehead. He looked completely absurd. His features were undistinguishable. Nem Brito she did with three downstrokes from the eyes to the chin on each side, in green, and then used the metallic silver to make a mask that completely distorted the shape of his eyes.

She motioned to Steel to come over.

"No," he said. "I hate that stuff. It feels bad. I'll wear the mask. I paid for it anyway."

Dona Elena looked slightly perturbed. Zaide forestalled any emotional scene by sitting down in front of the older woman. Dona Elena studied her face carefully. "I want to make you look pretty, like Iemanja."

After serious consideration, Dona Elena started painting out Zaide's entire face in white, including her eyebrows. She then applied the green around her eyes and on her lips, like exaggerated movie makeup. She painted thin, high brows on Zaide's now clown-white forehead. The effect was eerie and startling, but also raggedly seductive. "Go look," Dona Elena said when she was finished.

Zaide went to the small bathroom and looked in the chipped mirror. She looked like something dead, like a picture she had seen once of the *candomble* gods. She looked like she had thought of herself in the Wave.

There wasn't time for much speculation. Francisco rapped loudly on the door. "Come on, twilight is the best time to go. . . ."

And he was right, she knew. When the light was changing rapidly it was hard for people to see at all well. They had about a fifteen-minute window of twilight before it became dark enough for the street lights to come on. The harsh artificial glare would pick them out quickly in the crowd. They grabbed noisemakers and started the long climb down to the street.

Below it was like Carnival. There were empty bottles stacked against the pilings of the building. Although it was far too early, the barzinho was open. No way the owner would pass up the profits to be made today. And his take must be good. Everyone was standing around with a glass in his hand, drinking toasts and healths and falling down dead drunk in the dry red dust.

No one noticed them. More important, here surrounded by Bakunin's neighbors, no one recognized them. People called out and invited them to join in a drink, a toast, a victory song but it was just a politeness to strangers. The four of them blew their noisemakers and strolled through the crowd as if they owned it.

It took nearly an hour even with the powerbikes to get through the city. Even though the streets were designed for ground flow and there was never a traffic jam for normal reasons, the soccer fever was highly abnormal. The last game of the season didn't always end in this kind of joyous frenzy. There was the year that the Rio club had swept all the awards and no one in Brasilia cared. There was the year the São Paulo team took the title when they hadn't won anything since the last century. And there was the year the team from Belém lost and their supporters rioted in the streets. It had been nearly as bad as when the Forestation Acts went through. Martial law had been declared and half the Gilberto Salomao was looted before troops brought the disgruntled fans under control.

But this time it was a happy win for the underdog Palmeiras, a cause of celebration and good will. And so even on powerbikes they couldn't ignore the shouted invitations to drink or taste some candy or grilled beef and relive the best moments of the game. Even on the Esplanade and into the Northern Commercial District the street party was going strong. They leaned on the bikes' horns for protective coloring as motorized fans played a cacophony in honor of victory that would have horrified the Roman emperors who had begun the practice. Green and white confetti made the black pavement festive, while the parties in various superquadras could be heard past the lawns and hedges that shielded them from the street.

It was already full dark by the time they arrived at the Vielho-Markowicz building in the commercial district. The front doors were locked and the place was deserted. No doubt everyone had left the moment they could join the merrymaking.

Zaide pressed her palm against the night lock, and the doors swung open immediately. Lights came on, illuminating deserted corridors and offices secured for the night. She went behind the deserted reception desk, found the garage line, and requested a comfortable passenger vert for herself and friends on voiceprint authorization.

Authorization came through immediately. A distant computerized voice informed her that her vehicle would be waiting for her in the priority circle on the roof. She signaled the others to follow her to the lift.

The vert was waiting for them, a sedate metallic graphite luxury model with white leather upholstery and full audio that was grinding out soccer chants at three-quarters volume.

"Change the music," Nem Brito groused.

Zaide smiled. "Bleakhouse," she said, and abruptly the soccer chants were replaced by harsh discord that reminded her too sharply of Paulo. She never would have heard this if he hadn't introduced her. Somehow the pain was new again.

She forced herself to open her eyes and start the ignition sequence. "Would you prefer full automatic?" the luxury vert asked her. It must be one of Uncle Victor's or Sonia Leah's orders, a machine that took care of such mundane functions such as getting home.

She nodded through the tears that threatened to fall. "Automatic, please," she managed to say before her throat closed up. The vert lifted. The pain closed around her like a warm cocoon and held her gently as the vert took her home.

It was not home. From the air the place seemed different, changed. The big house sitting white and solid in the middle of the carefully manicured lawn, the tennis courts and playing fields out to the back, the field house and garage and stables and other outbuildings hidden by flowering hedges that were newly trimmed, all of it was the same. And yet it wasn't. The house, though utterly familiar, seemed completely alien at the same time. It was as if her real home had been replaced during her absence. She knew that it was still the same, that it was she who had changed. She hesitated, and then keyed the manual controls.

"We're going to the village," she announced.

"What about the infirmary?" Nem Brito asked quickly.

"I don't trust it," she muttered. "I don't trust anything." She veered away through the trees over forested land, the fazenda proper. The canopy below was brilliant emerald, spotted bloodred where parrots roosted in the branches. And yet they, too, seemed wrong, as if the parrots she had always loved had died and been stuffed and set up in the branches.

The village was well away from the big house and separated from it by rough country. The growth here was so thick that even a machete wouldn't open more than a few meters a day, and that would all grow back almost overnight. The forest below was not just a collection of passive trees. It was an entity in itself, and the fazenda families were both its owners and its slaves.

Zaide brought the vert down outside of town, to a little parking area fenced off from the residential streets. They had to walk through the village, and Francisco had never seen anything like it. He had always lived in the city. This was like something out of a storybook, something that should not exist at all in the real world.

To Francisco, it looked more like the center of a prosperous satellite city than a village. The plaster houses were all enclosed by high walls painted pink and aquamarine and yellow. There was a church in the center of a paved plaza that had a tiled fountain and neat benches. Growth spilled over the high walls of the private dwellings, hinting at lush gardens and comfort beyond. There were street lights every three or four meters and the houses seemed well-lighted and prosperous, but there were very few people in the streets. Those few sat on the benches and chatted and smiled at the strangers, but never took their eyes off the children in the plaza playing pick-up soccer with the church door as a goal.

The streets and the houses were well-scrubbed, the children all seemed well-fed. There was an air of contentment in the village that eluded Francisco. He didn't trust it at all.

Zaide walked purposefully through the plaza, stopping to chat with some of the people briefly. One woman held up an embroidered shawl and Zaide admired it, then told some joke. The women on the bench laughed. Then she told them goodbye, kissed the older woman on both cheeks and moved on.

She led them down what looked to be the main street. There was a small market and bakery and a hardware-paint store. Across the street was an imposing cinema and what appeared from the outside to be a very respectable corner bar. No one emerged carrying glasses and there were no tables set up outside, but the windows had been recently washed. Through the plate glass Francisco saw a tray of snacks set out on the bar, slices of hard-cooked eggs with olives and sardines on bits of toast. He remembered that he hadn't eaten in a long time.

But Zaide didn't stop. The commercial street ended and there weren't as many lights as before. Zaide led the way through what seemed to be a maze. The narrow lanes twisted and ended suddenly, Francisco thought, unlike all the nice straight lines of the city. This entire village could fit into his supermanzana back home, but it would be frighteningly easy to get lost here.

"Where are we going?" he demanded sharply.

Zaide just shook her head. "We're almost there," she said, and then she led on. Two turns to the left and they entered a gate in a bright blue wall. The gate had been left ajar and Francisco, Nem Brito and Steel slipped through. Then Zaide bolted the heavy iron gate behind them.

The garden was dark, and from behind a second wall Francisco heard drumming. It was the call of the *candomble*, the ritual drumming that beat the heart of the earth, that called down the sacred trance of the gods. The scent of incense permeated the small yard. It seemed to billow out of the windows and fuse with the ragged vines that clung to the walls.

"We're safe here," Zaide said softly.

Francisco shook his head and started to back away. This was worse than he had suspected. It was one thing to hide out on the fazenda, even in the village. But in an *axe*, that was not something he could accept. He did not believe in these gods, in these rituals. They were something left over from a distant and distorted past. They were part of what had made Brazil and what had destroyed it. His revulsion for the *candomble* was surpassed only by his fear.

An old woman wearing a red turban came to the door of the house. She smiled broadly and beckoned them, waving as if she wanted to call them over to talk. Francisco resisted. This could not be the same old woman, that was not possible. But he knew that it didn't matter whether she was the same or not—she was the priestess of this *axe* and that was enough. They were all the same.

Zaide went over and folded her hands and bowed in front of the old priestess. The priestess pulled out a length of bloodred cloth and wrapped it around Zaide's head. Then Zaide turned and smiled at Francisco. "What are you waiting for?" she asked.

Francisco could do nothing but stare. "You?" he asked hoarsely. "Let me back onto the street."

Zaide only laughed. "You wanted to ride the Wave, didn't you? But the Wave is only power. Whatever you call it, however you interface, it is still power." She turned and took a handful of something from the old woman, put it in her mouth, and then swallowed it with the *pinga* the woman gave her in a glass.

Francisco shook his head in horror. "No," he said in denial. "No." He moved back and tried to unbolt the gate.

Nem Brito stopped him. "We can sit in the garden here," he whispered. "It's probably safer than any other place we could be."

Francisco took long seconds to make up his mind. The drumming never stopped. Zaide stood as if frozen in front of the door, half-turned, her eyes beckoning. "The Wave is nothing new," she said softly, but her voice was firm in the gentle drift of incense. "It always has been, it's a shift in perception is all. It's the baseline, the quantum reality. Do you know how many different phrines can open the interface? It's all in control. The secondaries and relays through the monitorboards just give us more control, reinterpret the reality in a way our minds can comprehend it. Change it. But you can live there anyway—all the data in the Wave is moving through you all the time, encoded in the electron stream.

"How is that different from all knowledge coming from the gods? Don't you know people always say that the gods are forever? That time means nothing to them? Doesn't that remind you of the whole universe on the subparticle level? There is no time at all, there is nothing but the chaotic flow of existence-nonexistence. And that's all."

Francisco sank down, his arms crossed across his chest. "Fine. Do whatever you want. I'll wait here."

"You mean you're not going to help?" the old priestess chided. "You're going to leave her to fight that bad Julio all by herself and you won't give her no aid? I am ashamed of you, boys, I am ashamed."

"What do we have to do?" Nem Brito asked, leery.

"Just come in." The old woman beckoned. "Just come on in."

Francisco remained unmoved, but Steel and Nem Brito

followed Zaide and the old woman into the house. The drumming never stopped, and there was a little nip in the air now that the sun had been gone for hours. There was still warmth in the concrete wall and he pushed his back hard against it.

Time passed and then there was silence. The garden was dark, and above Francisco could see the stars, millions of them massed the way he had never seen them in the city. The way Paulo had shown them to him out in the cerrado. The thought of Paulo made him sad and he felt deeply lonely.

The door to the house was open. He could see nothing and there was no longer any sound from inside. He waited. He told himself that it did not matter, not at all. And he knew perfectly well that he was wrong. And then he couldn't wait anymore and very quietly he went in the door.

The inside of the house was dark, but since he had been sitting in the dark he could make out shapes well enough. There was Zaide seated in a thronelike chair with quick code flashes from microwave interface chips. Steel and Nem Brito were both lying in the middle of what seemed to be a picture drawn with sand on the ground. Both of them wore virtual reality caps just like the ones in the games arcade in the Gilberto Salomao. The lines leading from the helmets snaked to the structure where Zaide sat and ruled, a fully interfaced Carnival Queen and her court.

He could not possibly resist and she knew it. She put the gauntlets on him, and settled the helmet over his head. The screen encompassed his face, the gloves were stiff against his skin. He always felt slightly claustrophobic in the VR fields, which was why he avoided them for pleasure. There was only so much the small game machines in the realities could re-create, and then it got far too complex and began to break down.

The face screen seemed to melt away. He knew he was merely seeing readout, but this was like nothing he had ever experienced on the Gilberto Salomao, not even for double price. This was more intricate, more real than that, and somehow he understood that he was seeing his mind's recreation of the reality it now perceived and had not understood before.

He was in a current in the sea, deep in a great flow of sparkling green-blue energy, which danced in a pattern that disintegrated and reassembled at will. The current itself was strong, and he was one of a mass of lights gathered to the side of it, exerting influence, changing it as it moved. And he could see down into the current as if he were over it at the same time, and see how the change in the nexus of light diverted its course and re-created the pattern. The old pattern still existed underneath and there was no time, no cause and no effect. There was only movement, there was only beingness in this energy mass.

Somehow he felt silent approval surround him. The feelings solidified and resolved into Zaide, into Paulo. Both of them looked beaten and worn. They were covered with blood as if they had been in a fight, and it looked like they had not won. But neither were they defeated.

Zaide turned away from him and walked out into where the current was the strongest. It whipped the red turban from her head and started to unwind it, a single ribbon in the vast dark blueness of the sea. He reached out and grabbed the turban, and inside himself he heard voices echo, telling him to push, to hold on to the red fabric, which seemed to disintegrate around him and become blood. Zaide was still dancing in the current before him, merged with the energy field and directing it.

Then he heard the laughing again in his head. Laughing that was harsh and a little mad, that was deep and familiar. *Paulo?* he thought. But Paulo was dead.

And here everything existed at once. There was no past, no future, no cause or effect. There was no time. There was no death, just the way the priests always said.

He had never believed in the priests, in the Church, in the gods of the *candomble*. He believed in reason and logic and order. And here it seemed that the two were the same.

Come, the echo of Paulo told him. There was little choice. Much as Francisco distrusted the familiarity, he was unable to do anything here on his own. He didn't have the knowledge he needed, didn't have the passwords or keys. And so he let the voice take him and gather up all the parts of him that were spread through the glittering Wave.

Then the perspective changed, although he did not feel himself to move at all. He was in a place that was dark and cavernous, far from the energy nexus of the galaxy. From here he could see the patterns unfolding over millennia and light years, configurations that were grand and simple and utterly familiar.

He knew their name and it was chaos. Perfect and utterly precise, the giant butterflies stretched across the universe like on a Ming bowl. All that activity, all that movement, none of it repeated exactly and yet all of it following a non-linear logic that was perceptible though disturbing.

The longer he studied the patterns, the more he could discern. Embedded in these structures were others, different, the movement of nascent consciousness and not the stars.

He concentrated on these, and they, too, resolved into patterns. But these patterns were less fluid and organic than the immense butterfly matrices of the galaxies. These were defined and rigid and followed each other over and over again, repeating instead of varying and moving on. Human history did follow the whole reality of the rest of existence, and this made Francisco overwhelmingly sad.

Then he was in it, *was* it, unified with all the formations that comprised the whole of human life. It was wrong, too structured to breathe, too severe to encompass necessary change. But he just had to give it a little push, just a small adjustment, finding the kernel that was the original attractor and freeing it from its muffling bonds. Wondering, he found it as easy to do as to think.

Around him the energy seemed to flutter with newfound freedom. A sigh rippled through the matrix and then the newly chaotic butterfly emerged from its cocoon. He was filled with wonder and joy at the transformation, and with a protective love for this new entity. Which was not new, but only a thing waiting, implicit in the design.

The upwelling emotion thrust him back into identification with the pattern. He found himself conscious of being human again, of being flesh and mind, an identified unity in the quantum universe. Liberation of spirit poured through him.

And around him there was laughter. Not Paulo's laughter this time, but something more bitter and triumphant. Exu Tiriri, the trickster god, was reveling in victory.

Then Francisco saw it and the realization made him ill. Exu Tiriri wore a face that he knew. It was the face of Julio Simon.

It had already happened in quantum time, but that did not make it any easier. Zaide knew that she was only seeing, reinterpreting and making the experience more familiar so that her brain could make sense of what it was being fed. The drugs and the secondaries and all the surgery, the VR helmets for the others, all these were only the tools of translation. Deep down reality was inviolate; they were its byproducts and sometimes its victims and very very rarely its masters. Zaide Soledad knew that, just as she knew that the great river below the flood plain was only an image and not a reflection of reality. It was a medium for her to cope, that was all.

And so she took the step into the dark cold, into the abstraction where existence was and was not all at the same time. Where there was only brilliance and darkness, all of it unified into a great singularity of meaning. And then she felt a great wash of despair.

She was the only consciousness in this place and she was alone. Terribly alone, the way no person ever could endure being. The bright energy dance was alien to her, a thing that was governed by conditions she knew she was not meant to see. There was nothing here for them. Why had men ever come into the Wave at all? Except that men always trespassed on the territory of the gods.

We are the gods.

The words formed inside her, but a voice she knew had made them. She recognized the arrogance and she knew the unquestioning assumption of her acquiescence. This was the thought of Julio Simon. And she acknowledged that his thought was the truth.

As she recognized him through the matrix of the Wave, she felt a cohesive identity vibrating in the dark void. He was the dark, he filled every ripple and eddy of it. Every shadow identified in him, as him, and responded to his trembling. Though if it was excitement or fear, Zaide Soledad could not say. Only that she knew him and in that moment he was all things that were not bright, that were not movement, that were not complete and perfect in their own spheres of being.

Julio Simon was the dark. But without the dark there would be none of the glorious sparkling dance of energy that surrounded her. Without the darkness there would be nothing at all.

She acknowledged this as the truth and bowed before it. It was not a force she could eliminate. Julio Simon was as much a part of the necessary real as she.

But he was not Julio Simon alone. He was not a single identity, but all identity that was one with the null, with Exu Tiriri through all time. He was all things *ex nihilo*, the cold wind of the abyss that sometimes wore the face of a man. And sometimes wore the form she knew as Julio Simon.

She could feel him like a vacuum, a great void in the heart of beingness. And like a vacuum, he drew her in toward himself. He needed her, she realized. He was trying to absorb her the way he had tried with all the living things he had killed. The way he had tried to kill Paulo.

But she had saved Paulo from him.

Now he wanted her. He wanted them all. He wanted all existence, all life, all the dancing patterns of the universe. He needed to dictate their movement because the reality of the universe was madness. He only worshipped what he perceived as order because he could not see the greater organization that held no order he could accept. He held on to those things firmly because the patterns of consciousness were fixed and held in the minds of men who were afraid and were part of the void. Patterns that repeated themselves without freedom, that could be predicted, because men valued what they could predict.

Then the Wave must be even more terrifying to them than to herself, she thought. She loved the great chaotic choir of being. The particle universe was a collection of insanity against which the bulwark of reason seemed weak and obscene.

No one can make you free.

How little Paulo had known when he had said that. Indeed, no one could make anyone else free. It was such a small and simple thing, the actual realization that she did not have to accept the paradigm anymore. That it had always been her choice to accept the reigning patterns of existence or change them to suit her own truth, her own needs. It was a simple thing.

The rigid structure dissolved before her and she felt an influx of energy. Someone else with her, someone else who chose freedom, who rejected the stale hegemony of the mass. And the unyielding construct with its solvable mathematical equations shattered in her mind and re-formed.

Consciousness opened into chaos and spread its wings. Thought was freed and followed new patterns, never repeating for as long as being existed.

She moved like an angel of liberation through the knots of thought and carefully loosened them one by one. Especially the dark nonbeing molds she touched. With those, she was gentle and tender because they had the greatest fear, fear that Zaide Soledad saw as very strange and painful.

Bit by energy bit, she tried to teach the void-being freedom. It resisted, drew back from her, shielded itself. It tried again to be negative and draw her into its being to devour her, but this time she had given up all fear and all need. There was only the new emancipation that guided her, the butterflies of open thought emerging from the chrysalis of reason and despair.

She flung the new into his greedy heart, the pulsing undeniable energy of liberation, of chaos. It was an act of joy, a small child throwing flowers into the sky.

And it burned through him. The realignment of reason and order denied all its basic precepts of existence. Zaide did not know how he could have spent so much time in the Wave and still have remained so ignorant of its basic design. But there was no doubt that Julio Simon was burning, burning, his own rationality fighting beyond death to assuage his sense of logic.

She felt the immense resistance and the energy that, once released, could not be bound up again. Not even in Julio Simon's mind. He had seen the true foundation of the universe and it had appalled him beyond belief. Beyond sanity.

Twenty-four

THE *axe* was silent. Francisco, Steel and Nem Brito were unconscious. The old priestess nodded toward them, and Zaide knew that she would take care of things. They would sleep.

Sleep was a luxury Zaide could not afford. She stood up and stretched. The ornate chair she had sat in all night seemed to have carved ridges into her back and her neck, and her left shoulder was miserably stiff. She forced herself to the door and out into the yard. The sun was just rising, such a different dawn than the last.

The old woman took her hands and kissed her cheeks three times. Then she patted the red turban that still sat on Zaide's head. "Keep it," she said. "You have the power."

Zaide blinked. "But it's just the Wave." She dismissed the irrationality of the *candomble* gently.

The old priestess patted her hands and pressed them between gnarled ancient ones. "Power is power," the old woman said, and her voice was steady and low. "And you say the truth—anyone can walk in that place and meet the ghosts. But not everyone can stand up to Exu Tiriri. Or whatever you call the trickster. But there always is one, even in your textbook world. Now, go. There is someone from the big house come to get you."

Zaide was surprised. She was even more surprised when the old woman opened the garden gate and there stood Manuel Leal. "Uncle Victor wants to see you," he said, and dropped his eyes to the ground.

Somehow she was not worried. Maybe she was just too tired to care. That seemed more likely.

Manuel flew the vert competently, quickly, saying nothing at all. Things looked strange as they approached. She could see the field house and the lawn, but there was an acrid smell in the air and the house looked lopsided and blackened. Ravaged.

"What happened?" she asked, abashed.

Manuel Leal shook his head. "I don't know. Only that in the middle of the night for no reason Julio Simon went crazy and tried to burn it down. They took him to the infirmary, but the doctors here don't specialize in psychiatric cases. He'll be moved to the hospital in São Paulo later today."

He set them down at the garage behind the house. Zaide could see that only the north wing had been burned, as if Julio Simon had started the fire in his own room. Without thinking, she walked across the lawn to the blackened scar on the family home.

With her eyes on the damaged house, she didn't notice the people coming across the lawn. Uncle Victor, Sonia Leah and Susana converged on her.

"What did you do to him?" Susana blurted out. "He went completely crazy."

Zaide didn't looked at Susana. She looked straight at Uncle Victor, at the approval in his expression. "What did I do?" she asked softly. "I won."

Breakfast was set out like a picnic, on the lawn. The veranda furniture had been brought down so there were chairs and small tables, and a single long serving buffet had been set up with coffee service, bowls of mangoes and papayas, a tray of fresh rolls and butter. The silverware had been wrapped in oversized dinner linens printed with an informal pattern of parrots and leaves.

Zaide took a large cup of white breakfast coffee. She wasn't hungry; the night and the morning had taken too much out of her.

It was over. She had won. Somehow the realization of that didn't quite hit yet. Maybe she was simply too exhausted to feel it.

"The one thing I don't know is how he knew," Zaide said, sipping her coffee. Susana sat with her at the table, along with Sonia Leah. Uncle Victor had a table to himself, and honestly Zaide was just as glad. She might no longer have quite the fear of him she had earlier, but he still wasn't a comfortable presence. Especially when she hadn't showered or changed her clothes and smelled of incense and sweat. "I didn't even know."

Susana shrugged. "It's the series thing, you know. Even I felt it. I knew what was going on, even if I couldn't intervene. It was between the two of you. You are really a hell of a lot alike, you know, you and Julio Simon. Bottom line all the way, play to the max, and no hard feelings."

Zaide looked at Susana without speaking. Susana could be right. She didn't harbor any anger about her cousin's siding with Julio Simon when things had gotten rough. It was the rational thing to do.

Only Susana was not in love with rational order. She was more creative than that, more flexible. And then Zaide saw how similar they all really were. Her attitude about order was different only because she had seen how there was structure to chaos as well, a pattern that was more complex than the rigidity embraced by Julio Simon, but no less perfectly organized. Merely different. Bottom line.

And then she caught herself with those words. Bottom line. She'd lived with them like punctuation all her life. But what was the bottom line, anyway? She had always assumed it meant profits for the fazenda, the family.

That wasn't enough anymore. The bottom line was something more difficult to describe, like the great butterfly patterns she had seen in the Wave. Only it had a face, now. Paulo's face.

And she remembered a story about someone who had gone into the underworld to retrieve someone dead. She had not gone looking for Paulo, but he had followed her back. Now everything was under his scrutiny and it had all changed.

The bottom line was not the fazenda, not the family. It was down in the south sector of town. Only now there was something she could do. Power. It didn't matter what you called it. *Candomble*, the Wave, the fazenda. Power was meant for changing things. The old priestess had been right.

The hammock swung gently under him, cooler than a bed would have been. It had been a very long time since he had slept in a hammock, was Francisco's first thought on awakening. Then he realized that he was in fact awake, and opened his eyes. He was in a small house with walls painted different colors, two of them aqua, one orange and one pink. The pink one had a large glass door open to a breeze redolent with flowers and sun and the end of winter. A flutter of gauze at the window in one of the aquamarine walls caught the draft.

He swung one leg over the edge of the hammock carefully and steadied himself. Outside the door he could see a flawless blue sky and a garden full of late flowers. He didn't know where he was, or, more precisely, he was in a place that was so infinitely right he did not question it. There was brightly colored pottery on a shelf on the orange wall along with holy pictures tacked up with yellowed tape. Everything was scrubbed and sparkling in the morning light. The smell of coffee prompted him to the door.

He was wearing loose cotton pants, the kind that Paulo used to wear for *capoeira*. They were gray with black and yellow stripes and very soft. They were not his pants, he had never owned a pair like them. And these were old and well-washed and smelled of soap and sunlight like the rest of the place.

The door over to the right of the orange wall was the bathroom, he knew, and it was as perfectly clean as the rest of the house. The tile was old and some of the painting on it worn, but it was cool and ornate the way it was supposed to be. The way a house in the village should look.

The coffee smell was coming from outside. He ventured out of the room to the walled garden. A link unit was set into the wall, framed with green and orange tile, but it was turned off. There was a patio with a small fountain set to the side. The fountain was tiled in blue so that the water looked cool and fresh and inviting. Next to the fountain was a small white iron table and matching ornate chairs. Steel and Nem Brito were seated, drinking coffee and cutting up mangoes. Nem Brito had a blue parrot on his shoulder.

"We have a bet going on how long you would take," Nem Brito said, smiling. "And I win. Steel now owes me five hundred centavos, and if anyone else had owed it to me, I wouldn't have a chance to collect. But Steel, I expect Steel to make good on the bet."

Francisco poured a cup from the highly decorated pitcher. It was weak white coffee, morning coffee, and it tasted as good as it smelled.

"What happened?" Steel asked. "You were out way longer than us."

Francisco sat down, sipped his coffee. He accepted a mango from Steel and peeled it. The succulent orange fruit dribbled over his hand. He took a bite and it was sweet, sweeter than the generously sugared coffee. The mango strings caught in his teeth.

He remembered the Wave. The memory did not have the quality of a dream, and he was certain that there was something true in what had occurred. But it seemed very distant from the sheer new physicality in this garden on this morning, as if he had entered another universe where history had run differently and he had never enjoyed the comforts of this village home. Which he knew was not true.

And yet there was an echo in his thoughts, a strange double image of who he was and where, which was confusing. He knew he was in the Vielho-Markowicz village and that he belonged here, and that soon it would be time to meet Zaide at the big house. Soon.

Absently he went over to the link and brushed the painted controls on the tile. The screen flickered alive and he requested update before it queried him. Brasilia flickered to life before him, nothing changed. The southern sector was still ugly and run down, the bureaucrats with their soft cases still marched into the matching Ministries at eight in the morning, the Northern Commercial District still held the Vielho-Markowicz and Cadea and Alado headquarters.

And the rain forest was still there on the screen. Beautiful, lush, fragile, it lay untamed and inviolate.

"It's time to go to the big house anyway," Steel said to no one. And there was nothing at all to indicate the time. "The old woman said that we might want to start over when we finished eating."

But there wasn't any time, Francisco remembered. There wasn't any time at all, and cause and effect were merely functions of time. There was only the order of chaos, the infinite variety of quantum anarchy.

"Last night seems so unreal," he said.

Steel snorted. "Last night? Make that two days ago."

Nem Brito poked him playfully with an elbow. "Come on. We were out until yesterday ourselves. Anyway, we got you cleaned up and everything. And the old woman came in and told us that maybe we should go by the big house this morning. Otherwise, it's pretty dead around here."

"That's the truth," Steel agreed. "There is absolutely nothing at all to do. We spent a little time on the link last night and that was it. This is really the boonies. There isn't even any arcade out here. If I didn't know better, I'd think this was the phrine-free farm. But I guess not."

Francisco shook his head and turned away. Somehow Steel's bitterness hit him wrong. "Let's go," he said softly. "I guess we take the vert we came in?"

Both Steel and Nem Brito shrugged. Obviously they hadn't been told any differently.

The village was very different during the day. There were people in the streets now, stopping to chat over a glass of *guaraná* or a cafezinho in the plaza. A group of old men played chess and read the newspaper aloud near the fountain and a few children kicked around a soccer ball until one of the men said something about them being in school. Then the kids took off down one of the side streets.

People looked at them and smiled politely, but seemed uncertain if they should be greeted or not. They weren't known in the village, but manners dictated greeting everyone, and the locals were obviously uncomfortable.

Francisco found it both awkward and fascinating, as if he weren't really there himself at all. This was a place out of the past, a society that he had read about but didn't believe existed outside the entertainment industry in the city. And then he realized that a large part of the growing unreality in his mind was the environment itself. He had no place here. He did not belong in a village with scrubbed steps and tiled window frames and women talking over the garden walls. He needed to return to Brasilia.

They found the vert where it had been left. A group of young boys gathered around and loudly demanded money for having watched the fascinating machine and made certain that no parts took off in the night. Francisco glanced at Steel, who came up with enough dinheiro to satisfy the urchins.

They sat at the controls. "I don't know how to fly this thing," Francisco admitted.

Nem Brito shrugged. "I don't either. But I know there's an autocontrol on it, and it's always set at prime base."

Steel ignored both of them. He shouldered Nem Brito into the back seat and his fingers flew over the controls. The panel lit blue and red and amber; then one of the lights began flashing. Steel hit it again and the vert quivered and rose.

"This should be the autodirect," Steel said. "I hope so. I don't know where this big house is from here."

"But when we escaped before," Nem Brito said slowly,

"then we were able to get home with no problem. You just touched the thing and it took off."

"It was primed for us and programmed to go to Brasilia," Steel said. "There was even the message on the screen for us, remember? It's the kind of arrogant thing you'd expect from the fazenda crowd, assuming that we couldn't possibly take the thing ourselves."

Nem Brito shrugged. "But they were right."

Francisco thought of telling them to cut the bickering, and then thought better of it. If they were occupied with each other, they wouldn't be wondering about him. He only hoped that the vert and the autopilot program were not a trap. On the other hand, he didn't have any choice.

Obviously the vert had been primed. It swung around and headed straight across the forest that unfolded beneath them. It was a magnificent sight, Francisco thought. And though it was perfectly innocent and pristine, perfect in itself, he wondered how it could have caused so much misery and still remain so untouched.

If he could drive, Francisco thought, he'd take the vert across the great expanse and head for home. For the city. He wanted to see Zaide, to talk to her, but he didn't trust the fazenda at all. The vert was flying and he wanted to bring it to his own territory.

The flying might be easy enough, but he had no idea of where they were in relation to Brasilia. And he didn't know if the vert had enough fuel to make the trip. The idea of running out of fuel was less than attractive, and so he gave up on the fantasy of running off with the machine.

And then they were landing at the garage. He assumed the large white house with part of the top story on the left side burned off was their destination. Other than the charred roof and remains of a wall, the house looked perfectly serene. The only people out on the lawn wore the uniforms of Security and Service. The valet checked in the vert without question.

Then Francisco hesitated. He wanted to see Zaide alone,

to find out what had happened in the Wave as much as what their status was here. Surely they were not prisoners. But what else they might be was unclear. He didn't trust the memory of the Wave and the feeling of victory that had filled him there. He'd had enough VR games to be careful.

As he considered the options, the autovalet chimed softly. "Seu Francisco, Dona Zaide invited you and your friends to take coffee with her on the porch. If you would be so kind."

"Nothing ever talked to me that polite before," Nem Brito commented.

"Maybe I should wait here and secure another vert to go home," Steel offered.

It was a good idea and Francisco told him so. But Zaide knew how many of them there were, and by now so did the entire fazenda. Including the valet, which most likely was programmed to stop any unauthorized attempt to take a vehicle.

Zaide Soledad stood at the top of the stairs watching for them. She was dressed in a fine ice-yellow linen dress and matching sandals. As they approached, Francisco could see that she wore gold earrings and bracelets as well. She looked rich. She looked like she belonged here. She did not look like the girl who had sat on Paulo's lap in the barzinho drinking aguardente out of a jar and laughing at crude songs.

He mounted the stairs and saw, seated deep in the shadows under the awning, a gray-haired man in an elegant Italian silk suit, watching them. Zaide greeted each of them, Francisco, Nem Brito and Steel, as old friends, kissing them on the cheek and chattering about how good it was that they could come and how rested they all seemed to be.

Then Zaide invited them to sit on overstuffed porch chairs and a sofa, and went about pouring coffee from a silver service. They made small talk about the village, the big house, carefully not mentioning the burned section or Julio Simon. Francisco kept watching the man in the suit.

After the conversation had drifted enough that everyone felt manners had been observed, Zaide brought a cup of coffee to the older man. "This is my Uncle Victor," she said simply. "I told him that you brought me back."

"Seu Victor," Francisco said formally, inclining his head slightly.

"Seu Francisco, I am very grateful to you for having returned Zaide Soledad to her family," the gray-haired man said, his voice low and assured. "I am sorry that my nephew Julio Simon caused you so much grief in the matter of your friend. However, you have impressed me greatly. I would like to ask you to join the family."

Francisco felt his body go rigid and his mouth dry. "What do you mean, join the family?" he asked, gaping.

"Precisely that," Victor said. "To be adopted as Vielho, work in your area of competence here. We are now in need of a Security Chief, and I believe that you are qualified to fill that position."

Francisco was stunned. In all the universe this was the one thing he had never expected. Nor did he trust it. These people did not give their family name so easily, nor did they divide their profits so readily. He glanced at Zaide to see how she was reacting to the offer. She smiled at him faintly.

"It isn't gratitude only," she added. "I want you on my team."

The older man nodded. "Indeed. Zaide has done very well. It will take a period of training, but I believe that it would not be premature of me to tell you that she is my first choice to inherit my post one day. She will need people she can trust in key positions."

Francisco Pope studied them both carefully. "You're trying to corrupt me," he said quietly. "You know precisely what I mean to do, and Paulo's death hasn't changed that. So you're trying to bribe me, get me to stop."

Zaide stood up. She looked very sad, and there was thought in her face when she spoke. "I know what you want," she said slowly, as if weighing each of the words. "And I don't think you trust me, but I have learned some things from you. From Paulo. Anyway, you could do a great deal from this position. We have a great deal of power here. Isn't that what you wanted? Power? And between us, you and me, we could recreate the city beyond your wildest dreams. We have the resources, and with the city we have the talent as well. Join me, Francisco. Think of what we can do, how much we can change."

Francisco put his coffee cup down on the glass table, got up and leaned on the nearest pillar. "And what if I don't?" he asked arrogantly.

"What will you do with your life if you don't?" Zaide demanded furiously. "Live in a favela and sleep on the floor in the dark your whole life? Spend your free time in the Gilberto Salomao and all your dinheiro on phrines? So what?

"Change doesn't happen overnight. At least not for the better it doesn't. You can destroy a place in a day—look at what happened with the Forestation Riots. But it takes a long time to build something, to prepare for the future.

"Besides, do you really think you can unite the tribes? You're crazy, you know that? The cadres are too territorial, too shortsighted. That was the whole problem with the Serps, and see what happens to the Jaguars without Aluizio at their head. Just wait. Or do you want to end up like Aluizio? He had the brains and the charisma and biggest, meanest cadre in the state. And he ended up as a road-kill. Is that what you want to be? A martyr?"

Francisco smiled lazily, just like Paulo would have. He didn't need to listen to her tirade. He had learned something in the Wave, that the Wave itself wasn't the key to any power at all. It was merely a power itself. One kind of power. What he wanted was another.

Instead he had come up with an idea, and it was an idea that pleased him greatly. He didn't look at Zaide. He looked at the older man. There was some wordless understanding between them, and strangely he found he trusted Seu Victor. At least to some extent.

"There was a pretty generous reward offered for our capture," he said softly. "I think that since we arrived on our own, we should collect the money. And further, in the elections . . . You did mention running for Congress as an option, didn't you?"

Realization dawned on Zaide. She gasped. "You mean you're going to run for Congress? Then, if you win you'll help us?"

Francisco couldn't stop grinning, but he shook his head. "Not quite. I'm going to win and you're going to pay for it. And then I'm going to fight you like hell. Because you people need a conscience, you know that? You need the opposition so you don't forget and start playing these games again. And if you get any ideas about making things more difficult for me, well, there is the matter of Julio Simon and a number of murders. Torture is illegal even now, and I'm sure the Swiss courts would look very unfavorably on some things the three of us know."

Zaide Soledad smiled slowly. "I think we will make very good enemies, Francisco Pope," she said very softly.

She watched him leave the porch, flanked by his lieutenants, and smiled. His back was to her and he never saw her expression. But she knew that in the infirmary lab the geneticists were working on a new series. The "P" series. There had been plenty of genetic material left.

She wanted to laugh, to tell Francisco that. To tell him that she was as much a street kid as he was. Probably more. Where the hell did he think they got the original material to breed the fazenda children? Only the toughest from the street could stand the pressure.

"We'll make very good enemies, Francisco," she whispered. "But what will you do with Francisco Paulo and Linea Pui and all the others?"